# PRAISE FOR THE MAID

Dr. Osborne's and Kay Bowling's novel *The Maid* exposes the great complexity and pure evil in the world of human trafficking. The novel tells the story of children lost in a lawless world, yet with great fortitude, one young woman saves the lives of others. It is a must-read for anyone!

—Major Marc Nichols (Ret) NCSHP
Federal Criminal Interdiction Instructor
NC Human Trafficking Commission,
Chair of the NC HT Public Safety Committee.

*The Maid* is a captivating narration of the most undetected, unnoticed, and unreported crime against humanity that will tug at your heart and will forever linger in the back of your mind. This story will instill a new and informed awareness that causes you to start to notice little things, situations, and family dynamics that you never paid attention to before. Reading this book should make you want to speak out to your family, friends and others you come across in life about the realities of how our most vulnerable are being exploited.

—Aaron Kahler, Found and Chief Executive Officer of
Anti-Human Trafficking Intelligence Initiative

Prepare yourself to be taken on an emotional journey in Dr. Osborne and Kay Bowling's novel *The Maid*. The tragic, vile and revealing truths about human trafficking will leave you in tears but this story will undoubtedly inspire you to fight. Fight for the most vulnerable and innocent, our children.

—Kellie Hodges, NC SBI,
Special Agent In Charge of Human Trafficking

*The Maid* by Michelle Osborne and Kay Mann Bowling powerfully combines real-life stories into a fictional accounting that gives readers an inside glimpse of the horror of human trafficking happening every day, not only in far-off lands, but right here in our own communities. Awareness of the problem is the first step in bringing this travesty to an end.

"God [then] revealed to Anna that she should go public with her story to appeal to people everywhere to help stop human trafficking."

This is a thought-provoking novel that will not easily let go of your conscience. Perhaps the message in *The Maid* will move you to take one step forward in the battle to save others from this detestable fate. And then another.

*The Maid* exemplifies that every single life is precious beyond measure.

—Jodi Burnett, author of
*Concealed Cargo (FBI-K9 Series, Book 3)*

# THE MAID

# THE MAID

MICHELLE FLYNN OSBORNE

*and*

KAY MANN BOWLING

Durham, NC

*The Maid*

Michelle Flynn Osborne
chopinbachbeethoven@gmail.com

Kay Mann Bowling
kmannbowling@nc.rr.com

Published 2021, by Torchflame Books
an Imprint of Light Messages Publishing
www.lightmessages.com
Durham, NC 27713 USA
SAN: 920-9298

Paperback ISBN: 978-1-61153-421-4
E-book ISBN: 978-1-61153-422-1
Library of Congress Control Number: 2021912909



This book combines true stories of human trafficked victims into one dramatized novel. The names and details of individuals have been changed to respect their privacy.

*The Maid* is dedicated to all human trafficked victims around the world.

We earnestly pray for their freedom, continued healing, and full restoration.

We pray especially for the children, the most innocent victims of all.

# ACKNOWLEDGMENTS

*THE MAID* IS BASED ON TRUE STORIES obtained during doctoral research conducted in Costa Rica—research that could not have happened without the help of local missionaries who gave us insight into the depth and breadth of human trafficking in the area. We thank them for their association with us because it put them in a potentially dangerous position. So, at their request, we withhold their names to ensure their safety. We also thank God for their work in rehabilitating and ministering to rescued victims and pray for their continued success.

Writing this book was difficult. Due to the subject matter, we struggled to abide by the rules of decorum. To be realistic without being offensive, we leaned heavily on the wisdom of trusted friends. We are especially grateful for award winning published author Nancy Panko. With her longsuffering support, we finally made it to the finish line. We also owe a huge debt of gratitude to those who gave their precious time to read or edit the manuscript. In the order that it evolved, we thank beta readers Jackie Buckner, Carolyn Stern, Susan Nester, Sherri Hubbard, Angela Hatchell, and Patty Poole.

Believing the stories of these victims needed to be published and believing we were capable of getting the job done, family and friends encouraged us on a near-daily basis. A special heartfelt thank you goes to (alphabetically) Tess Brewer, Linda Farrell, Maxine Love, Lynn Stoeckel, and Suzanne Walker.

Next, we thank all the people at Torchflame Books for bringing *The Maid* across the finish line and into the marketplace. As first-time authors, our book could have sat on the sidelines for years. But as God would have it, He allowed the timely message in this book to come to the forefront through them. We appreciate the core values of Torchflame Books and the high quality of their work on all levels.

Of utmost importance, we thank you, our readers. You didn't have to buy the book. You didn't have to take the time to read it. But you did, and we are grateful. It is our prayer that you will spread the message of awareness and accountability—weapons of war against one of the most sadistic crimes on earth. Listen to the voices of human trafficked victims—especially to the voices of the children.

# INTRODUCTION

*All that is necessary for evil to triumph*
*is for good men to do nothing.*

—Edmund Burke, 1729–1797

DO YOU HAVE A CHILD, or know anyone who does? If the answer is yes, this is a book you must read. Your reward will be information—shocking information—that you will not read in the newspaper or hear on the news. It could mean that you will save someone's life. That is precisely the intent of this book. *The Maid* brings awareness to the pain, suffering, and sometimes death, inside the dark and desperate underworld of human trafficking.

*The Maid* begins with two fifteen-year-old girls, Anna and Rosa, who work side by side with their families, picking coffee beans on Nicaragua's mountainous terrain. One day, the girls learn of a high-paying job in Costa Rica, where work conditions would be less strenuous and dangerous. Unaware of the hidden dangers, the girls' parents permit them to take advantage of what appears to be a once-in-a-lifetime opportunity.

Twenty years later, Anna courageously shares the harrowing details of the new job—that of imprisoned, human-trafficked sex slaves. Because Anna's story involves other victims, you will also hear their stories. *The Maid* combines true stories of human trafficked victims into one dramatized novel. Although the authors conducted research and interviews in Costa Rica, they have changed the names of some places, and the people interviewed, to ensure their protection.

Today, Anna recounts her story as an urgent plea to you, the reader: "Please listen to the voices of these children. Share their stories with others. And listen to the millions of children worldwide who remain in modern-day slavery of the worst kind. Carry the message of awareness and accountability everywhere. Take part in saving our children!"

# CHAPTER 1

## A NEW DAY'S COMING

It was a typical day for Anna. Her jet-black hair glistened under the blazing sun, and sweat trickled down her bronzed face as she picked coffee beans from bushes growing on a craggy slope. It was backbreaking, tedious, and sometimes bloody work, especially for a fifteen-year-old girl.

Anna and her best friend, Rosa, didn't make two dollars a day like the older workers, but that wasn't unusual for the children of farmworkers. At least she was with her family: father, Carlos; mother, Juanita; and seven-year-old sister, Maria.

The family lived and worked in a mountainous region of Nicaragua known for its coffee beans. At the time, this rural area had no electricity for lights, refrigeration, or other such conveniences. So life at home had little to offer after a hard day's work.

Carlos hated to see his family live under such harsh conditions, but he never gave up hope that things would one day be better for them. He searched continually for different work, but there were few opportunities for farm families. Then one day, good news arrived.

"Good morning, my friend!" Rosa's father called out, as he rushed over to where Carlos was picking beans. "I heard in town last night about a job opportunity where Anna and Rosa could work in a luxurious hotel, doing less physical labor, and earn fifteen dollars a day. And guess what else...the girls could live and work together!"

"What?" Carlos replied. "There are no luxurious hotels around here."

"I know." Rosa's father kicked a clod of dirt with the toe of his boot. "That's the *only* problem—the job is in Costa Rica."

"Costa Rica!" Carlos removed his straw hat and wiped away sweat with his red bandana. "That's another country, hundreds of miles away! It *sounds* like an excellent opportunity for the girls, but I need to know all the details. And then Juanita and I will have to think and pray about it before we agree to let Anna take a job so far away from home."

This job opportunity was bittersweet to Carlos and Juanita because the family was close. All they had in life was each other. On the other hand, picking coffee beans was not only hard on the body, it was life-threatening. The fields were abundant with poisonous snakes, and disease-carrying mosquitoes swarmed overhead. Not to mention the long-term effects of pesticides and backbreaking labor.

Days passed while Anna's parents contemplated the idea of her moving so far away. She not only contributed to the family income, but she was an energetic girl who always saw the bright side of things. Everyone would miss her happy presence, but it would be especially difficult for Juanita to see her daughter leave home. The two of them had a tight bond.

Every day, after working in the fields, Anna would help her mother cook and then clean the house. As they worked together, they would talk about life. Anna would express her hopes and dreams, and Juanita would listen and offer encouragement.

But Carlos and Juanita finally made an unselfish decision: Anna should take the job. The temporary sacrifice would be worth it in the end.

# CHAPTER 2

## SAD GOODBYE

"HURRY! HURRY!" ANNA CALLED OUT. "We can't be late. We just *can't* be late."

Dressed in their finest, Anna and Rosa walked the three-mile dusty road to town, eager to catch the bus for their job in Costa Rica. Sweat soon soaked the girls' clothing in the dense, humid air, but they didn't seem to care. In their heads were visions of grandeur about their new life.

This occasion was the closest thing to a party Anna had ever experienced. Her and Rosa's family members walked the distance with them and kept them company. Everyone laughed and celebrated the incredibly good fortune the girls had in finding a job with great pay. Their hearts were full of hope.

Anna flipped the skirt of her red and white polka-dot dress from side to side, in rhythm with her steps.

"Rosa, can you believe it?" she said. "A whole new world has opened up to us."

"No, I still can't believe it. We're going to see the real world, outside of our boring little village."

"I know!" Anna replied. "I've always dreamed about riding on a bus and seeing the world...experiencing new, beautiful places...something different from coffee-bean fields—"

"That's right," Rosa said. "There are *no* cute boys in the coffee-bean field...or our village. I will *never* meet my handsome, dream husband if I don't get out of this place."

Anna huffed. "That's for sure. I can't wait to get married and have children. That's what I want. I want to be a mother, just like my mom. That's *my* dream."

The girls continued their journey to the bus stop, but their pace gradually slowed. Somber silence crept in. Occasionally, Anna or Rosa would glance over her shoulder at their loved ones who followed closely.

"Rosa," Anna said after a few sad minutes of thought. "We'll need to write to our folks every day. Maybe we'll meet someone on the bus—someone who travels back and forth between Costa Rica and home. Maybe they'll be willing to carry our messages."

"Yeah, you're right." Rosa nodded. "Even if we don't find someone to relay our messages, we'll save up money so our families can come to see us. Maybe they'll be able to stay for free in the hotel where we work."

The reality of separating from the people they loved so much caught up with them and dampened their spirits. Gloom now tainted the once happy faces of both girls. Separation for Anna meant it would be impossible to hear her mother's sweet, comforting voice. She would also miss the constant support of her father. Even though the family lived in near-poverty, he never once allowed them to feel afraid or desperate. The family always had a sense of love and security.

"I think we'll be happy once we get there," Rosa said. "We'll never have to pick another coffee bean. And we can send our families lots of money so they can live without worry."

"I know." Anna tried to control her emotions. "But saying goodbye is *so* hard."

"I-I'm a little bit afraid," Rosa said.

Anna reached for her hand. "Rosa...no matter what, we'll *always* have each other."

After an hour's trek, the exhausted group made it to town and approached the bus stop, which consisted of a wooden ticket booth and platform. But as soon as the girls bought their tickets, their world turned from sunshine to rain. And as the old folks would sometimes say...a case of nerves set in.

Everyone huddled and hugged to comfort each other.

Carlos said, “Anna, this is the hardest thing your mother and I have ever done. Life just won’t be the same until you return. Please, please take care of yourself. And please let us hear from you as soon as you can. We need to know that you are safe and happy.”

Anna’s father was a large, muscular man accustomed to hard labor. Often, he took odd jobs to make extra money. And Juanita worked hard around the house every day, after returning from picking coffee beans in the hot fields. Hearing her father say that sending her off was the hardest thing they had ever done was beyond Anna’s comprehension.

Juanita sucked her breath in and began to sniffle as she drew her daughter into her warm embrace.

“Oh, Anna. My dear, dear Anna. I will pray for you every day, until I see your sun-kissed face again. Never, never forget how much you are loved.”

All the while, Maria stood in the background, dwarfed in all the commotion. Mustering a smile, Anna reached down and lifted the chin of her sweet little sister.

“Okay, sis. I’ve taught you how to braid your hair all by yourself. Do you think you can do that every morning?”

Maria nodded. “Yes, but do you *have* to go? *Please* don’t go, Anna. I’ll miss you too much.”

Anna choked back tears. She didn’t want to upset Maria any more than she already was, so she winked and flashed a slight smile.

“Now don’t you get used to sleeping on my side of the bed, ’cause I’ll be home before you know it.”

“Yeah.” Carlos squeezed Anna in a tight hug. “Come home quick as a wink. Mother, Maria, and I will miss you so much while you’re gone. We’ll leave your little room just as you left it.”

The rusty old bus bound for San Jose, Costa Rica, pulled up to the platform. While the motor rattled in the background, the girls said their final goodbyes. They wanted the new job, but taking that first step onto the bus almost didn't happen.

"I'll be back." Anna wrapped her arms around her father's waist.

Tears flowed as she hugged her sobbing mother.

Rosa, being an only child, huddled with her father and mother in one big hug.

"As soon as I save enough money," she said, "I'll buy a ticket to come home for a visit. I promise."

The bus driver, tired and impatient, honked the horn and motioned for his two passengers to end their farewells. The girls climbed aboard and found a window seat next to the platform where their loved ones stood with long faces.

As the bus pulled away from the station, Anna looked through the dusty window to see Father waving his tattered white handkerchief. Mother was blowing her kisses, with tears streaming down her face, and Maria was bawling.

Anna managed to get the window opened wide enough to wedge her upper body through so she could frantically wave to her family as she memorized their faces.

"I love you! We'll be back soon!" She waved until they disappeared in a trail of dust.

As the bus rumbled along the washed-out roads, the girls' spirits improved, and they began to joke and giggle about the new lives they envisioned. Then, gloom returned as they thought more about all they had left behind. They leaned on each other for support.

These alternating spells of high hopes and deep sadness continued the entire trip. At least they knew that, no matter what, they had each other. Their families had always been together, and the girls were sisters in their hearts, if not by blood.

As the ride continued, more people climbed aboard, packing the bus beyond its legal capacity. People were even standing in the aisle, trying to keep their footing as the bus rocked back and forth. Body odor saturated the hot, stifling air.

Anna and Rosa encouraged each other, but the farther they traveled, the more anxious and nauseous they became.

An intense wave of fear rolled over Anna. She wrapped her arms around herself, trying desperately to calm her shaking body and conceal the tears. She turned to her friend, gasping for breath.

"I...I can't breathe. I can't breathe."

"It's okay, Anna. You're gonna be okay. There's enough air for everybody. Let's trade seats. Then, when we talk, you'll be looking out the window and not at the other people. Here, let me fan you with my diary."

"Rosa..." Anna still gasped for breath, "...I-I wish I were back home in my little room, lying on my bed."

# CHAPTER 3

## COSTA RICA—END OF THE LINE

IT WAS WELL AFTER DARK when Anna and Rosa finally arrived at the bus station in San Jose. Looking out the bus window, they saw a Latino man standing under the dim light of a pole lamp. Over his head, he held a cardboard sign with both their names written on it in bold black letters.

Her hand trembling, Rosa grabbed Anna's as they stepped off the bus and inched toward the stranger. Despite trying to conceal it, Rosa's face showed fear and anxiety. Anna, on the other hand, managed to disguise her worries. She approached the man with all the confidence she could muster.

"I'm Anna, and this is Rosa. Who are you?"

The man forced a grin that flashed a gold upper cuspid.

"I am Jose. You will not forget my name."

He pointed to a shiny black pickup truck and directed the girls to follow him. They had never seen anything like it. The only trucks they ever knew were old, beat-up ones used to transport coffee beans.

The girls climbed inside, wondering if this man might be their new boss. If so, maybe one day they would become rich just like him. Their case of nerves abated a bit, and slight smiles crept across their faces.

Jose remained silent, but the truck's luxurious leather was intoxicating. Rosa and Anna settled in, propped snugly against each other. In the silence, they dozed off from time to time, headed to what was supposed to be their new home.

After an hour or so, Jose turned the truck off the road in front of a beautiful hotel with modern signs and lights. The girls were excited to think that this was where they would live and work. But the man didn't stop there. Instead, he drove around back and rolled to a stop in front of a dingy white, single-story concrete block building. Overhead hung a lopsided old sign with missing lights. It read, *Bar & Motel.*

"Get out," Jose said.

Wide-eyed, Rosa and Anna stole a glance at each other in disbelief before they got out and followed the man. He unlocked and pushed open the squeaky motel door. Reluctantly, the girls entered a musty, dark lobby. Neither of them had ever set foot in a bar or motel, but their instincts told them something was wrong—very wrong. This place was not what they had expected. There must be some kind of mistake!

Trembling, they tried to hold each other up.

Jose slammed the door behind them and flicked on an overhead light.

"Give me your passports." He held out his hand. "I'm going to put them up for safekeeping."

The girls could not understand why this man would want to keep *anything* that belonged to them—especially their newly acquired passports.

"Sir," Anna said, her voice trembling. "We...we will not be able to go back home to see our parents without passports. *We* need to keep them. They are *ours*."

Jose bellowed with laughter. "Is that right? Well, there's something you two need to know. *This* is your new home, and *you* are my new girls. From now on, *everything* you have is mine."

Everything. Everything. That word, and the sinister way he said it, would ring in their ears for a long, long time.

# CHAPTER 4

## PASSPORTS CONFISCATED

JOSE PROCEEDED TO SEARCH THE GIRLS' BAGS and confiscate their passports.

"Follow me. I'll take you to your new rooms."

Jose then took his unwilling guests down a back hallway, opened the door to Room 117, and motioned for Rosa to go in. When Anna tried to follow her, he grabbed her arm and yanked her back.

"You two will not be staying together."

The girls hadn't spoken since they got into the truck back at the bus station, but their eyes said more than words could ever express. They realized they needed each other more now than ever before.

Again, Anna dared to speak up. This time, out of pure desperation.

"Please, please, let us stay together."

He snapped, "You will *not* be staying in the same room."

With that, he slammed the door and secured it with a padlock.

Anna kept looking back over her shoulder as Jose shoved her forward down the hall to Room 120. He opened the door and pushed her into the room like he had Rosa, but with even more force.

"You seem to be very high-spirited." He flashed his gold

tooth. "But that will only get you into trouble here. I'll be back soon to take you both to the dining room. After that, you will return to your *separate* rooms."

Jose backed out of the room, padlocked the door, and laughed as he walked down the long, deserted hall.

As promised, he returned in a few minutes to take Anna and Rosa to get something to eat.

The concrete dining room, painted dismal gray, was poorly lit and had no windows. Except for a dozen metal tables with chairs, the room was bare and smelled of garbage. It was now late, and the girls were the only people present.

Jose pointed to a table near the entry, so Anna and Rosa took a seat across from each other. Immediately, someone from the kitchen served them beans and rice—the typical Costa Rican meal. The girls were weak from a lack of food and water, but they were too heartsick to eat. So they just moved the food around their plates, afraid to even lift their heads and look around.

"Girls, girls...what? Don't you like my food? You know, it hurts my feelings when my guests don't like my food. But no worries. You will learn to love it. You will see that you need the energy to work."

After they forced down a few bites of food, Jose took them back to their rooms. Rosa paused before entering her room. She looked at Anna with tired, sad eyes and mouthed, *I love you.*

Anna yearned to comfort her dear friend, but she couldn't.

# CHAPTER 5

## FIRST NIGHT

JOSE WALKED ANNA DOWN THE HALLWAY and returned her to Room 120.

"Breakfast is served at six o'clock sharp. A guard will come to get you. Make sure you're ready on time."

Jose stood in the doorway, glaring at Anna. After a minute or so, he pulled the door closed and padlocked it.

*A guard? Why would I need a guard to come and get me?*

Anna turned to survey the room again. It was about ten-by-ten feet, constructed of bare cinderblock walls and a concrete floor. In the corner was a little restroom with a shower, sink, and toilet. Straight in front of her was a single bed with a side table and a small lamp. The wall beside the bed had a small window covered with ragged, dark-brown curtains.

When Anna pulled back the curtains, the sight of bars on the window shocked her.

*This place is some sort of prison! What have we done? What's going to happen to us?*

Exhausted, she collapsed on the old metal bed, topped with squeaky springs and a worn-out mattress.

Anna tried to look on the bright side. She was happy to have running water. Back home, she never had access to indoor plumbing. But at this point, the security of her tiny Nicaraguan home was better than any place on earth. Running water could not compare to Father's love and Mother's comforting voice. And Rosa, who was now a few feet down the hall, might just as well be hundreds of miles away. Oh, how she yearned to go to Rosa so they could comfort each other.

It was late when Anna turned off the little bedside lamp, but sleep would not come. Tears rolled down her cheeks and soaked into the pillow. She desperately wanted to go home.

An hour passed before she pulled the sheet up to her chin and closed her eyes. That's when she heard the padlock rattle and click open. The doorknob squeaked slightly, and the door swung wide open.

Anna's heart raced as she turned her head toward the door. From the backlight of the hall, she saw the dark form of a man standing in the doorway. Looked like the same form she had seen waiting for her and Rosa at the bus stop.

He took a few steps forward and stood beside the bed. With his gaze fixed on her, he stared for a minute, breathing heavily. A sinister grin spread across his face, and she saw the flash of his gold tooth again.

"Take your clothes off...all of them," Jose said.

Anna gasped. "Please, please, sir. Please let me stay dressed. Pleeease."

Jose remained silent as he tore off Anna's clothes. She struggled against his brute strength, kicking and screaming.

"Stop! Stop! You're hurting me. Get off me. Get off! Don't hold me down. I can't breathe. I can't breathe!"

Jose slapped her across the face. "Shut up! If you don't shut up and lie still, it's going to hurt a lot worse."

Gasping for breath and shaking in fear, Anna stopped struggling and endured the pain. When her captor finished, he simply redressed, slapped her on her backside as a gesture of his pleasure, and left the room.

Anna lay on the bed in a fetal position, shivering and bleeding from the trauma. Jose had taken something he didn't deserve, something no one could replace—her innocence and purity.

Deep despair overcame her.

*Rosa! Oh no! Did Jose assault her, too? Seems like he was in my room forever. Did he go to her room after he left me? Could he assault both of us in one night?*

Anna jumped out of bed and tried to open the door, but Jose had secured it with the padlock. She rushed to the window and tried to push the bars out, but they wouldn't budge. There was no way to escape her prison to check on dear Rosa.

Completely drained, Anna slumped to the floor and curled into a ball. Her dreams of a new life were shattered, replaced with shame and terror.

At the first hint of daylight, the persistent crowing of a rooster in the distance awakened Anna. Physically sore and emotionally spent, she dragged herself out of bed. After bathing again and again, she put on the clean clothes her mother had washed and packed for her. The familiar scent of laundry soap brought comforting thoughts of home and courage. Somehow, she and Rosa were going to get out of there and go back home.

# CHAPTER 6

## DAY TWO

IT WAS STILL EARLY MORNING when someone removed the padlock on Anna's door. Her heart pounded with fear at the thought that it was Jose returning to assault her again.

The door swung open, and a heavyset guard stood in the doorway. He reminded her of Goliath, the giant King David killed when he was a shepherd boy. So from then on, she thought of him by that name.

"It's time for breakfast," he grunted. "Follow me."

Anna wanted to see Rosa, so she jumped up and followed him. When they arrived at the dining room, she paused in the doorway to survey dozens of faces, looking for Rosa. Her heart sank when she realized her friend was not there.

*Where could she possibly be? Maybe she's late. Maybe we're eating on different shifts.*

Trying to encourage herself, she kept conjuring up excuses as to why Rosa wasn't there. But the thought that Jose had possibly gone to Rosa's room during the night to violate her friend tormented Anna's mind again.

"Sir, can you tell me where the girl in Room 117 is this morning?" she asked Goliath. "We got here late last night, and I would like to see her. Her name is Rosa. Would you know where she is?"

"I don't know of any such person."

"Oh please, sir. You must know who she is. Please tell me where she is."

"I told you already," he growled. "I don't know any such person."

Even though Anna was probably half this guard's size, she stretched herself upward to appear menacing.

"Sir!" she yelled. "I *demand* to see Jose. Someone better tell me what you've done with Rosa!"

The guard got down in Anna's face and snorted.

"If you know what's good for you, you'll be quiet and never speak to anyone here in that tone."

"Please, please help us." Anna dropped to her knees and begged. "I don't care what you do to me. Just tell me what you have done with Rosa."

He grabbed Anna by her shoulders and stood her up.

"Your friend is gone," he whispered. "Jose took her to another place on the other side of town. That's all I know. Now, if you care an ounce about your life, you better sit down and shut up."

Anna cared nothing about her life. She began to scream and cry, causing everyone to stop eating and stare at the commotion.

"If you hope to live long enough to see your friend again," Goliath said, "you better shut your big mouth!"

The guard let out a string of words that Anna had rarely heard. Her father never allowed foul language around his family, and she could only imagine what he would do to this man if he were here. But her biggest concern was not for herself. She now feared that she might never see Rosa again.

Anna turned and took a seat at the table where she and Rosa sat the night before. She chose that seat because it brought a sense of comfort.

Jose entered the dining room and sat without saying a word to anyone. The sight of him made her sick. She couldn't eat the dry cereal and toast, so he came over to her table.

"Eat every bit of your food, my dear." Jose sneered down on her. "I told you already. You will need energy for work."

"Where have you taken Rosa?"

"I don't know anything about a person named Rosa."

Anna jumped up and shouted, "You are a liar!"

He unfastened his belt buckle and whipped out the thick leather strap. With repeated thrashings, he blistered the entire backside of Anna's body. Crouching in pain from the stings, she put up her arms to shield her face. She lay limp on the floor, quivering in pain when he finally exhausted himself. Jose cracked the belt one last time in the air as though he were punctuating his actions with an exclamation point. He then ordered her to get up and eat her breakfast.

Somehow, Anna managed to drag herself back to the table and into the chair. The pain that racked her body did not compare to her heartache at the thought of never seeing Rosa again.

Piece by piece, she ate the dry cereal. Each bite of food transformed her feeling of sadness into hatred down deep in her soul—something she would never have thought possible.

# CHAPTER 7

## THE NEW UNIFORM

After breakfast, Jose took Anna back to Room 120, where she discovered new clothes laid out on the bed. There were three skimpy red dresses, a pair of sequined red high heels, and a pair of strappy black high heels. In addition, there was a generous amount of makeup, perfume, and cheap jewelry.

"Whose stuff is this?" Anna said. "What is it doing in my room?"

"This *stuff* is your new clothes. Think of it as your new uniform for your new job."

"What is my new job? You promised Rosa and me good jobs with good pay. Now, I don't even know where Rosa is, or what my job is supposed to be."

"You are about to find out, my dear." He smirked. "Now put on something that fits, and doll yourself up with makeup and perfume."

As soon as he left, Anna tried on the super revealing red dresses, which were not her style. And the high heels were so tall that she found it impossible to balance herself. Every time she tried to walk, her ankles turned over, casting her to the floor.

She finally tried walking with one shoe on and one shoe off. By alternating this procedure, she eventually managed to walk with both shoes on at the same time. No one would ever mistake her wobble for swagger.

Anna had always wanted fashionable clothing, but these outfits were not those of her dreams, and did not represent the person she was. Instead, they represented the person Jose was forcing her to become.

She looked at herself in the half-glazed mirror and saw a new Anna—an Anna her parents would have never approved. The image of someone even she hated.

A sudden wave of nausea swept over Anna. The sight of herself in those hideous clothes made her sick on her stomach, so she rushed to lie down before she threw up. After about thirty minutes, she calmed down and managed to fall asleep. When she awakened, she vowed never again to look into that mirror.

Jose returned later to take Anna to meet the other girls who would train her for her new job. He took her down the hall to a room where a few chairs lined the wall. Several girls, who were also all dolled up, were standing around talking.

"Girls, come. I want you to meet Anna, the new maid. I want you to teach her a few tricks of the trade." Jose snickered. "I'll be back in a few hours. Do a good job. I'm expecting big profits from this one."

*Maid? I thought Jose offered Rosa and me jobs working in an office.*

Anna had never been inside a hotel or motel to know what type of work maids did, but it was evident that this work would be a lot harder than she'd expected. Dressed the way she was, Anna hoped she wouldn't be on her feet all day.

Jose introduced Anna to the four girls. They were about her age, but they looked tired and worn out. They were kind to her at first, but after Jose left, they began to tease and laugh at her naivete and lack of sex appeal. One by one, each girl took her turn, prancing around the room in exaggerated movements to demonstrate her sensuality. They taunted Anna, telling her to *strut her stuff.*

Shy and embarrassed, Anna shook her head and refused. One of the girls stepped up and began pulling the neckline of Anna's dress down over the shoulders.

"Come on, girl. You've got to show off your goods. You're young, curvy in all the right places, and very well-endowed."

"Yeah," another girl said. "You'll make a lot of money if you ever learn to walk."

They all burst into laughter, making jokes about Anna's modesty.

The oldest girl said, "Look, let's get busy. We've got to teach this girl how to walk and talk and entertain the clients. We've got a lot to do before Jose comes back."

The girls became more serious about teaching Anna her new role. And they warned that if she didn't conform, Jose would make sure she would regret it.

Anna was so sore from her earlier beating that she could hardly bear the touch of clothes on her back, and she sure didn't want another one. When the girls noticed her bruises, they showed her sympathy and began to befriend her.

One of the girls said, "Look, kid, you can't fight what's going on here. You won't survive unless you conform."

Anna didn't understand what was going on there, but she did want to survive. So she tried hard to act like the girls, even though she was sore and humiliated.

After a while, she started asking them personal questions while they trained her.

"How long have you girls lived here?"

Their answers varied, as some had been there since they were fifteen years old, while others could not remember any other way of life. One girl had no recollection of her parents at all. Another girl said she wished she could forget her parents.

"How often does Jose bring in new girls?" Anna said.

"He brings new girls in when he knows many tourists are coming to town," replied the oldest girl. "Sportfishing seasons are one of those times. One is coming up soon, so men from around the world will come to catch marlin and sailfish."

"Yeah, a lot of these men want personal entertainment on their vacations," said another girl.

"How many more will he bring in?" Anna said.

"As many as he can get."

# CHAPTER 8

## JOSE'S DISAPPROVAL

"ANNA, LET ME TELL YOU SOMETHING," Jose said when he returned after the first training session. "First, you must learn to smile and be happy with your employment. Think about it. I have taken you out of the coffee bean fields, where you worked in the boiling-hot sun while being eaten by mosquitoes all day. Now, I have given you a private suite with three meals a day. And I've given you beautiful clothes to wear. And this is the way you repay me? You're nothing but an ingrate!"

Though anger raged inside Anna, she stood silently before him. What he had *given* to her could in no way compare to what he had *taken* from her.

Jose continued, "Second, you look like an escort, but you still don't act like one. I've tried to train you, but you're not getting it. You've got to loosen up. But don't worry, sweetie. I have something that will help you loosen up."

He went to his office and came back with a pill, and demanded that Anna take it.

"Please, Jose," she begged. "I promised I'll do better. Give me another chance. I just need to practice. I will go to my room and practice. Please, just give me a little more time."

Jose forced his will upon her again. Shortly, her anxiety and guilt faded, replaced with a warm, euphoric sensation. It was the first time she'd taken drugs, and it was something she would always regret.

Again that evening, Jose forced Anna to take her *medication*, as he called it. Afterward, he ushered her from the rundown motel out back to the lovely new hotel that she and Rosa had seen when they first arrived. In the lobby of that hotel, Anna met her first client. Jose proudly introduced her as *the maid for the day*. At that moment, she realized her new job was that of enslavement—she was nothing more than a sex slave.

*I don't know where you are, dear Rosa, but I'm so glad you're not here. I couldn't bear to see you suffer this imprisonment and cruelty. I hope and pray that you have made your way back home, and that one day we'll be back in the coffee bean fields, working with our families. Wherever you are, I miss you.*

That day, the day Anna serviced her first client, was the day something about her changed. Her subconscious began to exude a defense mechanism to protect her emotions, as an oyster protects itself from an irritant that gets into its shell. Her life became less and less like the real Anna. More and more, she became an actress playing a role. The girls finally accepted her, but she never considered herself as one of them. She was just following rules, obeying what Jose told her to do, trying to stay alive.

The following years of enslavement molded Anna into a new person, someone even she didn't know. Her need for drugs and alcohol grew as her shame continued to increase. The hopes of ever seeing her family and Rosa faded. She believed that she would remain imprisoned for the rest of her life, known only as *the maid*. She had not found one person who was a real friend, so she continued to withdraw from everyone, even from herself. It was the only way she could cope with the things she endured.

As sex slaves, Jose's girls never knew what the clients would do to them. The clients often raped, sodomized, or slapped them around. Sometimes, clients forced them into relationships with multiple sexual partners, or even married couples.

Forced abortions were common. Every day, Anna looked forward to getting her drugs or alcohol to numb herself from feeling anything.

As so often is the case when you think things can't get any worse...they do. After almost ten years of enslavement, one evening around midnight, a commotion outside Anna's window awakened her. Out of curiosity, she got up and peeped out the barred window that overlooked the backside of the motel. Four cars had pulled up, and the drivers had left the motors running. Anna could not believe her eyes. A group of men were pulling children out of the cars. Even out of the trunks! Altogether, she counted sixteen children: four boys and twelve girls. They looked younger than Anna was when she arrived.

*What in the world is Jose doing with these young children? I know it's about time for the sport fishermen season to begin, but he has never brought children into the hotel to service clients.*

Anna cried out to God for the first time in years.

"Dear God, wherever you are, please help these children."

She continued to watch the scene unfold. Her heart ached as she saw the children crying and clinging to each other. Jose ordered them to be quiet and to stop crying. Anna desperately wanted to comfort them, just as her mother had comforted her as a child.

After all these years, Anna began to care about someone other than herself. Perhaps something of her true self was still alive. She had a deep desire to meet these children and hear the stories of how they had ended up at this horrible place.

# CHAPTER 9

## MEET ISABELLA

THIS DAY WAS LIKE MOST SUNNY FLORIDIAN DAYS, but it was unusual in the sense that Frank, Isabella's papa, bustled about the apartment full of excitement. Even though the child was only six years old, she would never forget that day. Frank was never happy, but this day he whistled as he went about his business.

He pulled out his old brown suitcase from the attic and dusted it off.

"Isabella, today is your lucky day!" he said, with a big grin and chirpy tone.

Frank bent down and looked her squarely in the eyes.

"Today, you're going on your first airplane flight. You're going on a vacation to see your mama in Nicaragua. Also, you're going to meet other children at a special summer camp."

*What! I'm going to fly on an airplane! Why does he want to send me to visit Mama? And what is a summer camp, anyway?*

Isabella's mama had left her papa when she was four years old, so memories of her were vague. She did remember that her mama spoke Spanish and English, and that she was from that place called Nicaragua. Both of her parents were bilingual, so Isabella was as well. Whenever she asked her papa anything about her mama, he would never say a word.

Isabella also had memories of her parents arguing, and

they did that a lot because both of them drank a lot. They were always broke and in need of some kind of fix. Then one day, her mama left home. Frank never explained why. All Isabella knew was that one morning, when she got up, her mama was gone.

Isabella loved her papa. At least he didn't take off and leave her. He only left her alone in their tiny apartment sometimes. Or he left her to play with other children on the sidewalk.

The child was now shocked and confused about her papa's sudden interest in her. And she wasn't sure she ever wanted to see her mama again. One thing she *was* sure about, though—she did not want to fly on an airplane all alone.

"Papa, do I have to go? I don't want to go. I don't want to leave you."

"Yes, Isabella, you *have* to go."

"But Papa—"

"That's enough, Isabella. You're going, and that's the end of it."

Frank gathered up the few clothes his daughter had and tossed them into the suitcase, assuring her that he would buy her pretty new outfits when she returned. Most of her clothes were too little, so she was happy with that idea.

While Isabella dreamed of new clothes, Frank opened one of the few cans of food left on the shelf and warmed it up for her. She was eating slowly, maybe because she was sick of eating pintos. Or maybe because she was still upset about leaving home. But for whatever reason, Frank became agitated. He raised his voice and began yelling, telling Isabella that she must hurry before she missed her ride to the airport.

The little apartment's atmosphere was never happy, but gloom and doom rolled in like a dense, heavy fog. As soon as Isabella forced down the last bit of food, someone knocked at the door. Frank jumped up and hurried to answer it. Standing before them was a short Latino man with a straight face and piercing eyes. He looked Isabella up and down in silence.

"My name is Javier," he said in a heavy Spanish accent. "I've come to take a little girl to the airport." He reached out and grabbed the suitcase that was sitting by the door.

Isabella burst into tears and rushed to hide behind her papa, clinging to his shirttail.

"Papa, *pleeease* don't make me leave. I don't want to go. I don't want to see Mama or go to a camp. I'm afraid of flying, and I-I'm afraid of this man. Oh please, please let me stay home."

Frank turned around and put a heavy hand on her shoulder.

In a voice she'd learned to fear, he said, "Isabella, stop this! I've worked hard to give you this opportunity. You better not mess this up."

*Why hadn't Papa told me before now that I was going away? Now I won't have time to tell my friends goodbye. They will wonder what happened to me.*

Frank gave Isabella a little shove toward the door and told her again to get going, or she would miss her flight.

"Wait, I've got to get something." She reached for the backpack that Valery, her best friend, had given her.

Inside were her most valuable belongings.

Isabella had no choice. She had to follow this stranger out the door. But tears streamed down her face as she continued to beg to stay home. Outside, Frank bent down, hugged Isabella, and told her to be a good girl. He then opened the door of Javier's old blue Cadillac and helped her get in. Out of the corner of her eye, Isabella saw Javier hand her papa a white envelope.

When Papa looked inside, Javier laughed and said in Spanish, "Don't worry, mister. It's all there."

As the car pulled away from the curb, Isabella saw her best friend playing on the sidewalk. Valery began to wave, and Isabella waved back frantically with tears still flowing down her face. The two friends stared at each other in disbelief.

*Who is this man, and where is he taking Isabella? She would never go anywhere without telling me first.*

Javier sped off, squealing his tires, but Valery ran after them to see where they were going. She hoped to catch up with them at the stop sign, but Javier was driving too fast. Isabella bawled as she looked back and caught one final glimpse of her friend.

"You better calm down and stop that crying." Javier jerked Isabella back around. "I will not have you showing to anyone that you are afraid or upset. Do you understand?"

Isabella tried with all her might to stop crying, but she couldn't. Her heart was pounding as though it would explode.

Trying to calm down, she reached into her backpack and retrieved a picture someone had taken of her and Valery playing at the local park. It was all she had to comfort herself. She tried to imagine that she was on a trip with Valery. With that thought in mind, she held onto the picture. She didn't quite know who she would miss the most—her papa or her friend.

# CHAPTER 10

## TIME TO FLY

JAVIER AND ISABELLA ARRIVED SAFELY at the airport, but the mass confusion brought on by jet engines, honking horns, and passengers scrambling about made the child even more upset.

"I'm going to park the car, and then we'll go inside to board the plane," Javier said. "If anyone asks, you are to tell them that I am your papa. Tell them we are going to visit your mama in Nicaragua."

"I don't want to go. Please, please take me back. Please!"

"Listen to me." Javier glared down at her. "If you do not follow my instructions, I will hurt you. And then I'll go back and kill your papa. Do you understand me?"

How *could* a child of her age understand? She had little comprehension of the danger she was in or what she should do to get out of the situation. She knew this was a mean man, but she thought she had to do what this adult told her to do.

Javier got Isabella's suitcase out of the trunk of the car, along with his bag. She carried her backpack and held onto the picture of Valery, pretending she was not alone. They walked through the automatic doors and headed to the airline counter, where a female attendant took their tickets and asked to see their passports.

Javier reached in his bag and handed over two passports. Isabella didn't know what the little book was, but she did wonder how this stranger had that thing with her picture in it.

Next, the lady asked Javier if Isabella was his daughter.

"Yes. Yes, this is my precious one and only child. Some people say she looks like her mother, but I think she looks just like me. Don't you think so?"

The lady smiled politely. "Yes, I can see the resemblance. Where is her mother?"

"She has to work. This is just a short trip so the child can visit my parents."

The attendant questioned the relationship no further because Isabella had brown eyes, dark hair, and olive skin, just like Javier. Isabella desperately wanted to tell the attendant that Javier was lying, but she was afraid to say anything because she believed, without a doubt, that this man would go back and kill her papa if she did not obey.

"Sweetie, give the lady your backpack." Javier looked down at Isabella.

She obeyed without saying a word. The attendant examined the backpack and asked Isabella if she wanted to check it in or carry it on board. Isabella looked at Javier to gain approval.

"Yes, you may keep it with you." Javier smiled and spoke in a kind voice.

But Isabella knew better, so she thanked him and walked away.

After they went through security, Isabella had an urgent need to go to the restroom. Her stomach was all in knots. She quietly asked Javier if she could go. He looked at her suspiciously and asked if she *really* needed to go.

"Yes," she replied.

"Well, you better make it quick. I'll be right outside the door. And do not talk to anyone. Do you understand?"

"Yes, I understand."

Isabella hurried into the restroom and looked around for a way to escape from Javier. There was no other exit door. Then she thought she could tell some lady in the restroom that the man she was with was not really her papa. Maybe they could tell the police.

She kept looking to see which lady might help her, but then wondered if any of them would even believe her.

*Even if I do get away from this mean man, he's going to go back and kill Papa! He might even kill Valery! What can I do!*

# CHAPTER 11

## A NICE LADY

ISABELLA STOOD JUST INSIDE THE RESTROOM DOOR, paralyzed with indecision. In a few minutes, a neatly dressed lady passed in front of her, headed toward the sink to wash her hands.

"Hello, dear. I hope you are doing well today." The lady adjusted her graying hair pulled back in a neat bun.

Isabella couldn't help but stare at her. She was wearing a floral dress tied with a sash, and her purse and shoes matched the blue in her dress. The thing that held Isabella spellbound, though, was her eyes. They twinkled and smiled like nobody she had ever seen.

Isabella thought this lady might be someone who would help her. But even in a normal situation, she was too timid to speak to a stranger.

*I'm too scared to just walk up to someone and tell them that a mean man has taken me and threatened to kill Papa. They can see that I'm here all alone. No one will believe me.*

As Isabella continued to hesitate, something inside nudged her forward. She slowly approached the lady, fully intending to plead for help. But all she could do was to stare up at her kind face.

The lady looked down at her. "Dear, are you okay? Are you lost?"

Isabella's mind whirled, trying to come up with the words to say. Finally, she snapped back to reality.

*How long have I been in here? Does Javier think that I'm up to something? I've got to go. This lady is so nice, she would never even believe that something bad is going on.*

Isabella turned to walk away. But again, something caused her to stop. She turned back and looked at the lady.

"I'm okay. Thank you. "I like your necklace."

The lady looked puzzled, as though she didn't believe her. But then, with a beautiful smile, the lady thanked her for the compliment.

*This lady is so nice. And she has a happy face. It would be wonderful to have someone like her for my mama.*

As soon as the lady left, Isabella could not restrain herself. She broke down and cried and cried, until she remembered Javier was still waiting for her. She hurried to use the restroom, washed her face and hands, then left.

Javier was standing next to the door, seething in anger. "What were you doing in there so long. And why were you crying? I told you not to show any emotion. What were you doing?"

"I-I'm sorry. I had a terrible bellyache."

She could tell he didn't believe her, but he couldn't do anything to her with people all around. Instead, he grabbed her upper arm and shoved her along in front of him until they came to some scary moving stairs. As soon as they stepped off the stairs at the next level, they saw lots of police officers. Some were walking around, while others stood against the wall with their gazes searching back and forth. Isabella thought they must be looking for something.

Then she noticed the lady from the restroom was talking to one of the officers.

Javier and Isabella continued walking until they got to the gate where they would board their plane. They sat down to wait. In a few minutes, the nice lady came over and sat in the seat beside Isabella. At first she acted like she didn't know Isabella.

But then she started talking.

"Hello, dear. How old are you? Is this your first time flying?"

Isabella looked at Javier to see if he had noticed that the lady was talking to her.

"She just turned six years old, and this is her first time flying," he replied. "We are going down to join her mama in Nicaragua, and enjoy a short vacation."

The lady continued to chat away. Isabella could tell Javier was getting mad with the woman's conversation, but he didn't say anything. Finally, the lady patted Isabella on the arm, telling them that she hoped they would have a good time on their vacation. She then said she was going to the restroom, and invited Isabella to go with her if she needed to.

"No. She doesn't need to go to the restroom," Javier said. "She's already been, and she won't need to go again for a long time."

As soon as the lady left, the officer she had talked with earlier came over and started asking questions. Javier seemed nervous now. First, the officer asked to see their passports. He examined them and asked if Isabella was his daughter. Javier convinced him that she was.

Next, the officer asked where they were going. Javier told him they were going to Nicaragua for a short vacation. The officer looked at Javier suspiciously and asked why the girl's mother was not with them. Javier told the officer that she had to cancel her flight at the last minute because her father had gotten sick.

Isabella recognized that the story Javier told the officer was not the same thing he told the lady who had checked their luggage. She hoped the officer would talk with that lady and discover he was lying.

Finally, the officer asked Javier if he knew why Isabella was crying in the restroom earlier.

Isabella met Javier's glare. She knew she was in trouble, and thoughts of what he might do petrified her.

"Sir, I-I was crying because I was sick on my belly. I'm afraid to fly."

The whole time the officer talked with Javier and Isabella, the lady stood at a distance, observing them with the same look of confusion that Valery had when she saw Isabella leave home. The lady must have told the officer that she had seen Isabella in the restroom and heard her crying. Or maybe she had noticed Javier's mean attitude toward her. Somehow this lady knew something wasn't right, and she must have reported it.

There was a great deal Isabella didn't understand about the events of that day. But deep down, she believed this nice lady truly cared about her. That thought brought some comfort.

# CHAPTER 12

## SURPRISE IN NICARAGUA

To Isabella's relief, Javier didn't speak a word to her about the officer questioning him. And he seemed surprised that Isabella had spoken up for him.

"It's about time you start behaving. You'll learn that life will be easier if you do what I tell you to do."

The announcement finally came over the speaker, saying it was time for them to board the plane. Javier ushered Isabella on board, putting her next to a window where no one could see or speak to her.

"You better keep on behaving," he whispered in her ear. "Accidents happen in the air all the time."

Isabella knew Javier was still angry with her for crying in the restroom. Even if he didn't take it out on her now, she wondered what he would do to her once they landed in Nicaragua.

*Is he still going to take me to the summer camp? What's at this camp, anyway?*

The idea came to her that maybe her mama would be at the camp.

*Maybe Mama paid for this trip. Maybe the envelope Javier gave to Papa was money from her to have me come visit only for the summer. That means I will go back home and be with Valery!*

The plane gained speed down the runway during takeoff, and the events of that long, sad day played in Isabella's mind. It was evening now, and as she looked out the window, she could see the lights of Miami below. It seemed like she was looking down on the stars against a deep blue sky. Any other time, she would have gazed with her usual vivid imagination. But right then, all she wanted was to be back down there. Back in the projects with Papa and Valery.

The cabin lights were off, and Isabella hoped Javier couldn't see the hot tears washing her cheeks.

Finally, she fell asleep, overcome by exhaustion and emotions. She didn't know how long she had slept before Javier awakened her, saying the plane was making its descent into Managua, Nicaragua. When it came to a stop, Javier grabbed his things and instructed Isabella to carry her backpack.

Inside the airport, there was a line at customs, where they stood for a long time. The crowd of people and commotion made Isabella more nervous, so she stayed close by Javier's side. When it came to their turn to go through customs, the man at the desk spoke Spanish.

"How long are you going to be in the country?"

"Forever," Javier replied in a disgusted tone. "We are from Nicaragua, and we plan to stay here forever."

Javier didn't know Isabella knew Spanish, so he unknowingly let the truth slip. Isabella's heart fell to the pit of her stomach.

*Forever? What does he mean?*

Isabella couldn't believe her ears. Her weak knees started to buckle, and the room began to spin. She wanted to shout for someone to help her, but she knew no one would believe her. If the officers in Miami believed Javier, the officers in this place would for sure believe him.

Everyone around the airport was happy and laughing, but Isabella stood alone—betrayed and desperate.

*What did Papa do? I was supposed to go to a summer camp. He was going to buy me new clothes when I got back. Did he lie to me because I'm really going to live with Mama? Was he ever coming to get me? Would he know where to find me?*

Isabella asked Javier to please let her go to the restroom. He pointed to it and said she had better come right back out. She ran into the stall and began to vomit. She hadn't eaten since Javier came to get her, so her sickness was merely a case of sadness and desperation.

Before returning to Javier, Isabella reached into her backpack to look again at Valery's picture. She noticed something glittering at the bottom of it. It was the diamonds in the nice lady's beautiful cross necklace! Isabella gasped for breath and quickly looked over her shoulder to make sure no one was watching her.

*How did this get into my backpack? What if the lady reports it to the officers? What if she tells them that I stole it from her? I'm in big trouble if anyone finds this on me. What can I do with it now? What will Javier do to me if he finds out that I have it?*

Isabella tried to calm herself. She held the neckless close to her heart, thinking about the nice lady.

*She must have slipped the neckless into my backpack while she was sitting beside me at the airport. That lady really liked me. But I don't know why. And I don't know why she would give me something that must have cost a lot of money.*

A smile slowly spread across Isabella's face. This neckless was her first piece of jewelry, and it was very special.

She quickly put the prized possession back in her backpack and returned to Javier.

"You know that I'm angry with you for crying in the restroom last time," he said. "You better not show anyone again that you are scared. Do you understand?"

Isabella nodded as he shoved her suitcase at her and said it was her responsibility to take care of her stuff from now on. Even as tired as she was, that was okay. She knew the necklace would remain a secret if all her belongings stayed with her.

# CHAPTER 13

## SUMMER CAMP

JAVIER AND ISABELLA WALKED OUT OF THE AIRPORT and into the darkness. She had never been afraid of the dark before, but this darkness had a creepy, evil feel.

Javier set his bag down, leaned his shoulder against the wall, and lit up a cigarette.

"A bus with other children on it will come by soon," he said, in a cloud of smoke. "When you get on, take a seat, and make sure you don't speak to any of the children. Make sure you behave."

Just as he had said, in a few minutes, an old bus pulled up. The faces of a dozen or so unhappy children looked out the windows. Javier, on the other hand, grinned as he surveyed his inventory.

"Remember," he said, "take a seat and do not speak to anyone. Do you understand?"

Isabella nodded as she climbed aboard the bus. It lurched forward, pulled onto a highway, and entered the dismal night. After riding a long while, the bus made a sharp right turn that nearly pitched her out of her seat. They continued on that bumpy dirt road for another hour or so.

Isabella could see by the moon's light that everything looked completely different from the way Miami looked. There were no tall buildings or sidewalks. Now and then, she saw patched-up houses that were smaller than her tiny apartment back home. She noticed dogs running around the yards. These dogs look even skinnier than those in the projects where she lived.

Her doubts about this summer camp continued to grow.

The bus finally arrived at its destination. As soon as it rolled to a stop, two men stepped out of the night. They herded the children into a small wooden shack and told them to lie down on the floor and go to sleep. They gave the usual order not to talk, which they followed with the threat of punishment if the children spoke to each other. Then the men slammed the door and secured it with a lock.

The children found themselves crammed into a hot, dirty space lit only by the moonlight shining through two small, barred windows. They were like caged animals. The dogs Isabella had seen earlier roaming the streets were better off than they were. There was hardly room to turn around, but each child found a spot on the floor and curled up.

From glimpses of the other children in the dim lighting, Isabella guessed the youngest child was about five years old. And the oldest looked about eleven or twelve.

From all around her came the muffled sounds of children weeping. The men had not given them blankets or anything to sleep on, so Isabella decided to use her backpack as pillow. Besides, she didn't want anyone to take her most precious processions.

The other children must have been just as tired because everyone quickly settled in and fell asleep.

Morning came, and Javier, who had followed the bus in his truck, awakened the children with banging on the door.

He opened the door and yelled, "Everyone, get up and follow me in a single line to the kitchen."

Once there, he yelled at everyone again, telling them to remain quiet and come through the line to get their grub. Standing in the dining area were the same two men who had greeted the bus the night before. Both men wore guns on their hips while they watched everything that moved. No one had to tell the children not to speak or misbehave. The sight of men wearing guns petrified them.

*Why would a summer camp need guards? Why do they have guns? I'm not sure this really is a summer camp. If it is, it sure isn't a fun place.*

Isabella took her food, consisting of a single slice of hard, crusty bread and one boiled egg, and sat at the end of one of the long, rustic picnic tables. Javier told the children to eat everything on their plates because it would be a long time before they would eat again.

Although it had been almost twenty-four hours since she had eaten, the thought of food made Isabella sick. There was a lump in her throat from her sadness. She missed Papa and Valery. She missed her home, her few toys, and even the canned food she ate for supper nearly every day. In a weird way, she missed Mama, though she never really knew her.

# CHAPTER 14

## FROM NICARAGUA TO COSTA RICA

In her stupor, Isabella hadn't noticed that another girl had sat at the table next to her, until one of the men wearing a gun yelled at the girl to start eating. Afraid to look up, Isabella peeped out of the corner of her eye and saw that the girl looked even younger than her.

*I wonder where she came from and how she ended up here. She looks too young to go to summer camp. Maybe her papa sent her away also.*

The girl was whimpering. Isabella wanted to hug her and tell her that they would be okay, but how did she know they would be okay? She was also homesick and afraid of these people.

A few minutes later, a young boy who looked several years older than Isabella came over. Frowning, with a glare in his eyes, he slammed his plate on the table. It was obvious—he was ready to fight.

Isabella kept her head down and slipped farther down the bench to get away from him. His attitude was going to cause trouble, and she wanted no part of it.

One of the guards rushed over with his chest puffed out and his hand on his weapon.

"Do you have a problem with your food, boy? Or are you just a troublemaker?"

The boy spun around and spat in his face. As quick as a

viper's strike, the guard slammed him to the ground. He put his foot on the boy's neck and held him down.

"So you want to play rough, do you?" The guard bellowed with laughter. "Well, I'm up to it if you are."

He kicked the boy in the stomach, causing him to cough and gasp for breath. He then whipped out his blackjack and gave the boy multiple whacks all over his body. Writhing in pain, the boy begged him to stop.

The guard finally allowed the beaten boy to get up, but Isabella could see that he was still fuming, and she figured he would probably cause more trouble.

"Let this be a lesson!" the guard yelled to everyone as he stood with his hands on his hips. "There will be more of this kind of punishment if you continue to misbehave."

After breakfast, Javier told everyone that they had to work for their food. So the guards put the children back on the old bus and drove them out to a coffee bean field. Isabella had never seen coffee beans, nor even thought about where they came from. It didn't take her long to learn, though, that coffee comes from a lot of hard work.

Some men at the field gave the children sacks and instructed them on how to pick the red, ripe beans. Nobody picked many beans, even though they worked hard, dragging their sacks through the field. After working hours in the hot sun, Isabella's back ached, and her fingers bled from pricks. Most of all, she was sad. She still missed Papa, and she wished she was back home playing on the sidewalk with Valery.

About midafternoon, the guards loaded everyone onto the bus to take them back to camp. As soon as they arrived, Javier said they would be leaving again in an hour. He told them to line up in a row so he could clean them up. A guard hosed them off with cold water while they still wore their sweaty clothes, and then took them back to the shack. Isabella put on her favorite T-shirt and shorts. The dry clothes brought warmth to her shivering body.

It was strange that none of the children ever spoke a word

or even made eye contact. She didn't understand it at the time, but years later, she would realize that all the humiliating, harsh treatment was part of the process of dehumanizing them to the point where they would offer no resistance to anything their superiors told them to do.

As promised, within the hour, four cars pulled up to get the children. The guards then divided the children into four groups. There wasn't enough room inside each car to hold four children, plus additional guards, so Javier said two children would have to ride in the trunk of each vehicle. When the guard put the angry ten-year-old boy in Isabella's group, she bristled.

*I can't believe this. That boy is going to get our group in trouble. I'm afraid to even be around him.*

Javier began loading the children into cars. He approached Isabella's group and ordered her to get into the trunk. She didn't know if he chose her because she was one of the smallest children, or if he did so out of spite because she had given him trouble at the airport. Whatever reason Javier had, she did not move. Riding in the trunk of a car was the only thing she could not endure.

"I said get in the trunk!" Javier yelled in her face.

She couldn't. Fear froze her feet to the ground.

Javier picked her up and tossed her forward. Her petite body hit the metal on the inside of the trunk, and she began to wail. She couldn't believe he was forcing her to ride in a smoldering hot trunk! But that wasn't even the worst of it. He then picked up the mean boy and threw him in on top of her.

The boy started hitting and kicking back. Javier punched him in the face. The defeated boy then lay motionless beside Isabella, and Javier slammed the trunk closed. In the stifling darkness, the odor of sweat and urine reeked from the boy's battered body. For the first time, Isabella thought about his pain instead of hers.

The cars pulled out of camp, and they traveled the rest of that day and into the night. With every bump in the road, the strong-willed boy groaned in pain. Isabella reached out to him in the darkness, trying to comfort him. His only response was to pull away from her.

"I know you're hurting," she whispered, "but I want you to know I'm your friend."

Finally, they arrived. But where, Isabella had no idea.

The car jerked to a stop. Doors opened and quietly closed. The guards opened the trunks and ordered the children to climb out and keep quiet.

Isabella got out and straightened her stiff, aching body. Looking around, she saw the other children were crying and clinging to each other. Strangely, though they had never even spoken to each other, she felt their sadness.

# CHAPTER 15

## ROOM 125

In a matter of minutes, another group of guards appeared out of the dark. They hustled all the children into what looked like the back of an apartment building.

Packed into a dark room, everyone stood silently, except for intermittent sniffles and shuffling feet.

An overhead light flicked on, causing them to blink and rub their eyes.

When their eyes adjusted to the brightness, they saw a short man with a muscular build and a rugged appearance. His dark-brown hair was pulled back in a scrubby little ponytail on the nape of his neck. A big grin flashed a dazzling gold tooth, but his scarred face and squinty eyes made him look meaner than anyone Isabella had ever seen.

"Welcome, my children," he said in a harsh tone. "My name is Jose, and you will be my guest here at the motel. While you are here, you will stay in your same groups, protected by one of my guards. Now, I'm sure you're ready to get some rest, so these men will show you to your rooms."

*Rest.* That word sounded like music to their little ears. They were so tired, their legs could barely hold them up.

Jose assigned one guard to each group, and the gigantic guard assigned to Isabella's group instructed them to follow him down the hall to Room 125.

The small, musty room had two beds, with a restroom in the corner. The guard told each person where they would be sleeping. He assigned Isabella to sleep with the boy who had ridden with her in the trunk.

*What! That's not fair. I had to ride with this boy in the trunk, and now I have to sleep beside him. How can I do that when he wouldn't even let me touch him?*

But then she noticed how badly bruised and swollen the boy's face and eyes were. Her compassion for him overcame her embarrassment and anger.

"You have fifteen minutes for everyone to freshen up, get into your assigned beds, and go to sleep. And don't forget, do not speak to each other. I'll be sleeping right outside the door, and I'll hear if you speak even one word."

The guard then took a padlock out of his pocket and dangled it in the air.

With a hardy laugh, he said, "Look, you cannot escape. There are bars on the window, and we always keep the door locked. If you try to get away, you will wish you were dead."

As soon as everyone was in their bed, the guard turned off the little lamp. In the dark, Isabella could still see that he watched them for what seemed a long time, before he backed out the door and locked them in. In a few minutes, she heard him pull a bed in front of the door and lie down. A few snorts later, he was sound asleep. The other children also fell asleep quickly. Or maybe they were like her, just lying quietly, afraid to move.

Isabella wanted to go to sleep, but thoughts of everything that had happened since her papa sent her away kept her awake. Questions filled her head, and sadness filled her heart. The only good thing that had happened was when she met the nice lady at the airport.

She thought of the necklace the lady had secretly given to her. Isabella reached out for her backpack, which now lay beside her bed. She quietly scrambled around the bottom of it, searching to make sure her prized possession was still there—but she couldn't find it!

Frantically, she kept searching until her fingers finally touched it, and the face of the lady came to mind. With that bit of comfort, the child fell into a deep sleep.

# CHAPTER 16

## CARMEN'S STORY

JACO IS A BEAUTIFUL COASTAL TOWN on the west side of Costa Rica. It's a favorite tourist destination known for its luxurious gated resorts—much unlike the poor little villages that exist for miles around. Carmen should know because she grew up in one of those villages. And by the time she was twelve years old, she had already experienced more hardship than most women living in developed countries experience in a lifetime.

Carmen's family consisted of her mother, a three-year-old half-brother, and a two-year-old half-sister. Sofia, her mother, had many different male clients, which accounted for her brother and sister. Carmen's father, whoever he was, never lived with them or contributed to the family in any way. So as a single parent, Sofia did whatever she had to do to keep the family of four alive.

One day, when Carmen was five years old, her mother took her aside and looked into her eyes with determination and sadness.

"Carmen, do you remember Mister Torres?"

"Yeesss! He's that rich old man who lives down the road."

"That's right. Well, Mister Torres stopped by the other day and said that if you visited him, he would send you home with a bag of groceries and a cell phone."

"He wants *me* to come to get the groceries and cell phone?"

"That's right," Sofia said. "He wants *you* to come. I can't go because I have to stay here and take care of your brother and sister."

"I don't want to go see him," Carmen replied. "Why can't he bring it to us?"

"I know you are shy, Carmen, but we need to take advantage of this nice man's friendship. We have already set a date for your visit."

Because everyone who visited Mr. Torres was well-to-do, Sofia told Carmen that she needed to make a good impression. So the day of the visit, Sofia had her daughter take a bath and spray herself with the perfume Sofia used only on special occasions. Carmen then put on her favorite outfit—a black cotton knit top and a skirt with three layers of red ruffles trimmed in black.

Next, Sofia fixed her daughter's long, chestnut-brown hair in curls and pulled them back on one side with a red hair comb. Carmen was so excited because her mother allowed her to wear her most expensive perfume and use one of her dazzling hair combs. She may have only been five, but in her mind, she felt like she was fifteen!

"Oh, Mother," Carmen pranced around, "I never, ever looked so beautiful. Thank you. Thank you! This visit *is* a special occasion."

When the time came for Carmen to leave, her mother hugged her tight. Sofia swallowed hard, took a deep breath, and told Carmen to obey everything Mr. Torres asked her to do because she needed to help the family. At the time, Carmen had no idea what her mother was saying. All she understood was that this rich neighbor would be giving her groceries, and even a cell phone to bring back to her family.

*How can it be hard to obey a man who is so kind? He's nicer than the men who visit Mother.*

As Carmen skipped down the road on her way to visit Mr. Torres, she was now so excited that she could hardly wait to get there. Most people in their village were poor, and their homes were not big like the one Mr. Torres lived in. The village homes had two rooms with an outside restroom because there was no inside plumbing. Some places had chickens running around the yard. And sometimes you would see a skinny dog roaming around, looking for food scraps.

*Today, we will not be hungry like these dogs. There will be enough food for all of us.*

# CHAPTER 17

## THE RICH NEIGHBOR

CARMEN CONTINUED HER JOURNEY until she finally arrived at Mr. Torres's spacious two-story house. Would he hand her the groceries and cell phone at the door? Or would he invite her inside? She was hoping to at least get a peep inside to see how rich people lived. Mother had told her that on the day Mr. Torres visited to say he would help their family. He even wore a diamond ring! Someone as rich as him just *had* to be kind.

Though Carmen had wanted to see the inside of the house, she now stood motionless, gazing up at such a big house. Her excitement had subsided, and she had butterflies in her stomach.

*I'm scared. What if I do something wrong? Will he still help us if he doesn't like me? Mom said I need to be good and do everything he says.*

Isabella stepped up on the porch and knocked so softly that even she could barely hear it. Instantly, Mr. Torres opened the door. He bowed from the waist at the sight of her, made a broad swoop with his left arm, and invited her in. Much to Carmen's surprise, he was dressed casually, with his shirttail hanging outside of his trousers. All other times she had seen him, he dressed like a businessman, wearing a shirt and tie. She felt more at ease since he dressed like a regular person.

"Welcome, my dear." He smiled and nodded. "Please, come

to the kitchen. I have some food prepared for you. I do hope you are hungry."

Of course she was hungry. She couldn't remember a time when she wasn't hungry. But she didn't want to appear like she was starving.

"Yes, sir." She blinked her dark, almost-black, eyes. "I would love to eat."

Mr. Torres had all sorts of food: ham, fresh vegetables, and even dessert. Carmen ate until she thought she could never eat again. She was so glad this nice man was her friend. Even more, she wished he were her father.

Mr. Torres put the dishes away and said, "Are you sleepy, my dear? After I eat a big meal, I often want to take a little nap."

"Oh no." She shook her head. "No, I'm not sleepy. I don't take naps now that I'm five years old."

"I know you're a big girl now, but you need to rest before you walk back home on such a full stomach."

Carmen remembered that her mother had told her to obey him and do what he said, so Carmen agreed to take a nap.

Mr. Torres led her to a room with a big, fluffy bed. Never in her life had she seen such a beautiful bedroom. It was like a dream. Carmen couldn't believe that she had just eaten the best meal of her life, and now she had the chance to sleep on the most beautiful bed she had ever seen.

Feeling like a queen, she climbed up onto the bed and snuggled into the covers falling asleep almost instantly.

Carmen's sweet dreams turned into a nightmare when she awakened to the touch of Mr. Torres stroking her hair and face. She lay perfectly still, pretending to be asleep.

*What's he doing? This doesn't seem right.*

Carmen's heart began to pound. She wanted to jump up and run away, but she kept hearing her mother's voice telling her to obey Mr. Torres. She continued to lie still, but he didn't go away. Instead, he climbed onto the bed and snuggled close behind her.

"Don't worry," he whispered, as he breathed heavily in her ear. "I won't hurt you. I just want to lie close to you." He reached over her. "Here, let me hold your hand."

He took her hand and put it on his naked body.

*Why's he not wearing clothes? I-I'm scared. I want to go home.*

"Would you please take off your clothes? We'll both be more comfortable then. Here, I'll help you."

Carmen did not respond, so Mr. Torres undressed her. And after he satisfied himself, he told her to go into the bathroom and clean up. She obeyed, but the water from fancy indoor plumbing did not wash away the sick feeling she had inside. Carmen was only five years old, and she was scared, hurting, and confused about what had just happened. She couldn't believe what this man had done to her. Yes, the family needed food, but hunger never hurt as bad as she felt.

# CHAPTER 18

## LIFE AFTER MR. TORRES

As promised, Mr. Torres gave Carmen a cell phone and loaded her down with all the groceries her five-year-old frame could lug home. But no longer was she that happy, carefree little girl skipping along the road. Every step she took was painful, inside and out. That was the last day of her childhood, and the first day of her sexual enslavement.

Once a week, as the eldest child, it was Carmen's duty to visit Mr. Torres. She needed to help support the family, and he faithfully loaded her arms with groceries to carry back home.

This relationship with Mr. Torres lasted until she was nine years old, when he suddenly became seriously ill and died. She never knew any details about what had happened to him. She only knew that he would no longer be supplying food to their family.

Sofia was distraught over the loss of Mr. Torres's provisions because she had given birth to another child. Also, she had become older, and her services were less in demand.

After Mr. Torres died, Sofia had no choice. She had to send Carmen out to market herself. She had grown up a lot in the last four years, but going out into the community to work would be hard, for Carmen was still a child.

A whole year passed, and Carmen was still unable to bring in a steady income to buy food for the family. There were just too many young girls working locally. So she began to listen to other girls in the neighborhood who traveled to Jaco to work. They told Carmen that rich men from around the world visited the area when the fishing was good. They also said that these men loved Latino women, especially the young ones. Going there to work sounded like a good possibility for her to find work. So one evening, Carmen approached her mother with the idea.

"Mother, it's getting harder every week for me to find work, and things here at home are getting more desperate every day. Some of the local girls have told me about the work they've found in Jaco, and they said I could go with them. What do you think?"

Sofia considered the idea because they did need the income, but she was concerned about Carmen's safety. Nightlife in a resort area with foreigners from all over the world would present dangers, and her daughter knew nothing about these situations. Jaco was not like their small village, where everyone knew and looked after everyone else.

"Carmen, you are too young to go to Jaco. Stay here to work until you get a little older. Everyone knows us here, so you'll be safe as long as you work locally."

Carmen knew her mother loved her, and that she might be right. But Carmen also knew they needed food. So she defied her mother and asked the girls if she could ride with them to Jaco one night. They agreed to let her come along, but she would have to wait for her turn to connect with a client. And they could not guarantee that she would find work. Nevertheless, Carmen jumped in the back seat and rode to Jaco, happy to have the opportunity.

Many tourists were in town at the time because it was sportfishing season. As night approached, the girls took their position standing outside an upscale hotel. One by one, they took a turn, asking men if they wanted an escort. Carmen watched them closely while she waited for her turn. When that time came, she imitated their method of solicitation and got her first tourist client.

# CHAPTER 19

## CARMEN'S JACO CLIENT

CARMEN, WHO LOOKED AND ACTED MUCH OLDER than her eleven years, liked her first client. He was a a rich young American. Best of all, he treated her like the beautiful lady she had become. From the moment they met, Andrew and Carmen enjoyed being together. He loved her spunky attitude, and she loved the way he made her laugh.

Andrew first took Carmen to a nice restaurant for dinner, and afterward he escorted her around the luxurious hotel where he was staying. She had never seen any place so spectacular. The possibility of her staying at such a hotel was beyond her imagination. Andrew seemed proud to escort her, arm in arm, through the gorgeous facility. He made her feel like she was classy enough to belong in such a place.

Later, Andrew took Carmen to his room, where they talked for hours. She had learned the more elegant ways of life during the years she had spent with Mr. Torres. The man had tutored her in a lot of areas. And taking advantage of his library, she had become an avid reader.

Reading was her only pleasure—the only escape from real life. So it wasn't surprising that Andrew would consider Carmen as someone as mature as himself, though no other client had ever made her feel that way.

Her heart fluttered, and blood danced through her veins. The two of them had such a good time that evening that Andrew approached her with an idea the next morning.

"Carmen, I know that you rode to Jaco with your girlfriends, and your mother is expecting you to come home, but would you consider spending the entire week with me while I'm on break here in Jaco?"

*Me? He wants to spend his entire vacation with me! I'm so happy. I would do that, even if he didn't pay me.*

"Yes, yes, of course," she replied. "But I'll have to find the girls I rode with to let them know. They will tell Mother that I'm fine, and that I'll be home at the end of the week."

That week was the most fabulous week of Carmen's life. Andrew had been exceptionally kind to her. Although he never mentioned additional pay, he gave her $500—the most anyone had ever paid her. She had enough money to catch the bus home, and it would go a long way in helping her family. Still, she was sad to see Andrew leave. Maybe it was her hopeful imagination, but Andrew appeared to be a bit downhearted as well.

His last words to her were: "I'll look you up next time I'm in town," which he punctuated with a wink and quick smile.

The bus ride home was an emotional one for Carmen. Already, she missed Andrew. So much so that she was beginning to wish she hadn't met him at all. Tears rolled down her cheeks. Her young heart had never loved before, and she was pretty sure she would never love anyone else. Most of all, she was mad at herself for feeling that way about someone she doubted she would ever see again.

*Mother was right. I should not have gone to Jaco. There's more than one way someone can hurt a girl. I'm so stupid to have fallen in love with the first American I met. Andrew probably knows how I feel, and he's probably laughing about the whole thing.*

When Carmen returned home, her mother was excited to see her, but she was also full of questions. Sofia wanted to know everything that had happened. She mainly wanted to know if this Andrew client had abused her in any way. Carmen assured her mother that she had never been in an abusive situation.

There was something, though, that Carmen did not tell her mother. She was concerned about whether she had been careful enough about using protection. That was something her mother always insisted on to safeguard against sexual diseases.

Sofia would be even more upset with her about not using protection if she knew that her daughter had started her period several months before going to Jaco. And it was possible that she could have gotten pregnant.

Carmen realized the last thing they needed was another mouth to feed. If this had happened with any other client, she would have been in a state of high anxiety. But she overcame the apprehension because she loved Andrew, even though she had only known him for a week.

# CHAPTER 20

## LIFE BACK AT HOME

TWO MONTHS PASSED, and Carmen began to suspect that she was pregnant. Without mentioning anything to her mother, she went to the local pharmacy to buy a pregnancy test. The lady behind the counter welcomed her and offered her help.

*Oh no! This lady knows our family, and I don't want her to know that I might be pregnant.*

"You know my mom, Sofia Moreno. Well, she wanted me to pick up a pregnancy test for her. She's watching my brothers and sister, and could not leave them."

"Sure, wait one moment. I'll be right back."

In a few minutes, the lady returned.

"Here are two tests. Tell your mother that the test results are not always accurate, so she needs to take the test twice to make sure."

Carmen was so anxious to take the test that she almost forgot to pay the lady. She didn't want her mother to know what she was doing, so she went to a friend's house. This older girl had tested herself many times and knew what to do.

The tests confirmed her suspicion—she was going to have a baby! Her mind whirled with the prospects of it.

*What will I do with a baby? How will I ever be able to face Mother with this news? How will we possibly feed all these children if I can't work?*

Carmen burst out in tears. She loved Andrew and desired to have his baby. Still, all the problems this pregnancy presented caused her emotions to swing back and forth. She just didn't know what to do. The local clinic offered free abortion services, but she had a deep desire in her to keep this baby.

Carmen not only loved Andrew, but she also loved having a part of him with her. Her heart ached with the desire to share the news with him, but he never told her exactly where he lived. He had promised, though, that he would find her the next time he came for sportfishing. Still, she knew there was only the slightest chance that she would ever see him again.

The one person Carmen dreaded to share the news with was her mother. Carmen knew she would be upset because they could not afford another child. Not to mention, there would be less income due to her pregnancy. Carmen also feared that she would be less desirable when she went back to work, whether in an upscale tourist resort or locally, in the village.

Several weeks went by before Sofia said, "Carmen, you seem distracted lately. Are you okay?"

"I guess so. I hope so."

"What are you talking about. Are you pregnant?"

Carmen said nothing. She just sat with her head hung down, staring at the floor.

"Answer me, Carmen. Are you pregnant?"

"Yes, I'm pregnant. I'm going to have Andrew's baby. I did a pregnancy test...twice."

"Oh, Carmen. I warned you about the need for protection. Do you realize the danger here? You are way too young to carry a baby, much less deliver it. And I'm not sure what'll happen if anyone finds out you're going to have a baby. You can't keep it, Carmen. You can't. I won't allow it."

Carmen's mother had little education, but it didn't take much knowledge to recognize the dangers of an eleven-year-old girl being pregnant.

Sofia paced with mounting anxiety as she recalled a midwife sharing all the complications that almost killed another eleven-year-old. In desperation, she pulled a chair up and sat in front of her daughter.

"Carmen, I want to explain why it would be so dangerous for you to keep this baby. First, a girl eleven years old would have great physical difficulty in carrying a child to term. The placenta takes nutrients from the young mother, who is still growing herself. Calcium would leach from her, which would greatly strain her overall health. Second, the pelvis of a young girl may not be wide enough for delivery. Or she may not have enough strength to push the baby through the birth canal. The likelihood of either the mother, the baby, or even both dying is very high."

Carmen sat sobbing, shaking her head. "I can do this. I am healthy, and I'm a big girl for my age. I will do whatever it takes to carry this baby to full term and deliver it safely. I just know I can do this. I *know* I can!"

"Carmen, you cannot have this baby! I can't lose you. I know what we have to do."

Carmen continued to sob, pleading with her mother to please let her have Andrew's baby. She knew that her mother hated abortion, so she argued the points of pro-life.

"Mother, I'm sure the clinic would give me a free abortion if I wanted one, but I want to keep our baby, not destroy it. Why should that innocent baby pay the price for what I did?"

"Carmen, you don't know what you're saying. You are merely a child yourself. Don't you understand what I've just explained about the danger you are facing? You could die! Adding to the danger is that you will have to have this baby at home. There will be no doctors around if there are complications. Even if both of you survive, how will we feed this child? Carmen, I hate even saying this, but you have to abort this child."

Carmen became so upset that she bolted out of the house. Sofia stood at the door, pleading for her to come back.

In a few minutes, she turned and looked at her other children. The sight of them reminded her of how excited she had been while she was pregnant with Carmen. Sofia recalled how people had tried to talk her into an abortion, and how thankful she was that she had not listened to them. She also thought about all the ways she had put her firstborn in the worst possible situations. The guilt was overwhelming, and she desperately wanted Carmen to know how much she loved her and only wanted the best for her.

Late that evening, Carmen silently opened the door and crept inside. Sofia was sitting in the dark, waiting for her. Still furious, Carmen strode past her.

Sofia whispered, "Carmen, I will let you have the baby. But we must keep it concealed as much as possible."

Carmen rushed to her mother and gave her a tight hug.

"Thank you, Mother. I so want to have this baby. We will be fine. I promise."

The following seven months were tough as the family lived sparingly. They were thankful for the extra money Carmen had made that week in Jaco because she lost work during her pregnancy. But contrary to what Sofia feared, Carmen's pregnancy went better than expected. And Carmen forgot all the difficulty and anxiety that existed during the pregnancy when the most marvelous thing she had ever experienced happened—she gave birth to a baby girl.

The baby didn't have the typical Latino dark hair and eyes. Instead, she looked more like Andrew, with his blue eyes and blond curly hair. So Carmen named the baby Andrea, after her father.

Now, the question was, how could she make a better life for her daughter? She loved her baby more than anyone or anything in the world, and she would not allow Andrea to live her life selling her body to survive.

The day Andrea turned three months old, Carmen said, "Mother, I need to go back to Jaco to work. I can earn more in one night working there than I can working a whole week here. Andrea is old enough now for you to take care of her overnight. I don't want to leave her one second, but we have to eat."

"No! I will not allow it, Carmen. There are reports that drug cartels have moved into some tourist areas. These places are not as safe as they were even one year ago."

"I have to go. I want a better life for my child."

# CHAPTER 21

## CARMEN'S SURPRISE

CARMEN FELT SHE HAD NO CHOICE about whether she should go outside her village to find work. Again rejecting her mother's advice, she went to Jaco the next evening with the girls she had traveled with before. To her dismay, there weren't as many Americans in town because it wasn't sportfishing season, so business was slow. Only one girl at a time took her turn strutting in front of the luxury hotel where they usually had good luck.

Hours passed before it was finally Carmen's turn to solicit a man. She still hoped to make big bucks before the night was over. All alone now, she walked the street for over an hour, before a late-model car pulled up. The driver's side window rolled down, and a man whistled at her. To her disappointment, she saw he was Costa Rican and not American. Deep inside, she had hoped Andrew would return for her.

"You're a nice young chick." The man looked her over. "I'll pay you twice the normal amount for one night."

*Only double the regular price. Maybe I should wait for a better deal.*

"Make up your mind, chick. I can't wait all night."

Carmen agreed to the deal because it was late, and she knew she had to bring home some amount of money.

She stepped off the curb and got into the passenger seat. As soon as she slammed the door shut, the automatic lock engaged. Carmen heard something move, so she looked over her shoulder. In the back seat, a man was holding a gun. Carmen screamed to the top of her lungs as she beat on the window with her fists, trying to break out and somehow escape.

The car sped through the streets until it reached a deserted area on the outskirts of town, where it came to a screeching halt. The driver leaned over and took Carmen's face in his hand.

"Now aren't you a young one." He cackled. "You'll make us a lot of money."

Carmen kicked, scratched, and screamed, "Let me go! Let me out of here!"

Again, the man took her face and came so close that his nose touched hers. His breath reeked of cigar and liquor.

In a raspy voice, he snarled, "Shut your mouth, you little slut. Shut your mouth, or I'll slit your throat and leave your bloody body in the dust."

All Carmen could think of was her precious baby. She didn't care about herself, but she couldn't bear the thought of Andrea growing up without a mother. So she stopped resisting and got quiet. The two men bound her hands and legs with rope, and taped her mouth shut. They got on the road again and traveled for miles in the darkness. She couldn't tell where they were going, only that they had left the lights of Jaco far behind.

When the car finally stopped, it appeared they were at a campground of some kind. Two guards appeared out of nowhere. They removed all restraints and took her to a shack where children lay sleeping on the floor. She couldn't see well in the darkness, but the children looked to be of all different ages. The men ordered her to find a place to lie down and to keep her mouth shut.

As Carmen lay in the darkness, the reality of what had happened overwhelmed her. The men had kidnapped her and these other children, intending to sell them into sexual slavery. Most of all, she feared her mistake would cause her family to fall deeper into poverty.

Carmen knew her mother would try to find a way to take

care of Andrea, but at what cost? That cost could mean another sibling forced into sexual slavery.

Carmen had to find a way to get back home. She could not bear the thought of being away from her precious baby girl.

# CHAPTER 22

## CHILDREN OF THE NIGHT

ANNA AWAKENED from a restless night with little sleep.

The night before, Jose had hustled children into the back of the motel, under the shroud of darkness. The sound of them crying, and the pitiful look on their faces, had haunted her all night. She just couldn't believe such a thing was happening.

Jose was now getting involved in something more than his usual sadistic operations. He was trafficking young children for sex!

Still in bed, and unable to face the reality of what he was doing, Anna heard the rattle of the padlock, announcing the prospect of more trouble.

Jose barged into the room. "Get dressed and follow me. And be quick about it. You have work to do."

Anna hurried to change clothes, and followed Jose down the hall to Room 125, where he asked the guard standing by if the children were ready. With a nod, the guard opened the door, and Jose ushered Anna into the room. In front of her stood a young boy with two black eyes, a swollen lip, and bruises that seemed to cover his body. There were also two girls clinging together. The youngest girl, who appeared to be American and not more than six years old, stood with her head hanging down, scared to even look up. The other girl, who appeared to be Costa Rican and several years older, looked sad and desperate. Anna recognized them as some of the children Jose had smuggled into the back of the motel in the middle of the night.

"Who are these children?" she said. "What are they doing here?"

"That's none of your concern," he snapped. "You'll get all the details you need soon enough."

Anna's instinct was to reach down and wrap her arms around the children to calm their fears. But she knew she had to pretend as though she had no feelings for them at all.

*How can I help these petrified children? Especially the young boy? These injuries can't be from an accident. Obviously, someone has beaten him. What could a young child have possibly done to deserve such treatment? Wonder if he has serious injuries. How can I get him some pain medicine?*

"Anna, it's your job to look after these new residents." Jose gestured toward the children. "You know the rules around here. See to it that these newcomers obey them. Now, follow the guard to the dining room for breakfast."

Reluctantly, the children followed Anna and Goliath, the guard who was also assigned to watch over the *new residents*. He seated the four of them at a table. Anna and Isabella sat beside each other, while Carmen and Marcos sat opposite them. The other children sat at tables with the people in charge of their groups. Another guard stood at the entrance, watching all activity.

Up to this point, the children had sat quietly, fearing punishment. Anna was careful not to express any compassion toward them because she didn't want to be the cause of any further mistreatment. She could only glimpse into their eyes occasionally to express her concern.

After breakfast, Jose led them back to Anna's Room 120. To her surprise, the guards had set up three more small beds while they were at breakfast.

"The children will be staying with you, Anna. It's your responsibility to make them understand their new roles in life. First, these newcomers should understand that they will be entertaining guests at the motel. Second, they better obey everything we tell them to do without any resistance. Third, if they do not obey these instructions, I will punish them severely."

Jose looked at Anna over his nose for a minute, observing her reaction, and then abruptly turned to leave. He padlocked the door behind him.

Anna now had an intense craving for drugs, alcohol, or anything that would help her cope with the knowledge of what faced Jose's latest victims.

For several long minutes, Anna and the children stared blankly at each other in silence. She remembered how overwhelmed she was when she first got here. But what could she say or do? Somehow she had to help these innocent children understand the importance of Jose's words. But how could she tell them that they would never see their families again? They would never again play outside, go on trips, eat good food, make friends, or get an education. How could she tell them they were about to experience unimaginable pain and suffering? Adding further grief was the knowledge that Jose was forcing her to take part in this great evil.

"Come." Anna took a deep breath and forced a smile. "Let's sit here on my bed and talk. I would love to know all about you."

The girls complied, but the boy went to the room's farthest side, where he collapsed on one of the beds. Lying motionless with his face turned to the wall, he refused to interact at all. Anna feared he was in a state of physical and emotional shock.

"Whatever your name is," Anna said to him, "you have to believe that I don't like this place any more than you do. Please let me help you. I can put a cold washcloth on your head. It will make you feel better."

"No! Leave me alone. All of you, just leave me alone."

Anna's heart was conflicted because she did not want to get attached to these kids. She had finally become numb to her imprisonment and abuse. Year after year, layer after layer, she had developed a protective covering around her conscience, safeguarding against insanity. Now, Jose was forcing her to get involved in the trafficking of children. She was furious with him—and with God.

*It is just unbelievable, God, that you not only allowed these wicked men to destroy my life, but you have now allowed this to happen to these children. And I'm forced to train them in this. Why don't you just go ahead and take me? Please. I would rather die.*

# CHAPTER 23

## EVERYONE HAS A STORY

EVEN THOUGH IT WAS STILL EARLY in the day, Anna stretched out on her bed and turned her back to the children. She was tired from not sleeping the night before, and the last thing she wanted was to be in a situation that further complicated the sad state of her existence. Anna was praying and cursing under her breath at the same time.

*Whatever be the consequences, I will not be a part of this. I'm worth more to Jose alive than I am dead, and he knows that. He will have to get someone else to do his dirty work.*

As soon as Anna made this declaration, she heard sniffles coming from the youngest child. The sound was unbearable. At first, she put her hands over her ears to muffle the sound. She continued lying on her bed, self-absorbed in pity. But the louder the little girl cried, the more Anna's heart melted. Something within her started to come alive, and that spark of life grew with the child's every tear. Anna recalled her own childhood, and how her mother had consoled her when she cried.

*This little girl needs her mother.*

Anna also recalled what Jose had done to her on her first day in this place.

*I hope and pray Jose does not try to assault these children tonight. If he comes through that door tonight, he'll have to get past me first.*

That horrifying thought caused her to turn and look at the child. She had curled up in a ball on one of the beds, trying to hide under the sheet. Sympathy compelled Anna to go to her. When she sat on the edge of her bed, precious little eyes peeped up at her. They were so full of fear that Anna decided to try to talk with the children again.

"I guess it's a bad day for all of us. Can we start again? My name is Anna. Will you please tell me your names?"

The girls remained silent, and the boy continued to lie with his face to the wall. They still didn't trust her. And so far, she had given them no reason to feel otherwise.

Not knowing what else she could say, Anna lay down beside the little girl. The child pulled away at first, but Anna stayed there for a long while, and the little girl gradually relaxed and snuggled closer.

Anna looked down with a warm smile. "I've told you my name. Won't you please tell me yours?"

"Isabella. My name is Isabella," she whispered, with a deep sigh.

She curled up into Anna's arms, and in a few minutes, she looked up into her face.

"You kind of remind me of a nice lady I met at the airport."

Anna giggled. "I can assure you that I am also a nice lady. And I can most definitely assure you that I am *not* going to hurt anyone."

Isabella jumped up like fireworks had gone off in her head. Frantically, she looked around the room, and then teared up again.

"Can you help me get my backpack?" she said. "The guards took all my stuff when we got here, and they didn't give it back. I *have* to get my backpack. Please help me get it back. Please."

How could Anna explain to this child that she was in the same sad shape they were in, and that she had no power to make these people do anything?

She chose her words carefully, not wanting to say or do anything that would cause any distrust.

"These people are not my friends," she said. "They don't like me, and I can't make them do anything. But I promise I will do everything I can to make sure you get your backpack."

As the hours passed, Isabella began to open up to Anna. She started by sharing how her papa had told her she was going on vacation to see her mama, and to go to a summer camp. But instead, some man gave her papa money and took her away to this place. She told Anna about the nice lady at the airport who had slipped her cross necklace into her backpack. Then she told her how the lady had tried to tell the policeman at the airport of her trouble.

Now Anna understood why Isabella's backpack meant so much to her.

After a few minutes of silence, Isabella began to cry so hard that she had to gasp for breath. Anna hugged the child tighter as she continued her story.

"I miss Valery, my best friend. She watched as that mean man drove away with me. She even chased after his car. I know she loves me and wonders where I am. I wish...I wish so much that I could see her again."

Anna whispered in her ear, "Isabella, I understand how it hurts to lose your best friend. Jose took my best friend away. Now I don't know where she is, or if I'll ever see her again. We just have to keep believing that we will get out of here and get home again."

Anna continued to hold Isabella while the older girl sat on the side of her bed, listening intently as Isabella and Anna talked. Her head hung low with sorrow as she thought about what she had been through at Isabella's age.

"I know you are hurting," Anna told the older girl. "Would you like to share with us how you got to this place?"

The girl shook her head.

"Will you at least tell us your name?"

"My name is Carmen."

"Carmen, you must trust me when I tell you that I care about you. Please tell me your story."

Carmen whispered, "It started when my mother sold me to an older man when I was five years old. My pay that day was a bag of groceries and a cell phone in exchange for sex with him. That job lasted until he died four years later. After that, I found work doing everything I could to help feed the family. I don't blame Mother for sending me out to work. She did what she had to do. Anyway, I got pregnant last year, and now I have a baby girl back home. I know Mother loves me. She had to keep our family from starving. That was the same thing I was trying to do when some men kidnapped me and brought me here. I'll do anything to get back home to my baby."

Before Anna could respond to this girl's story, the boy jumped off his bed and erupted like a hot volcano.

"My name is Marcos. And the only thing you need to know is that I'm not like you. My parents would never have sold me or let me go. They are American missionaries working in this country, and I know they're looking for me right now. They know plenty of important people, and I'm going to get out of here. Just you wait, and you'll see. And I will fight anyone who tries to lay a hand on me. I'll die fighting, and you all will burn in Hell! Do you hear me? You'll burn in Hell!"

The two girls sat wide-eyed and motionless. But Anna understood Marcos's line of thinking. He had come from another part of the world, and had little understanding of their culture. He had only seen poverty and hunger, but he had never gone hungry himself.

Most of all, Marcos didn't understand that poor or underprivileged people still love each other. They are still close. Their families have the same feelings that other families have for each other. No person wants someone to rip them from the people they love. No person deserves to be in slavery—including sexual slavery.

"Marcos, thank you for telling us your name," Anna said. "But you must understand that, regardless of who we are, we're in this together. And if we're ever going to get out of this, we're going to have to work together."

She made no further efforts that day to probe into the lives of the children Jose had thrust upon her. It was enough that the four of them had to adjust to living together in such a small room.

Each of them was glad when the sun went down on their first, torturous day together.

# CHAPTER 24

## MARCOS LEARNS A LESSON

THE NEXT FEW DAYS PASSED SLOWLY as Anna's young guests became even more tired and distraught. They were still in no mood to talk, and she had no means to entertain them to make them feel any better.

Then, late one afternoon, the sound of someone removing the padlock from the door startled the occupants of Room 120. The children recoiled on their beds.

Jose barged into the room. "Anna, our guests have rested long enough. You will begin training them tomorrow for work. Do you understand what I mean?"

Yes, she knew what he meant. And he knew that she despised him more than ever for kidnapping the children. Loathing for him showed all over her face.

"Anna, don't forget who you are. You are *not* their mother. And remember...you are *not* so innocent and pure yourself. You're nothing but a whore! That's what you were born to be, and that's all you'll ever be. You should be grateful that you have me to look after you."

*How dare he call me a whore. I hate him! I was a virgin until the night he raped me. And he's the one who made me into what I have become.*

Jose's words pierced deep into her heart and soul. Maybe she didn't deserve to be a mother. But for once, after ten years of stone coldness, she had a desire for companionship with these children. Jose knew this, and he was playing mind games, trying to make the children doubt her innocence in all of this. Anna's chest heaved heavily as her clinched fists hung by her side. She knew she had to outwardly submit to him, so she forced herself to quietly turn away. The children looked at each other with confusion. As she feared, it appeared Jose had just shattered the little bit of trust she had gained. She realized that, at some point, she had to tell them her own story.

Jose left the room, and the guard entered and ordered everyone to go with him to the dining room for lunch. The girls got up from their beds, but Marcos refused to comply. Anna put her hand on his shoulder and begged him to get up and go with them peacefully.

"I don't want to eat," he snapped. "Just leave me alone. I promise you, all of you will be sorry you messed with me."

The guard bellowed with laughter. He stalked over to Marcos's bed and slammed him to the concrete floor. His head hit the corner of the bed and put a three-inch gash in his forehead. Blood flowed from the cut, dripping onto the floor.

Dazed, Marcos stumbled to his feet and got in line. Blood continued to trickle down the side of his face, so Anna put water on a cloth and washed his forehead. The guard started cursing and slapped her across the face. She staggered back and landed on her bed.

"You should know by now that pampering these kids will get you in real trouble. Now get up and get out of here."

As bad as that slap hurt, there was one consoling thought: at least the children saw that Anna wanted to protect them.

The girls ate a little better than they had at breakfast, and she thought it was because they had seen how she tried to help Marcos. As for Marcos, though, he still refused to eat. Anna began to worry about how long he could go without eating before he became sick.

The guard didn't appear to care whether the boy ate or not—or even if he lived. Anna was somewhat thankful for the guard's indifference. Otherwise, Marcos could have gotten into trouble again.

They only had a few minutes to eat before the guard ordered them to follow him back to their room. Once there, he opened the door and shoved everyone in. And in a tone that revealed he enjoyed having some bit of authority, the guard issued a warning.

"Don't you forget, Anna. I'm warning you. Train those kids good, or I'll be glad to break them in myself."

The children returned to their beds, but Anna still stood at the door with her arms and head hanging limp like a ragdoll. Questions flooded her mind.

*How am I supposed to train these children to be sex slaves? How can I ever explain this to such an innocent child as Isabella? How can I prepare them for the unspeakable things that are about to happen? Why would the God of my childhood allow me to end up here in the first place?*

# CHAPTER 25

## ANNA BREAKS THE BAD NEWS

Anna found herself in a place of despair. She couldn't help but think about her sexual entrapment, about the family she missed, and about Rosa, who had just disappeared. She doubted God would ever deliver her or the children.

"Anna, are you all right?" Carmen said. "Did your food make you sick?"

"No, no. I'm not sick." Anna tried to shake off the gloom that shrouded her whole being. "Would you and Isabella come and sit with me? There's something I need to explain."

The girls did as Anna asked, but Marcos continued to lie on the bed, face against the wall.

Giving the children the details about their duties was awkward and emotional, but she had to prepare them. Anna began by explaining that guests from all over the world would soon arrive, and these guests would hire them for fun and entertainment. Carmen, whose mother had sold her for sex at the age of five, understood what Anna was saying. Isabella, on the other hand, began to ask questions.

"What kind of fun do they want from us? What will we be playing?"

Anna hesitated, trying to find the words to explain.

"Well, Isabella, the fun they want is considered adult games. Umm...ahh...nothing like what you would normally want to play."

Isabella blurted out, "Oh, I would like to learn new games. I love playing games!"

Marcos jumped up and yelled, "I know the adult games you're talking about, and I will never let a pervert touch me. If they even try, they will pay for it. Who do they think they are, kidnapping me off my bike and smuggling me into this horrible place? You all are going to burn in Hell."

He screamed so loud that Anna feared the guards would come back and beat him again. She begged him to calm down, but he refused. He started throwing everything he could get his hands on. He didn't seem to care that he already had a swollen face, blackened eyes, and a slash across his head from all his previous encounters with the guards.

Sure enough, the guard heard the commotion and came to take care of it. The harrowing sound of the padlock opening brought dread to Anna's heart. The guard rushed in and snatched Marcos off his feet. He threw him over his shoulder as if he were a piece of dead meat, and walked out.

Anna knew what would happen. The guard would give Marcos real-life job training.

About an hour later, the guard brought Marcos back, shoved him into the room, and secured the padlock. Bowed over with pain, the boy stumbled to his bed and collapsed. His little body shook uncontrollably from the trauma.

"Oh, Marcos, I'm so sorry," Anna said.

She took the sheet from her bed and wrapped it around him. For the first time, he did not pull back at her efforts to comfort him. Nothing was left in him. The fight was gone.

The sight of Marcos terrified Isabella. She was so frightened she cowered in Carmen's arms, clinging to her.

There was no training the children that day. What could Anna say to prepare them for the savage abuse they would endure?

Fear gripped their hearts. They had seen enough to know that their lives would never be the same.

# CHAPTER 26

## THE SIGN OF THE CROSS

One of the guards came to Room 120 early the next morning with Isabella's suitcase, backpack, and some bags of clothing for each of the children. Marcos got shorts and T-shirts, while the girls got short skirts and halter tops. In another bag were toiletries such as shampoo, toothbrushes, toothpaste, tissue paper, and aspirin.

Anna was happy to see there was some medicine to relieve Marcos's aches and pains. She wanted to do something to heal his wounds and lift his spirit. The abuse he experienced from the guards had broken him, and he was now ashamed and withdrawn. He went to breakfast with the girls, but he only went through the motion of eating to appease the guard. When they returned to their room, he lay on his bed with his face turned to the wall, silent. Something in him had died.

"Would anybody like to hear my story about how I got in this place?" Anna said, thinking Marcos would be willing to talk if she shared her story.

The girls responded in chorus, "Yes!"

Marcos never acted interested in anything Anna had to say, but he couldn't help but hear her since they were in such close quarters. So she went ahead and invited the girls to come over and sit on her bed. They intently listened while Anna gave them the short version of how she and her best friend had come to

Jaco. They had hoped to find a better job than the one they had picking coffee beans, but Jose brought them to this horrible place instead. When Anna finished her story, a sorrowful expression appeared on Isabella's face.

"Anna, a kind lady talked to me the day I left home," she said. "It's too bad you didn't have a kind lady to talk to you."

She jumped up and retrieved her backpack. Her hands scrambled around inside until she brought forth the beautiful cross necklace. She proudly held it up for everyone to see, and spoke again about the kind lady at the airport who had given it to her.

"What does this mean?" she said. "It must be important because it looks like it cost a lot of money."

"It has something to do with Jesus," Carmen replied. "But I don't understand either."

Anna knew what the cross meant. She also knew she had to answer them, but she didn't want to. Her own heart wrestled under conviction because of her hatred of Jose—and rage toward God.

*Evangelizing these children is the last thing I should be doing. But they have a right to hear the gospel.*

In obedience to her conscience, Anna reached down and pulled out from under her mattress the Bible she had refused to read all these years. It had been so long-forgotten that the pages stuck together as she turned to John 3:16.

"For God so loved the world, that he gave his only begotten Son, that whosoever believeth in him should not perish, but have everlasting life."

She explained to her small audience what the missionaries had taught her family long ago. They had explained how everyone born into this world needs to have God forgive them for their sins and make things right with the one who created them. To get forgiveness, though, someone without sin had to pay that debt to God. But there was no sinless person on earth who could do that. So God sent Jesus, His own perfect Son, to Earth to die on the cross of Calvary to save us from our sins. All anyone has to do is confess their sins, ask for God's forgiveness, and put their trust and faith in Jesus.

"Will God forgive anybody?" Isabella said. "Even people like that mean guard, or Jose?"

Anna replied, "Yes, Isabella. There is no person so bad that God will not forgive them if they trust in Jesus. He was innocent and did not deserve to die, but he loved even his enemies enough to die in their place so they could have new life. That doesn't mean that a child of God won't have trouble in this life. But when anyone accepts Jesus as their Savior, it means they can have inner peace and joy in this life, and eternal life in Heaven when they die."

"Anna, do you think this lady with the kind face loved Jesus?" said Isabella. "I wonder if that's why she was so nice and tried to help me. Is this cross on her necklace like what Jesus died on?"

"Yes! Isabella, this cross is truly a sign that God has not forgotten us. We must never give up hope."

"I love Jesus." Isabella said. "And I want to wear my beautiful cross necklace."

"Sweetheart, I know you love your beautiful necklace. But I think you should keep it tucked away for now."

"Why? I never had anything so beautiful, and I can't wait to wear it?"

"It is beautiful," Anna said, "and that's exactly why it's best not to wear it in this place. Jose doesn't like Jesus, and he would take it away from you. Also, I'm quite sure it's made of real gold, and we know how much Jose likes gold."

"Yeah," Isabella said. "He's not going to make another gold tooth with my necklace."

# CHAPTER 27

## MARCOS DENOUNCES FAITH

"YOU DON'T KNOW WHAT YOU'RE TALKING ABOUT!" Marcos shouted, as he rose from his pretensions of being asleep.

He had been listening all the time Anna and Isabella were talking about Jesus.

"All that stuff about the Bible is nothing but garbage. There is no God. If there is, he sure doesn't care about any of us. And there is no Heaven or Hell. If there is, Hell is where we are right now. I've gone to church all my life. We were good people, but look at me now. If there was a God, and if he cared about me, I wouldn't be here. Can't you people see? Don't you get it? I'm not like you. I don't belong here. So just you shut up about Jesus. All of you, just shut up!"

Marcos lay back down and pulled the sheet over his head again. Isabella, Carmen, and Anna stared with wide eyes at the form of Marcos's body curled in a fetal position under the cover. The girls were confused, but Anna's heart convicted her. She had accused God the same way Marcos did. The difference between them was she had hidden her struggle with God. Marcos openly expressed his.

She said, "Marcos, I have experienced sexual abuse just about every day. Sometimes many times a day. I wanted to blame somebody. I didn't blame myself. I trusted God as a child, and I was a good girl who tried to do right. I couldn't blame Father or Mother. They unselfishly sent me to Costa Rica, thinking my life would be better here. They earnestly prayed about it. So I believed in my heart all those years that my abuse must be God's fault. The evil in this place caused me to doubt God, but Isabella has caused me to recall my faith as a child. I want to renew that faith and trust in God's care."

That confession brought peace to Anna, but she still had a long way to go to understand why bad stuff happens to good people. Even more so, she couldn't understand why the most innocent and precious people seem to suffer the most. But at that moment, compassion for Marcos gripped her heart. She wanted him to know that she understood his frustration.

"Marcos, you are absolutely right about one thing—you don't deserve this cruel treatment. No one does. But as bad as it is here, I've heard that some slaves are chained to the wall like a dog, beaten daily, and sometimes starved. Marcos, if you don't become more compliant, I'm afraid Jose might sell you off to one of those other places."

Marcos remained silent, but Anna thought she heard a sniffle from under the sheet.

Room 120 remained unusually quiet until later that evening, when Jose charged into the room and announced that clients from America would arrive the next day.

"Anna, you've had enough time to train our new guests. Are they ready?"

"As ready as they can be."

"They better be. And they better not complain about it." He noted their startled faces.

"Jose, please don't do this," Anna said. "Sell me a thousand times—but not them."

Jose slapped her again across the face, and stormed out the door.

That night, groans punctuated the stillness as the children tossed and turned in their sleep. Everyone needed rest, but rest had not come.

Anna was still lying awake at the first hint of morning light.

Trying to look on the bright side, she concluded that a night with no sleep was better than one filled with nightmares about the children's first day of work. Still, she couldn't believe the horrible day had dawned when Jose would prostitute children, especially the three who were in her care.

Before anyone else stirred, Anna gathered her clothes to prepare herself for the man who would choose her as his escort for the day. She stood in the shower for a long time. Water poured over her, but there was a sense of guilt that would not wash away. Anna would rather die than be a part of child prostitution, but she could do nothing to save these children from it.

Weeping, she turned off the water and fell to her knees. *Dear God, I have given the gospel to the children, but I know I have grown cold to the truth of it. Right now I surrender to you, asking for mercy and forgiveness for blaming you for the evil that is happening in this place. Please, please help us today.*

As Anna got ready, she reasoned with herself. She knew that a god who loved her enough to die for her would not afterward hurt her. No. All evil had to be the result of human choice, not God's will.

She remembered her mother telling her that God allows people to make their own choices. That he will not force people to do right. She couldn't understand why these innocent children had to suffer this abuse, but she knew she had to trust God to help them.

*Lord, the Bible says that faith as small as a mustard seed can do great things, like move mountains. With the little faith I have, I trust you to deliver us from these evil men. I must trust you. You are our only hope.*

With a renewed spirit, Anna awakened the children to get them ready. Oh, how she wished she were getting them ready for school, the place they should be going.

She gently placed her hand on Marcos's face, and softly asked him to awaken. He remained unresponsive, though Anna knew he was awake.

Next, she went to the girls and rubbed their backs to wake them. Isabella rolled over and again began asking questions about what they would be doing.

Anna took Isabella's little face in her hands. "I can't tell you what this day will bring, sweetheart. But do you remember the adult games I mentioned earlier?

"Yes." Isabella rubbed her eyes.

"Well, the men who will come today to play these games are a lot like Jose and his guards. They are men who want children and adults to do things that might hurt. But no matter what these people tell you to do, you must obey. But just remember, little one, God sees and cares. He's only a breath away, so don't hesitate to pray. Just remember that we'll be back together again tonight. Now, let's get dressed."

*Never, never would I have imagined that one day I would dress and put makeup on a child so someone could sexually exploit her. But this is what Jose has forced me to do. May God deliver these precious children.*

# CHAPTER 28

## CINDERELLA AT THE GRAND BALL

In Anna's mind, dressing Isabella for her first day as a child prostitute was unspeakable. Something she would not have done, even if it meant her death. But she feared what Jose would do to the children.

To make the situation as easy as possible, Anna suggested they play a game.

"Isabella, you said you loved to play games. So let's play a game of pretend. We'll pretend that you are Cinderella, and you are getting ready for the Grand Ball. First, we must shower and shampoo your hair."

As Anna dried and brushed Isabella's hair, they entered the world of make-believe. Carmen understood what they were doing, and she began playing along with them. Until then, Carmen's focus was all about getting back to her infant baby. But now that she saw Isabella's desperate situation, she joined the game to help Anna dress Isabella and apply her makeup.

When they had put on the final touches, they stepped back and oohed and aahed over her. Delighted with all the attention, Isabella continued to pretend she was a princess. Although she wore only a candy pink top and blue denim shorts, she giggled and began twirling around as if she were wearing an elegant princess gown.

It was now time for Carmen to get ready for her day of

work. As she passed by Marcos's bed on her way to the shower, she tapped him on the leg and told him he better get up before he got into more trouble.

Marcos threw back the sheet and shouted, "You just keep on playing games and mind your own business. Nobody's going to tell me what to do. They'll have to kill me first."

Carmen didn't want to make matters worse, so she just shrugged and headed to the shower. After she dressed, she twirled around the room like a ballerina.

"Look, Isabella, I'm also wearing a princess gown. Do you think there will be a prince at the ball for each of us?"

After they danced around the room for a while, Carmen saw that Anna had gone over to get Marcos up. So she continued to pretend she was going to the Grand Ball, trying to keep Isabella occupied. In the meantime, Marcos refused to get up, only making things worse for himself. Fearing the guards would beat him again, Anna encouraged him to be agreeable.

"Marcos, I'm sure God has a plan to help us. But until then, we can't lose hope. We *will* get out of here one day."

He crawled out of bed, grabbed his T-shirt and shorts, and headed for the shower. A wave of relief swept over Anna because the children were up and dressed before breakfast.

Five minutes later, the guard opened the door and called for them to come to the dining room. Isabella ran to Anna and grabbed her hand. Then she was too scared to move, so Carmen grabbed her other hand. Together, they followed the guard out the door, and Marcos reluctantly fell in line.

This morning, all the children and their supervisors were present, packing the dining room. In the ten years of her imprisonment, this was the first time Anna had seen everyone together. Before, Jose always had his sex slaves—*escorts*, he preferred to call them—eating in shifts to isolate them further and keep things under control. So the sight of all the escorts and the many children together at one time shocked Anna. She wanted to bow her head and pray, but she knew that would bring the wrath of the guards upon her.

The crowd also upset Isabella. She couldn't eat for looking at so many sad faces.

Anna leaned over and whispered in her ear, "Let's pretend that you are Cinderella at the ball, eating delicious food."

Isabella looked down at her plate and paused for a moment, then whispered back, "Yes, I am Cinderella, and I am hungry."

Even more concerning than Isabella not eating was Anna's fear that she might never see these children again after this meal. She couldn't believe how attached she had become to the three children assigned to her. Her heart had changed not only toward God, but toward others as well. The bitterness she had held for so long was melting away. She was finding something greater than herself.

Before anyone had time to finish eating, Jose came into the dining room and made an announcement.

"I want all of the new residents to get in line. The guards are going to take individual photos. Make sure you give a big smile in the picture so the clients can see how happy you are. And we want to show them what a good variety we have to offer them."

After the guards took pictures, Jose went over the rules they had to follow on their new jobs.

"First, you are not to talk to anyone except the person who requests you as their escort for the day. Second, you are to be happy and agreeable to everything your client asks. If you do not, the guards will severely punish you."

Jose paused to survey his audience. Staring back at him were faces of fear, girls of various ages—except for Marcos, the only boy.

Jose dismissed everyone, telling them to go back to their rooms until someone called them to the motel office.

# CHAPTER 29

## FIRST CLIENTS

AFTER JOSE FINISHED HIS SPEECH, the guard took Anna and her children back to Room 120 to wait. She didn't know how long the wait would be—minutes, hours, or even days. The anxiety she felt was not for herself, but the children.

As time ticked by, Carmen continued to entertain Isabella with fairytales, which they acted out before Anna. Marcos paid no attention to them. He just paced beside his bed, his face distorted with anxiety.

Hours passed before a guard came to the door. "The boss wants to see Carmen in the office. A client has requested her for the day."

Carmen got busy packing a few essentials in a travel bag. Holding back tears, she looked at Anna, and then back to Isabella. She wanted to cry, but she didn't want to upset the child.

During the last few days, Carmen had transformed from a victim to a caregiver. She desired to protect Isabella, just like she would want someone to protect her own baby. For Isabella's sake, she had to be brave.

*I wish I could help Carmen—to rescue her. But I can't.*

When Carmen left, Isabella continued to pretend, acting as though Carmen's departure was part of her fantasy.

"Anna," she called out, "Carmen's prince has come for her

already. Will you play with me until she comes back?"

Time continued to tick by as they waited, fearing the guard's return. Then, shortly after lunch, another guard unlocked the door and ordered Marcos to come with him.

"You all are crazy!" he shouted. "There's no way I'm walking out that door. You'll have to kill me first."

The guard punched Marcos in the stomach and dragged him out the door. Marcos kicked, clawed, and hollered. Jose ran from his office to see what was going on. One glance, and he knew what he had to do.

"The boy's not going to calm down unless he's drugged. Go to my office and get the stuff."

"Which one do you want?" the guard said. "Xanax, the happy pill, angel dust, or Versed?"

"You know I don't like using Versed unless I have to, but this is the only way to get this boy to do what anyone tells him to."

Jose grabbed Marcos, slammed him against the wall, and held him there by the throat.

"Look, kid, I'm finished with your defiance. You will do your job agreeably, or I will use methods I only use as a last resort. I would rather do this the clean way. But if you don't cooperate, I will do what you force me to do. Do you understand me?"

Marcos continued to struggle until the guard returned with a bottle of Versed and a syringe. At the sight of it, Marcos spat at Jose. Stone-faced, Jose injected him, and in a few minutes, Marcos became sedated and compliant with his new role.

The guard had unwittingly left the door to Room 120 open, and the whole scene unfolded right before Anna and Isabella's eyes. A frightful sight for both of them. But most of all, it broke Anna's heart to see Marcos injected with drugs. She felt like this was the first of what would be many times of Jose drugging the boy. He would never willingly give in to Jose's demands.

*I know where this is going to lead. Marcos is going to get addicted to drugs or alcohol. I first took drugs, and then became addicted to alcohol. God, help this boy.*

Time dragged by until, at last, the sun went down and the

room grew dim. Anna was glad the day was over, but her heart was sick with worry, wondering what had happened to Marcos. She was also worried about Carmen. Her client had requested her for the day, and the day was over.

Though Anna was sick with worry, she was thankful that Isabella had survived her first day on the job, with her purity and innocence preserved. And she was thankful that no client had requested herself, allowing her to stay with Isabella to keep her calm.

# CHAPTER 30

## MARCOS AND CARMEN ARE MISSING

NEITHER MARCOS NOR CARMEN HAD RETURNED by morning, and Anna was worried.

*What type of client has them? Where have they taken them? Are they hurt? Something most definitely has gone wrong.*

Anna had to get herself and Isabella ready for clients, but she was reluctant to awaken Isabella. This little girl had an overload of curiosity, and she would ask lots of questions about Marcos and Carmen.

Anna gently stroked Isabella's face while whispering in her ear that it was time for her to get up. Isabella stretched, reached up, and hugged Anna around her neck.

Slowly, Isabella got out of bed to get ready for the day, pretending she hadn't noticed that Marcos and Carmen were missing. Anna didn't know if the little girl didn't say anything because she didn't want to believe it, or because she didn't want to upset Anna.

After Isabella had gotten ready for breakfast, she said, "Anna, can you pray for Marcos and Carmen before the guard comes?"

"Why don't you and I both pray for them."

Isabella lowered her head. "I don't know how to pray."

"Of course you do. You know how to talk, don't you? Prayer is just that. You're talking to God."

Isabella stood with her head still hanging down, thinking about what Anna had said.

After a few moments, she looked up. "How do you know he can hear you? Where is he?"

Anna wondered how she could describe the Almighty God in terms simple enough for a child to understand.

"Isabella...when you go outside and look up, what do you see?"

"Oh, I see lots of things. I see trees, birds, and butterflies."

"If you look up higher, what do you see?"

"I see the sun, but it hurts my eyes if I don't squint."

"Yeah, it hurts mine, too, if I don't squint." Anna chuckled. "What about when you look up in the sky at night. What do you see then?"

"I see the moon and the stars."

Well, that's as far as we can see with just our eyes. But if we could see farther, we would see where God is. He is in the highest part of the sky, called Heaven."

"What's he doing there?"

"From there, he rules the heavens and the earth. He made everything, and he keeps his eyes on everything. He especially watches over people because he loves them very much. People are the highest form of all his creation because he created us in his image. And when we accept Jesus as our Savior, he becomes our very own Heavenly Father. Do you remember the Bible verse I read to you before?

"Yes, I remember," Isabella said. "And I believed it. It's in the Bible."

It said that God so loved the world—that is the people in the world—that he sent his son to earth to die for our sins. And after we become his children, he wants us to love and obey him.

Isabella's face began to show some understanding.

"Do you mean that sin is like when I didn't obey *my* father?"

"Yes, that is a good way to describe it," Anna said. "No matter how old God's children are, he is happy when we read the Holy Bible and obey him."

Isabella looked up at her. "I want God to know that I love him. I want to be able to talk to him and make him happy."

"Would you like for Jesus to forgive you of your sins so that you can know that you are a child of God?"

"Yes, yes, I would!" Isabella said.

"Wonderful! If you truly believe in God and ask him to save you, this will be the best day of your whole life."

Anna and Isabella knelt beside Isabella's bed to pray, and the child talked to God. She asked for forgiveness of her sins, and invited Jesus to come into her heart.

God was most definitely watching and listening to Isabella because as soon as she said "Amen," the dreadful sound of the padlock rang out. God had deliberately kept the guard from interrupting Isabella until she had become his child.

# CHAPTER 31

## THE HOSPITAL

THAT MORNING, ONLY A FEW CHILDREN ARRIVED to eat breakfast—a big contrast in attendance compared to those usually there. Their absence meant their clients had retained them for the entire night. That further disturbed Anna, but she couldn't let Isabella know. The child was at peace with everything because she was still so young and innocent.

Anna gazed at her while she ate breakfast, silently begging God to have mercy and spare her from sexual abuse a second day.

Isabella and Anna returned to their room to discover Marcos lying motionless on his bed, covered from head to toe with the bedsheet. Anna rushed to his side to check on him.

"Marcos, are you okay?"

He turned over and replied in a weak voice, "Just leave me alone."

His quivering body, slurred speech, and dilated eyes could only mean one thing—Jose had given him more drugs. And it was plain to see that he was struggling with too much of it.

"Marcos, what happened?" Anna said. "I want to know because I care."

He ignored her and pulled the sheet back over his head.

*What have they done to this poor boy? I have to know.*

Anna banged on the door, yelling for help and demanding to see Jose.

The guard opened the door. "Shut up! You better mind your business if you know what's good for you."

Anna got in his face, demanding to know what they had done to Marcos. The guard backhanded her in the face. She stumbled backward, trying to reorient herself.

Anna wiped the blood from her busted lip and screamed, "I will not shut up. I demand to see Jose. This boy is heavily drugged and needs help."

The guard pulled back his hand to hit Anna again, but she turned her face away from him, receiving the brunt of his blow across her ear and nose. Blood dripped from her nose, and her ear was ringing. She couldn't hear what he said, but she read his lips as he told her again to shut her mouth.

She was ready to hit him back, but then she caught a glimpse of Isabella cowering in the corner. Anna again realized that she was only making things worse.

As soon as the guard left, Marcos stammered, "Don't try to help me. It's useless. They will only beat you more."

Anna knelt beside his bed and cried. "Marcos, I'm so sorry. I wish I could somehow take this from you."

"You can't, so don't try. Don't worry. One day, I'm going to kill them."

Emotion charged the atmosphere in Room 120. Anna tried to calm down and keep a positive attitude for Isabella's sake, so she sat on her bed, thinking about what she could do.

Gradually, a smile crept across her face as an idea came to mind.

"Isabella, would you like to play hospital with me?" she mumbled through swollen lips.

"Hospital? I never played hospital before. Can I be a nurse?"

"Yes. Yes, you can." Anna nodded, relieved at Isabella's positive response. "We're going to pretend this room is a hospital, and Marcos and I are your patients. First, I need you to get a wet cloth and put it on Marcos's forehead. He's not feeling well this morning, and a wet cloth on his face will make him feel much better."

Anna was sure Marcos was listening, but she wasn't sure how he would react to this game of pretending. To her surprise, he had no objections. It looked as though he genuinely cared about Isabella, after all.

"Nurse," Anna called out. "Oh, nurse, can you help me now. I seem to have fallen."

Isabella rushed to her side. "Yes, you sure did. How did this happen? Don't worry, I have some medicine for your hurt nose and lip. Just stay still. I will make you well."

Anna lay back on her bed, assuming the position of someone lying on a hospital bed. She then requested Nurse Isabella to get another wet cloth to clean her wounds.

Isabella quickly took on the task at hand as if her patient were at death's door. She began bossing her, telling her to get plenty of rest, and demanding that she be more careful walking down the stairs.

Anna was amazed to see how quickly this child had slipped into the world of make-believe to escape her painful situation.

"Next time, be more careful," Isabella said. "You could break something, and we don't have any doctors to help with this right now."

Isabella wanted to apply some medicine to the wounds. Since there were only a few toiletries in the room, Anna suggested that she get a small tube of petroleum jelly from her purse. While Isabella rummaged through the purse, she found a little picture of some woman.

"Who's this?" She held the picture up.

"She is my mother." Anna tried to suppress her emotions.

She never allowed herself to look at the picture because sadness always overwhelmed her at the sight of her mother.

"Where is she?" Isabella said. "Do you have a father?"

Anna didn't want to talk about the past, and she didn't want

Isabella to leave her world of make-believe, so she continued pretending.

"Guess what. I am a real princess—the daughter of the richest king in the world. And one day, I will take you to a faraway land where you will personally meet my mother and father."

"You will?" Isabella jumped up and down, clapping her hands.

"Just you wait and see." Anna winked. "Just you wait and see."

# CHAPTER 32

## CONFRONTATION OVER CARMEN

SEVERAL HOURS WENT BY, AND ANNA RESTED, at ease in Isabella's world of make-believe. But there were in-between-moments when her mind continued to worry about what had happened to Carmen.

Before she realized how late it was, the guard came to take them to lunch. Regardless of the beating she had gotten from the guard, she still intended to find out when Jose expected Carmen to return.

When they arrived in the dining room, Anna saw all the children were there—everyone except Carmen.

*What has happened to her? She should be back by now! Why is Jose not mad? Even though he keeps everyone against their will and sells them for sex, he brags about his business practices, that he is better than any of the pimps. He prides himself on taking care of his* employees. *But I'm afraid someone has hurt Carmen. Or even worse, Jose has gotten rid of Carmen, like he did Rosa.*

A flood of emotion swept over Anna at the thought of Rosa, and tears welled up in her eyes. After all these years, she still missed her as though Jose had taken her away just yesterday. She could not bear the thought of Carmen going missing as well.

On the way to the dining room, Anna had noticed that Jose was in the motel office, where she used to work sometimes before he assigned her to take care of the children. She wanted to confront him about Carmen's whereabouts, so she told Isabella and Marcos to stay seated at the table and not to move until she got back.

Marcos, who was still dazed by the drugs, complied with the request. But Isabella begged her not to leave. As Anna stepped away, she tenderly patted the child's shoulder, assuring her that she would be right back.

Anna walked past the guard at the door, but he grabbed her by the arm, demanding that she go back and sit down.

"I need to speak with Jose!" she shouted.

The guard again demanded that she go back to her table.

Jose overheard the commotion and told the guard to let her come. Anna entered his office with trepidation. Nevertheless, she demanded Jose tell her where Carmen was.

Reeking with the smell of alcohol, he flipped his hand in the air as if to dismiss any concerns.

"Jose, one of the children you gave me to take care of is missing, and I have a right to know where she is. Will you please tell me when she's coming back?"

"Anna, Anna. Mother of many, but none of her own. You forget they are not your children. They are mine! I bought them, and I can do whatever I want to with them."

Anna softened her tone. "Jose, where is she?"

"Are you jealous? Or are you just plain nosey? Look," he flipped his hand in the air again, pretending to dismiss Anna's concerns, "Carmen knows how to take care of herself. She's been around the block, you know. But for your information, I gave her to a client who will spoil her as no one has ever spoiled her before. Right this minute, she's living it up, getting everything her heart desires."

Jose's tone of voice and actions were so nonchalant that Anna doubted he was being honest.

"And just how do you know this?" she said.

Jose let loose a long string of curse words. "You should know by now that I know what I'm doing. The Americans spoil my escorts, and this man can keep Carmen for as long as he wants.

Now don't ask me again where she is or when she's coming back. That is my client's decision, and not yours. Just remember, I'm not going to keep telling you what I do. From now on, you better leave me to take care of my business, and you take care of yours."

Anna turned and left Jose's office, confident that Carmen's client was one of the Americans who had come for sportfishing. She walked away, feeling somewhat relieved, believing that Carmen was with someone who would take care of her.

As Anna left Jose's office, she noticed some colorful marketing brochures and magazines on a table by the door. It dawned on her that these publications would be perfect for making Isabella some paper dolls.

Risking the wrath of Jose, she reached down and grabbed a handful to take with her. Of course, he noticed what she did.

"And what are you planning on doing with my brochures?" He smirked. "Are you planning on going someplace? Maybe you're planning on taking a little vacation. Is that it?"

"I-I only wanted to look at them while we wait for clients."

Jose had observed over the years that Anna only stuttered when she was nervous about something. He leaned back in his chair and crossed his arms over his chest.

"While you wait?" he said. "Keep in mind, Anna, that you won't need that stuff to entertain you while you wait because you won't be waiting long. It won't be long before a client comes for you *and* Isabella."

Anna's heart sank. She couldn't bear the thought of Jose selling Isabella, but she tried not to allow her mind to go there. Instead, she consoled herself with the good news that Carmen was with someone who would treat her well.

Jose wasn't the only person who took notice of Anna taking the publications. When she left Jose's office, the guard glared at her. He knew her well enough to know that she had something else in mind for the brochures. Though he could do nothing to her in front of Jose, he decided to keep a close eye on her.

Anna went back to the dining room, content to focus on

Marcos and Isabella. Unsure of where Anna had gone, the child was afraid she would not come back to her, or that maybe she would come back with even more cuts and bruises.

"Anna, please don't leave me. Don't ever leave me again."

"Isabella, you know I can't be with you every minute. But if I do have to leave, you must have faith that I'll get back as soon as I can. This time, I was just in Jose's office, checking on Carmen. And I'm happy to report that she is doing great, having some time away at a nice vacation spot. She won't be back for a while, but she is just fine."

Isabella looked up with a big smile and sparkling eyes.

"Well, if she gets hurt on her vacation, we can fix her up in our hospital."

"Yes, nurse. Yes, we sure can."

When they returned to Room 120, Marcos lay back down and continued to sleep off the effects of the drugs Jose had given him. When Anna saw Marcos in that condition, she felt more passionately than ever to protect all the children from Jose. But, as often was the case, Isabella's cheery disposition helped dispel Anna's gloom.

"Wow!" Isabella picked up one of Anna's brochures. "What are these?"

"These little pamphlets show pictures of people visiting beautiful vacation spots. And we're going to tear out the pictures of the people."

"What? Why are we going to tear up the beautiful pages?"

"We are going to tear up the pages because we are going to use the people as paper dolls."

"Paper dolls?" Isabella said. "I've never played paper dolls. Are paper dolls like Barbie dolls?"

"Yes, exactly. You choose the people you want to play with, and we will have a whole bunch of new patients that need help in your hospital."

Isabella beamed as she began to treat the brochures like toys. They didn't have scissors, so Anna instructed Isabella to be careful as she tore around each of the people.

"But if we tear off an arm or leg," Anna said, "that will be a good reason why you should treat them in your hospital."

Anna and Isabella fell backward on the bed, giggling. They spent the rest of the day creating a whole collection of paper dolls. With all the bad happenings, there was still a thread of happiness in Room 120.

As hard as Anna tried, though, anxiety persisted. She was afraid that if a client asked for her, there was a possibility that neither Carmen nor Marcos would be in the room to stay with Isabella while she was away.

The days of Carmen's absence continued to drag on, and Marcos was gone all the time since he had become more compliant. Though she was deeply concerned about Isabella being left alone in the room, Anna was grateful to God that no client had yet requested her.

Anna and Isabella continued to play paper dolls, although they had become worn and tattered from the various roles of make-believe. And during that time, Isabella became happy. She began to love Anna as the mother she'd never really had.

# CHAPTER 33

## CARMEN RETURNS

An entire week passed before the guard finally returned Carmen to Room 120. Isabella leaped from her bed and ran to welcome her home.

"I've missed you so much! Why did you leave us for so long?" Isabella said in a tone that mixed joy with scolding. "Where have you been?"

Carmen paused, not knowing how to answer that last question.

"I've been on vacation, and I've brought souvenirs for you," she replied.

Isabella said, "Who went with you? What are souvenirs?"

Carmen, wanting to spare Isabella any details of her absence, replied with excitement.

"I went with a super-nice friend down to the beach, where there are beautiful hotels and nice shopping. And I have some toys for you."

"Really? Let me see!" Isabella clapped with anticipation.

Carmen handed her a sack filled with all kinds of candy and small toys that she smuggled in for her. She had worried that Jose would confiscate them before she could get them into the room, but new clients coming into the motel had sidetracked him entirely. Neither Jose nor the guards realized Carmen had gifts inside her travel bag, and she managed to slip them into the motel, right under their noses.

As Isabella pulled out each gift from the sack with shrieks of joy, Carmen and Anna looked at each other with a sense of relief. Entertainment was just the thing this child needed during her confinement.

With Marcos away, and Isabella distracted with her new stuff, Anna and Carmen pulled aside.

"Anna, I can't wait to find out—has a client requested Isabella? The whole time I was away, I couldn't stop worrying about what was going on back here?"

"No." Anna shook her head. "It's unbelievable. Marcos is the only one who has received requests. He's gone almost all the time, but God has spared Isabella and me so far. Please, tell me about where you've been and who you were with."

Carmen was reluctant to say much about her absence, only revealing that the client was handsome, kind, and generous. Anna desperately wanted to learn more about Carmen's time with him, but they couldn't talk about it with Isabella around.

"I did enjoy my time with this man so much that I begged him to keep me," she finally admitted.

Anna suspected that Carmen might try to escape.

"Do you think you can trust him?" she said. "Please be careful."

"Yes! I know I can. He cared about me more than anyone has ever cared."

"I'm glad you were safe and happy. Isabella and I prayed for you every day. And thank you for getting these gifts for her."

Carmen gave Anna a big hug. "I could never forget you and Isabella. Not even Marcos. Where is he?"

"He's with a client again." Anna released a deep sigh of sadness.

"Is he still fighting them?"

"Jose is keeping him on drugs. Without them, I don't think he could survive."

Carmen shook her head. "Can we blame him? You do what you have to do to survive this place."

Later in the evening, Carmen fumbled through her suitcase and pulled out a manicure set and fingernail polish.

"I thought we girls would enjoy doing nails to get ready for the next princess ball." She dangled them in the air.

"Carmen, how clever!" Anna looked down at the suitcase. "What else do you have in there?"

Carmen smiled as she pulled out another gift.

"Look what I got for Marcos to defend himself. You can't tell anyone that I gave this to him."

"A comb? You bought him a comb to defend himself?" Anna nearly laughed out loud.

"It's a comb that flips open and becomes a knife. I have one also."

"Carmen! Are you crazy," Anna shouted. "If anyone here catches you or Marcos with that, you know you'll be in more trouble than anyone could imagine. Are you sure you want to give Marcos something like this? I don't even want to think about what he would do with this."

"But nobody will know it's a knife until the time comes when he needs to use it."

"Carmen, did your client know you got these things?"

"Yes, he knows. He's the one who bought all this stuff for me. The man said he liked me, and he wanted me to protect myself if I had to. Even if Jose or the guards saw these combs, they wouldn't suspect they were weapons."

Shaking her head in disbelief, Anna couldn't imagine that the guards or Jose would not be familiar with these gadgets. She was pretty sure they knew every kind of weapon sold anywhere.

"Carmen, I'm happy that this man likes you and wants to protect you. But people on the outside, even the clients, don't understand what it's like in places like this. They don't understand the danger of crossing a man like Jose. Just don't play games with Jose, or you may pay with your life. People in this place have gone missing before."

# CHAPTER 34

## MORE TROUBLE IN ROOM 120

About midnight that same day, there was a scuffle in the hallway, followed by the padlock's ominous clinking. The door swung open with a bang against the wall.

"Get in there and shut up!"

One of the guards pitched Marcos into the room, and the boy's frail body landed hard on the floor. The guard then slammed the door and snapped the padlock in place.

In the dim light coming from the window, Anna could see Marcos repeatedly stumble, trying to stand on his feet. Finally, he just crawled to his bed, cursing, waving his arms in the air, and mumbling something about killing all of them. It looked like he was hallucinating from some drug Jose had given to him.

The commotion awakened Isabella, and she cried out in fright. Carmen comforted her while Anna tried to restrain Marcos. When she put her arms around him to keep him from hurting himself, he looked at her with the eyes of a raging animal. He stared her down for almost a minute, before he lunged forward and began choking her.

Anna tried to pry Marcos's fingers from around her neck, but his grip was so firm she couldn't budge even one of them. She went limp and dropped to the concrete floor, hitting her head. With blurred vision, she saw Carmen's legs wrapped around Marcos's body, and her arms around his neck, trying to pull him off.

"No, Marcos! No!" Carmen screamed. "Stop it. You're choking Anna, not one of the guards. You don't want to hurt Anna. Stop before you kill her."

Two of guards returned to the room and separated the pile of tangled bodies on the floor. They pulled Marcos off Anna, beat him with their leather blackjacks until he was unconscious, and dragged him out the door. Carmen raced to the door and shouted to the guards that she needed help with the blood flow from a cut on Anna's head. They returned and carried her to Jose's office.

For once, Anna was glad to see Jose. He sat her in his office chair, where he stopped the bleeding and bandaged her head wound. He had always claimed to be a paramedic, but she knew his training was merely the product of surviving on the streets. From what she had heard from clients, Jose had a reputation in town of someone you wouldn't want to fight.

Anna was shocked at how attentive Jose was in treating her wound, but she still feared he would blame her for the brawl. Instead, he acted halfway kind, not in his usual cold and calloused manner. She allowed him to believe that she wasn't pampering the children as much as he had thought.

"I've stopped the bleeding, so how's your head feeling now?"

"Fine. Thank you," Anna said with apprehension, knowing he wasn't a nice person unless there was something in the deal for himself.

"You don't look so fine," he replied. "You'll stay here with me until you're better."

Jose put his arm around her waist to steady her walk as he ushered her to a bed over to the side of the office. Frequently, when he worked late, he would sleep there instead of going to his room in the fancy front hotel where clients met their escorts.

He turned back the sheet and helped Anna lie down to rest. She had doubts about the motive behind Jose's kindness.

Nevertheless, it felt good to lie down and let her aching body sink into the soft, downy mattress.

Anna felt as though there wasn't an inch of her that Marcos hadn't kicked or punched, and her head was still throbbing from hitting the concrete floor with such force. But the worst thing of all was her concern for her children back in Room 120. They had to be frightened for themselves and worried about her. She was especially worried about Marcos.

*What will Jose do to him now? Will I ever have the chance to let him know that I don't blame him for what he did in his drugged state? Will he even remember what happened?*

She finally worked up the courage to say, "Jose, what's going to happen to Marcos,"

"Don't you worry about him." He nodded in a manner that was supposed to reassure Anna of her safety. "It will be a long time before he hurts you or anyone else."

Jose got up from his desk and came over to sit on the side of the bed. With a soft touch and a glint of his gold tooth, he began to stroke her hair.

The man hadn't wanted her intimately since the children had come to the motel. But she knew by the way he stared at her lying on his bed that his intentions were more for her to service him than to help her.

After a few minutes, he went to his desk for something and returned.

"Here, take this. It'll help you rest." Jose handed her a shot of tequila to wash down a pill.

She didn't want to take that stuff, but she knew he would get mad if she didn't agree to it. So she took the pill and pretended to swallow it. She barely took a sip of the tequila, keeping whatever he had given her under her tongue.

Fortunately, one of the guards called for him to come at once. Jose rushed out the door and locked her in his office.

Before the children had arrived at the motel, she would have drunk all the alcohol, hoping it would make her intoxicated before he returned. But this time, she needed to hear everything and know all that was happening. It was more apparent than ever that she must find a way to escape and save as many children as she could.

Anna knew Jose could come back at any moment, so she ran to the restroom, spit out the pill, and swished her mouth with the tequila so he would smell it on her breath when he returned. She then poured the rest of the drink down the drain and ran a wee bit of water, hoping Jose would not hear the faucet running. Anna remembered all too well the loud, squeaky sound of the plumbing.

She then rushed back to Jose's bed and pretended she was asleep.

*This night, of all nights, I will just have to suffer through Jose's sexual advances so I can watch everything that's going on in the office.*

# CHAPTER 35

## A REVELATION

ANNA DIDN'T KNOW HOW LONG SHE HAD SLEPT before Jose and Javier, the head guard, entered the office, talking about how Marcos had become so addicted to drugs that he was now a real business problem. Jose became irate, cursing to the top of his voice.

"That's why I never wanted to use hard drugs in this place. I need things clean around here. You should know this by now!"

"Look, that was the only way we could get him to cooperate," Javier said. "He wouldn't do what we told him. He fought us the whole way. Otherwise, we would have missed some of our biggest clients. They said they would take care of him. And it worked. Now he'll do anything for a hit. So what's the big deal?"

"What's the big deal?" Jose continued to spew profanity. "Look at him! He's a raging maniac, hurting my girls and costing me money to support his drug habit. I told you I didn't want that boy."

"Jose, you know there is an increasing demand for young escorts. And a lot of these customers want young boys. We need that business. We've already lost a lot of money because you won't also sell drugs."

Jose got nose to nose with Javier. "Don't you tell me how to run my business! I know what I'm doing. Get your nose out of my business, and leave my work to me."

"All I'm telling you is there's a growing demand for young boys and drugs. Think about it. And keep in mind that not one client has asked for the six-year-old girl. She hasn't gotten a single request."

"Shut up!" Jose yelled. "This a prime example of why I'm boss and you're not. Nobody has asked for her because I've set the price way up for that little virgin girl. You're a virgin only once, and someone will give me big bucks to score that opportunity. After that, I'll lower the price, but she'll still be in high demand. As for Marcos, just look at the trouble you've caused me with your great ideas. This boy has caused me nothing but trouble, and now I may have to dispose of him. And you need to remember that nobody—*nobody*—is indispensable in my operation."

*How dare these men talk about enslaved children as mere merchandise. These children are not a commodity. They're human beings. And how dare they talk about disposing of Marcos after they turned him into the monster he's become.*

It took everything in Anna not to jump up and tell them off. But the only thing she could do was to lie quietly and listen to the vulgar, pathetic conversation between these two men. No matter how often she had to listen to such talk, she never liked to hear it. But right now, she felt compelled to listen, hoping to pick up on some detail that would help her plan to rescue the children.

Anna began to pray, and amazingly the men's voices faded into the background. In that stillness, she recalled the days Jose had her working in his office. And she remembered Jose's safe, which was just inside the closet on the other side of the room. That's where he kept his money and other important things.

*Important things...important things...important things. Such as passports. Yes, passports!*

Anna felt that God was letting her know that Jose's safe held the passports he had taken from them years ago. She hadn't thought about it before, but getting those passports was crucial if they ever hoped to escape and go back home.

She lay on Jose's bed, thinking about the safe and the passports. Anna knew the safe must still be in the closet, but she didn't know how to get into it. And even if she got into it, there was no guarantee the passports would be there. Jose had no need to keep them. He certainly would never let any of his escorts leave the county.

Jose left the office after lunch to go somewhere, and it was almost midnight when he returned. In his drunken state, he began making his moves toward Anna. The touch of his hands on her body was hard for her to accept without the help of alcohol. But for the sake of the children, she had to act as normal as possible. Fortunately, he had drunk so much he would never know the difference.

# CHAPTER 36

## JOSE GOES INTO THE SAFE

THE NEXT MORNING, Jose went into the safe in his closet to secure the money he received the night before. Anna desperately needed to get into the safe to look for the passports, but she couldn't see how he opened it from where she lay on the bed.

He had always been careful not to let anyone see him go into the safe because he trusted no one. That he'd gone into it with Anna in the room meant only one thing—he was beginning to let his guard down.

Jose left the office and returned with breakfast for Anna. Even though she had a headache and her stomach felt nauseous from all the anxiety, she tried to eat while he made a few phone calls. After he took care of business, he came over and removed her head bandage.

"Well, it looks like you're going to get to spend another exciting night with me," he said, after examining her wounds.

It was clear Jose just wanted Anna for himself. He always preferred a more mature body over the younger girls. The thought of sleeping with him another night made her sick. But another day in the office was exactly what she needed if she ever hoped to get into the safe. Staying another night with him was something she had to do, but she desired to get back to Room 120.

*What is Isabella thinking? She must be overcome with fear, wondering what has happened to me. I don't dare ask Jose about her, or he'll get angry. May God spare her from evil another day.*

After Anna finished breakfast, Jose handed her a glass of rum and Coke.

*What is Jose doing? He usually wants me sober in the mornings to help with paperwork. Why is he giving me liquor so early in the day? I don't want to be on this stuff anymore.*

Jose kept sitting at his desk, watching her every movement. Anna had hoped he would become sidetracked with his work and not notice that she wasn't drinking it. But he didn't.

"I gave you something to drink. It'll make you feel better."

"I have a sick stomach. I-I'll drink it in a few minutes."

"What is wrong with you? Drink it now!"

Anna obeyed, all the while praying that God would keep her sober enough to carry out what she needed to do.

It wasn't long before she fell into a heavy sleep. When she awakened, she ran to the bathroom, vomiting.

"So I guess you have lost your tolerance," Jose snarked.

Still bent over and holding her stomach, she groaned, "No, I'm just sick on my stomach for some reason."

"Then you need to take this medicine." He handed her a little white pill.

*Medicine? Is this the kind of* medicine *he gave Marcos?*

Anna had never known Jose to use any drugs. Yet something had changed about him because was now popping pills. She didn't know what he was taking, but he kept a bottle of pills on his desk.

*What is he giving me? Is it the same drug he's taking? I can't take this. I have to stay awake and alert. If I spit it out this time, he will surely see me. What can I do?*

Anna took the pill and put it under her tongue. She pretended to be grateful for his help, climbed back into bed, facing the wall, and pulled the sheet over her head. When the pill softened, she scraped it onto the concrete floor, where Jose would never see it. He was talking on the phone the whole time, and never noticed a thing.

In a few minutes, she rolled back over, with only her eyes peeping out from under the sheet. She could now watch Jose while she pretended to sleep.

In the ten years of Anna's captivity, she had never caused Jose an ounce of trouble. It was to her advantage that she had gained his trust before this crucial moment. She could now observe everything that went on, without him being suspicious.

Another half-hour passed before Jose went into the closet and opened the safe. He put a key in the pocket of his trousers after he relocked it.

Anna realized that getting her hands on that key would take a miracle.

# CHAPTER 37

## THE SEARCH

As THE HOURS CREPT BY, Anna wanted to get up and tell Jose that she felt fine, and return to Room 120 to be with Isabella. But that would defeat her effort to get into the safe, so she continued to lie there, pretending to sleep. And Jose continued to work at his desk until the phone rang.

He listened in silence for a few minutes.

"Don't do anything!" he said. "I'll be there in a minute."

Jose rushed out of the room, and Anna jumped out of bed. With him gone, she took advantage of the opportunity to search for another key to the safe.

She scoured through the things on top of his desk, making sure nothing had shifted from its present location. All the while, she listened intently for any sign that he was returning.

*It's not just my life that's on the line here. If Jose catches me rummaging through his desk, he will surely take vengeance out on the children as well.*

There was no trace of a key on top of his desk, so she dared to search the desk drawers.

She opened the top drawer and nearly fainted at what she saw. There was a stash of pictures of females of all ages, each one marked with a price.

*I can't believe it. Jose is selling girls—not just their services.*

The realization that he was selling girls as sex slaves broke her heart. Through the tears that streamed down her cheeks, she recognized one of the faces—Rosa! She was alive. But Anna's heart sank when she saw how tired and older her dear friend looked.

By chance, she turned the picture over. To her surprise, she saw that someone had written, *The Hideaway,* on the back of the picture.

*Could this be the name of the motel that Jose sold Rosa to at some point?*

"The Hideaway. The Hideaway..." She kept repeating the name to make sure she wouldn't forget it.

Anna never had a chance to learn any other places in Costa Rica, but she now had another reason to get out of Jose's prison. She had to rescue the children *and* Rosa.

The silence was broken by Jose talking to someone as he came down the hallway. Anna hurried to put everything back as she had found it, and rushed across the room. The door swung open, and Jose caught her getting back in bed.

"What are you doing?" he said.

"Nothing, Jose." She bent over with her arms around her waist. "My stomach is still upset, and I went to the restroom."

He got in her face and spoke slowly. "You better not be lying to me."

Scowling, with his hands on his hips, he surveyed the room. Nothing appeared to be out of place. But he came over and demanded Anna to take more meds and alcohol. She obeyed, but knew that she had to remain sober enough to get that key. This night might be her last chance.

Another phone call sidetracked Jose. Still, she worried that he might notice she had moved something on his desk.

More calls and guards coming in and out of the office kept him busy. She tried to stay alert, but her head started to spin, and she fell asleep.

Anna didn't know how long she had slept, but Jose was standing over her, undressing, when she opened her eyes. After forcing himself upon her, he collapsed and fell asleep. The problem was that he was lying partially on top of her.

Anna wasn't thinking clearly, but something inside her kept driving her onward. She had to get into that safe.

She decided to get the safe key out of his pocket, where he had stuck it earlier in the day.

Anna had spent many restless nights awake in the past, hoping Jose would roll over or reposition himself so he would stop snoring. Strangely, even though his snoring rattled the room, the slightest movement or noise could easily awaken him. He seemed always to be on guard, even in his sleep.

No matter how uncomfortable she was, awakening him was something she tried hard to avoid due to the consequences. From his teenage years living on the streets, his self-defense reaction was quick and violent when anyone awakened him. And waking him this night could prove to be more consequential than ever before.

Jose's body was heavy. He smelled of sweat and alcohol, and he was breathing loudly in her ear. Anna was anxious to get up and get the key, but she needed to wait until he was sound asleep.

Fifteen minutes passed before a few short sputters erupted from his lips. Finally, his snoring was in full force, and it was music to her soul.

Little by little, Anna carefully moved Jose's arms from around her waist. It seemed to take hours to slip every part of her body away from his. She didn't for a second take her eyes off him, making sure he was still asleep. At the slightest twitch of his eyelids, she would pretend that she was turning in her sleep.

Inch by inch, she slipped to the side of the bed. She slowly reached out for Jose's trousers, now lying on the floor within arm's reach, and pulled them to her. The key wasn't in the front right pocket...nor the left pocket.

*Maybe Jose thought I was up to something, and put the key someplace else. Where could it be?*

Jose's body twitched, and he reached out for her. Anna slipped back next to him and waited for him to resume snoring. Then she went through the same slow process of getting to the edge of the bed.

She got hold of his trousers again and searched the back pockets this time. Again, nothing. No key in any of his pockets. There were rolls of money, but that wouldn't help her. He hadn't put the money up, so what had he done with the key?

Now what? Time was running out, and she had to locate those passports.

# CHAPTER 38

## THE SAFE

FINALLY, ANNA SLOWLY SLIPPED all the way off the bed. As soon as her feet touched the floor, Jose moved and mumbled something in his sleep. Anna halted, ready to act like she was going to the restroom. When he resumed snoring, Anna got down on her knees again and crawled around, searching for his shirt.

She fumbled around until she felt it in a heap beside the desk. It had only one front pocket, which was buttoned. But from the weight of it, Anna could tell something was in it. She undid the button, and sure enough, there was the key.

*Now what? How am I going to get into the safe in the dark? And how can I see what's inside the safe?*

Anna had only focused on getting the key. Now she had to think through her next move.

She remembered the closet had a light, but she dared not turn it on. Looking around, she noticed there was a crack under the office door, emitting a sliver of light from the hallway. It might be enough for her to examine the safe's contents. But to do that, she would have the fateful task of bringing the stuff from the safe to the crack in order to examine it in the light, and then return the stuff—all without awakening Jose or leaving any evidence that she had disturbed the contents of the safe.

Somehow, Anna got up the courage to keep going forward

with this plan. There was no turning back.

With the stealth of a mountain lion, she crawled to the closet, clutching the key. Her heart pounded so loud that she was sure it would jump out of her chest. If Jose awakened and found her crawling, she planned on telling him she was too dizzy to get on her feet to go to the restroom.

Telling lies was a common thing for her now, but it was something her conscience never allowed her to do before her imprisonment. Her parents had taught her the importance of honesty. But in Jose's clutch, lying had become a means of survival—a matter of self-defense.

Anna timed her every movement toward the closet to sync with Jose's inhaling and exhaling. Once there, she quietly opened the door. The outline of the safe was visible in the dim light. It was about four feet tall and smelled like old metal. The thing had a massive presence that stared back at her, daring her to approach.

Second doubts overcame her as she wondered whether she should even try to get into the old safe. Such a relic would likely squeak—a sure death knell.

*Why can't I remember if this old door makes a noise when it opens? I should have listened better when I worked in the office. I can't do this. I should stop before Jose kills me.*

Anna broke out in a cold sweat. She was ready to quit. Then, seeing the faces of the children in her mind, her heart argued back. She had to do this. If this were God's plan, he would help.

Finally, Anna reached out and turned the big knob on the safe's front, and the outer door swung open. A high-pitch sound rang out as though the safe had squealed with pain. She dropped to the floor and quietly crawled out of the closet, praying that Jose was still sleeping. She listened for the sound of his snoring. Instead, she heard him stirring.

*Did the sound awaken him? Will he grab me once I get back to the bed?*

Anna hurried back and waited for the sounds of his heavy breathing and snoring. She could not believe she had to chance a second attempt to make it to the safe. Her head and stomach were still feeling the effects of the alcohol, and fear overwhelmed her heart.

Retracing her careful movements, she crept back into the closet, and with trembling hands, inserted the big key into the inner lock. But the key stuck instead of turning.

*What more can go wrong! This has to be the key Jose used. God, you've got to help me if this is your will. Please help me.*

Anna kept jiggling the key to make it turn. After a few more tries, it fell into a groove, turned, and opened the lock to the inner door. She pulled on the handle, opening the heavy door inch by inch, when it suddenly swung open on its own accord and slammed back against the outer door, which then hit the closet wall. The chain of events caused a bang that sounded like an explosion.

Anna did not attempt to rush back to bed this time. Instead, she crouched down, fully expecting Jose's wrath to come upon her at any second. When he didn't jerk her up by the hair of her head, she knew he was still asleep.

In the past, this noise would have indeed awakened him. Evidently, the combination of drugs and alcohol had put him into a deeper sleep than usual. Or maybe there was an unseen force working on her behalf.

Now that the door was wide open, Anna squinted her eyes to adjust to the deeper darkness of the safe's interior. She could faintly see stacks of money, guns, and ammunition. For a moment, she thought about taking a weapon for the escape. Just as quickly, she reconsidered the thought, knowing Jose wouldn't hesitate to use it on her if he discovered she had it. Besides, she had never even held a gun. How could she possibly know how to use it?

The one thing Anna couldn't find was the passports. *Where could they be? All this was a wasted effort. It must not be God's will to deliver us.*

She decided to feel around the back and sides of the safe before closing its doors. And there, tucked behind the guns, was a small, slender box. Anna inched it open and felt inside. All she could feel was a batch of papers, but she couldn't see what they were. So she took the box to the light at the crack under the door and examined the contents.

Anna carefully opened a yellow envelope. Inside she found the precious passports. Her fingers quivered as she read the names on each one. Minutes dragged by until she finally found the passports belonging to Rosa, Isabella, and herself. Jose had not taken Marcos across the border, so she knew there would be no passport for him.

Anna hurried to replace everything else just as she had found it, closed the safe, and crawled out of the closet. In her haste, she bumped into the closet door, and it slammed shut. Knowing this unexpected noise would have aroused Jose, she snuck into the restroom.

*What can I do? I have the passports and Jose's key. He will not hesitate to kill me the instant he finds these things on me. Somehow I have to hide the passports and get the key back in his shirt pocket.*

Sure enough, Jose stirred and called out, "Anna, where are you? What are you doing now?"

"I'm in the restroom, Jose. I have a stomachache."

"You better not be lying to me. Now come back to bed."

Anna had to find a place to hide the passports. But where?

Looking all around, she noticed a crack between the ceiling and the wall by the barred window. She climbed up on the commode and tucked the passports into the crack. They fit perfectly.

Anna's joy was short-lived as she remembered that she still had Jose's safe key. He would need it to put his money in the safe first thing in the morning. Anna wanted to put it back into his shirt pocket, but she dared not take that chance now. There wasn't enough time to devise a plan, so she held the key and walked back to the bed.

Jose was lying on his side, facing her. So Anna climbed into bed, hoping that in his stupor, he would move back. He did precisely that, and she slipped in front of him. She could see the outline of the shirt at arm's distance on the floor in front of her.

Anna lay motionless beside Jose, staring at the shirt, waiting for him to resume his snoring. After about thirty minutes, she reached out slowly and drew the shirt closer to her. She managed to replace the key in the shirt pocket, rebutton it, and toss it back onto the floor.

She had no idea how long this daring ordeal had taken, but it felt like an eternity.

*Thank you, Jesus*, was Anna's last thought before she fell asleep.

# CHAPTER 39

## PASSPORT PROBLEMS

THE SUN WAS UP WELL BEFORE ANNA AWOKE the next morning. Jose had gotten up and left the office to take care of business without disturbing her.

As hard as she tried, she just couldn't seem to keep her eyes open. Anna felt awful. She had gotten little sleep, and her head was throbbing from her injury. It took several minutes for her to get her wits about her, but she slowly pulled herself up and sat on the side of the bed. As the fog in her head lifted, events of the night came into focus.

*Passports!*

She jumped out of bed and rushed to the bathroom to make sure her precious bounty from the night was still safe. The sight of the passports tucked away brought a sigh of relief.

Anna climbed onto the commode and pulled them out of the crack to examine them in the light. Her eyes filled with tears as she stared at Rosa's picture. It had been a long time since she'd seen her best friend.

"Oh, Rosa, Rosa. How could this have happened to us?" she whispered, clutching Rosa's passport next to her heart. "We didn't deserve this. Will I ever see you again? Will we ever be free?"

She heard Jose come back into the office. Quickly, she stuffed the passports back in their hiding place, stripped off her clothes, and jumped into the shower. As soon as she turned on the water, Jose opened the bathroom door.

"Hurry up! It's time for you to return to your room. I have business to take care of today. Also, a client has requested you."

Anna dried off and got dressed, hoping Jose wouldn't notice she had been crying.

She reached for the door, but hesitated.

*What about the passports? I can't leave them here. Jose will kill me if he sees them. I have to take them with me, but how?*

Not knowing what else to do, she tucked the passports in her underwear. Before she could finish dressing, two guards came into the office, talking to Jose about some missionaries, and how they were handing out flyers all over town, with Marcos's picture on it.

Jose started cursing to the top of his lungs. "They're going to keep looking until they find him. I don't know what we're going to do with that troublemaker. I want to see Marcos, now!"

As soon as Anna came out of the bathroom, Jose grabbed her by the arm. He hustled her back to Room 120 and pointed for the guard to unlock the padlock. Jose pushed her into the room and relocked the door. Anna stood motionless, staring at the shut door in front of her.

*Where could Marcos be?*

When she turned around, she saw Carmen and Isabella sitting on her bed. Isabella jumped up and ran to her with arms outstretched. Anna swooped her up and held her tight. Her concern for Marcos shifted to Isabella and her ever-present danger of becoming sexually abused.

"Where have you been?" the little girl said. "Please don't ever leave me again."

Anna smiled. "Isabella, as I told you before...I can't promise that I will never have to leave. But I can promise that I will always love you, and that I will come back to you as soon as I can. Remember, you are God's child, and your Heavenly Father is always with you, even when I'm not."

As soon as Isabella calmed down, Anna went to the restroom.

The walls, constructed of concrete blocks, had small gaps here and there. For the first time, she noticed a narrow space between two blocks where the mortar had fallen out. This spot was just like the place in Jose's restroom, right above the commode. She climbed up and placed the passports in the gap.

*Well, that takes care of that mission. But now I have to find a way for each of us to escape before Jose discovers the passports are missing. I must find the missionaries to tell them about Marcos. And I have to find Rosa. How can all this possibly happen?*

"Anna," Carmen whispered, when she came out of the restroom. "A new client has requested me for the afternoon and evening, and I'm nervous about it."

"I know that fear when you go out with a new client," Anna replied. "Did Jose tell you anything about him?"

"No. Like usual, it's a wait-and-see deal. I desperately want to get out of here, but Jose will never let us go. He tells us he will let us go one day if we behave, but I think he only says that so we will cooperate with his demands."

Anna rested on her bed for a while, reflecting on her little family there. Room 120 almost felt like home. There was a sense of structure, and a bond of love. Yes, things were looking bad, yet Anna continued to trust God to guide her with wisdom to plot their escape. She didn't know who she could trust to help her. Of course, no one inside Jose's operation would dare betray him. And from what her clients said, people in town looked out for him, fearing retaliation. Worst of all, there were rumors that some authorities in high positions were corrupt and part of the sex trafficking business.

In Costa Rica, the law permits prostitution for anyone fifteen years or over. But even for the officers who try to uphold the law, there was a problem. Escort services dress children up to make them look like they are of legal age. Without proper identification, it's nearly impossible to distinguish a child from an adult. That's why the police sometimes don't bother with the hassle of checking identity. To further complicate the situation, children sometimes want to work because they want to eat.

With so many people accepting their country's culture without question, there was no way for Anna to get the inside or outside help she needed to set these children free.

Still waiting for her client, Anna thought more about the morning events, including the news about the search for Marcos.

Then the answer came in one word: *Missionaries!*

She chuckled inside as she credited her enemies for speaking the word that was quite possibly the key to the escape plan.

*Didn't God speak through the mouth of a donkey when a reluctant servant of his refused to speak the truth? Doesn't he sometimes use his enemies to accomplish his will? Yes. I can surely trust those missionaries. I just need to find a way to contact them.*

Her contemplations vanished when Jose returned and said he needed to see her in his office. She followed him, wanting to find out more about Marcos.

Before she had a chance to say anything, Jose spouted off in his usual curt manner.

"First, the client who requested you today had to cancel at the last minute. Second, that European client who always requests you for several days is coming to town. He will come for you early tomorrow morning." Jose beamed. "Third and most important, some American men are arriving in two weeks, and one of them has requested a little virgin girl. That means Isabella will entertain her first client."

Anna's heart seemed to plummet to the pit of the earth, and her knees buckled. She knew the day would come when a client would request Isabella. But like death, you're never ready for the news.

"I told you not to get attached!" Jose blasted. "These are not your children. They are mine. And you better inform Isabella and have her ready to cooperate with her client. If she's not, she will suffer severe consequences. Oh, and make sure Carmen is ready today by two o'clock for her client."

Jose had never allowed clocks in any of the rooms, not wanting his sex slaves to even think about the time they spent in captivity. They only had an inner clock. So they made sure they got ready well before the appointed time, whether it was to eat a meal or meet a client. And Anna's inner clock was now telling her that there was a narrow window for the occupants of Room 120 to make their escape.

Anna would put her life on the line to escape and contact the missionaries. But she did not want to escape and leave anyone behind. She didn't even want Isabella left alone for one minute. So Anna begged God to allow Carmen to come back from her escort service before she had to leave early the next morning. If God truly wanted to deliver them from slavery, he would surely answer this much smaller prayer.

She decided not to tell Isabella anything about the client who had requested her. Anna would simply trust God to spare her.

# CHAPTER 40

## A HAPPY SURPRISE

WHEN THE GUARD RETURNED Anna to Room 120, she asked Carmen to come into the restroom. Whispering, Anna told her that a client had requested Isabella, and he would arrive in two weeks.

Carmen gasped. They wanted to cry together, but that would only arouse Isabella's curiosity.

Anna said she wouldn't tell Isabella. Hoping and praying that God would intervene, she would wait until the last minute to give the child details and further prepare her.

Anna also told Carmen about the European client that was coming for Anna early the next morning. This man came to Jaco once a year to take care of business, and when he was in town, he always requested her for the entire time. She never knew how long she would be away. Usually, she was gone several days. But a few times, she was out for the whole week.

"Carmen, I'm praying that your client will bring you back before I have to leave. Marcos is gone almost all the time, and I don't want all three of us gone at the same time. I don't want this child left alone."

"I agree." Carmen nodded. "I promise I'll do everything I can to get back as soon as I can. It's the same thing I would want somebody to do for my little Andrea. But we both know we have little control over when a client brings us back."

"Carmen, can you at least try to keep anyone from talking to her about a client coming to take her away? If someone should come in to take my place, tell them I will have enough time to prepare her when I return. Tell them the child will respond better for me than she will for anyone else."

Shortly, the guard came to take them to lunch. Isabella was happy to walk down the long hallway with Anna, but she knew better than to take hold of her hand. She had learned well that there could be no show of affection between them, but she still felt secure in Anna's love for her.

Their love was a mutual blessing. Isabella had filled a void in Anna's heart, and she would fiercely protect Isabella as if the child had come from her own womb.

Upon entering the dining room, the juxtaposition in the scene before Anna was heartbreaking. All the children looked like beaten dogs, with their heads hanging down and their eyes fixed in a daze. What a contrast to Isabella, whose eyes still had that sparkle of life in them. It was apparent that Jose's clients had already violated all the other children.

*Oh, how I want to save all the children. But that's impossible. You can't even save your skin.*

After lunch, a guard came to take Carmen to her client. She told Isabella goodbye, and to have fun playing with her dolls.

As Carmen exited the room, she told Anna, "I'll do my best."

Anna winked at her. "I know you will. Just be safe."

As soon as the door closed Jose came in. "There's a problem with your client's flight leaving London," he told Anna, "and the delay means he won't be here 'til tomorrow afternoon. Make sure you use this time getting Isabella ready for her first client."

*What? I can't believe my ears. This is such good news. I wonder what on earth could have caused the delay.*

Whatever it was, peace came over Anna's soul. That evening, knowing she would not have to leave Isabella first thing the next morning, Anna snuggled up against the child.

"I love you," Anna whispered in her ear. "No matter what happens, always remember that if I could have a child, I would want her to be just like you."

A curious look spread over Isabella's face as she looked up at Anna.

"Could you be my mother?"

"I would love to be your mother. But you can only call me that in secret. Remember, Jose would get mad if he knew I mothered you. Also, remember that I have to work for the next few days. But I will return. All you have to do is stay close to Carmen and play dolls with her."

Isabella began to whimper. "I don't want you to go. Please don't go."

Anna caressed her. "I don't want to go, but sometimes moms and dads have to work. That's just a part of life. You just have faith and believe that I will be back. Now let's get some sleep."

As soon as they went to sleep, Carmen returned to Room 120. The guards opened the padlock and shoved her through the doorway, obviously upset with her.

Carmen straightened herself up. "I may be in trouble, but I got back as soon as I could."

"Carmen, what did you do?" Anna said.

"Well," she flashed a sly smile, "let's just say it wasn't my best performance. I wanted to get back here to be with Isabella, even if it meant I would get a beating."

Carmen and Anna burst out in muffled laughter. Isabella joined, though she had no clue why they were laughing. She just enjoyed seeing them having fun.

# CHAPTER 41

## ANNA'S CLIENT

JOSE CAME TO ROOM 120 the next morning after breakfast to inform Anna that the European client had arrived in town, and she had one hour to be ready.

As she prepared for the day, she asked Isabella if she would like to help her get ready.

"I know a princess like you can make me look good for Prince Charming." Anna winked.

Isabella spread out all of Anna's makeup on the bed, then stepped back to survey the assortment of products, rubbing her chin as though she was making an expert decision about how she would proceed. Next, she carefully applied her selections of eyeshadow, mascara, and lipstick. Again, she stepped back and declared that the final product made Anna look just like a princess.

Anna's clothes, hair, and makeup looked fine, but the most important thing was still missing. She excused herself and went into the bathroom to retrieve the passports, and tucked them in her underwear, as she did before.

Anna wore a short red skirt and a black off-the-shoulder top that hung down below the waist on one side, so she checked to make sure no one could see any sign of the passports.

"You are beautiful, Princess Anna," Isabella said with admiration, when Anna came out of the restroom and twirled around. "What time will your prince bring you back?"

"Oh, I'll be back after the ball." Anna placed her arms around Isabella. "But it may be a few days. But don't you worry. And always, always remember that I love you like you were my very own."

Within minutes, Jose came to take Anna to the office to meet her client. Separation was incredibly hard, and Isabella tried with all her might to hold back tears, but her eyes filled to the brim.

Anna hurried out to keep Jose from noticing the child's emotional state. But she looked over her shoulder as she walked through the door, giving Isabella a wink and a smile. She had no choice but to trust God to get Isabella out of that place before her client came in two weeks.

Whenever Anna went out with a client, Jose was always agitated, strutting about like a male dog. His posturing rose to an even higher level with this important client, yet he never denied his request for her escort.

When Jose and Anna entered the office, the European man, whose name was Charles, rose to his feet and nodded at Anna.

Charles was a tall, slender, and distinguished gentleman with red hair and green eyes. Unlike most clients, he dressed impeccably. He wore a three-button gray business suit, a fresh white shirt, and a red-striped tie. Charles had been coming here for over five years, but only at random times due to his business schedule. It had now been over a year since he last visited Costa Rica, and he was eager to see Anna. And she, for once, was glad to see him. Hopefully, his visit at this particular time was a part of God's plan.

Charles had a cab waiting to take them to his hotel on the coastline. This place overlooked one of the spots most tourists flocked to for a vacation, catering to guests who preferred five-star hotels. Charles changed into casual clothes, and the couple went back downstairs for lunch. He wanted to stroll around the place with Anna on his arm to show her off. He was about twenty years older than she was, and he loved to show the other men that he could still get a younger woman.

Charles knew Anna loved the ocean, so they walked hand-in-hand on the beach, enjoying the sunshine and looking for seashells. One reason Anna enjoyed her time with Charles was that he took her to places that she liked. Other clients, even those who were kind to her, never took her anywhere special.

Later, while eating dinner in town, Charles ordered wine and asked Anna what kind she would like. Anna didn't want to drink, but she knew she had to play the game to keep him from becoming suspicious that something unusual was going on in her life. So she just sipped the wine, and Charles never noticed the change in her habit.

After dinner, he flagged another cab to take them back to the hotel. Their room overlooked shimmering waters and the moonlit beach. But as a world traveler, Charles wasn't interested in the romantic setting. He had seen it all many times. His only desire now was to retire early for the evening. Anna knew what he wanted, and what she had to do. She also knew that she needed to find the missionaries and give them the passports.

Anna felt safe with Charles because he had never abused her, unlike most other clients. But on the other hand, she didn't completely trust him either. If he found the passports on her, he would surely tell Jose.

Anna had no plan for how she could hand off the passports to the missionaries without Charles's knowledge, and she wondered whether she could even find the missionaries.

"Dear God, please help me. Please show me the way," she prayed under her breath, lying beside Charles.

# CHAPTER 42

## THE SLIP

ANNA CONTINUED TO LIE AWAKE, thinking about how she could find the missionaries.

Then her eyes sprang open. *Yes! I will slip out. Charles is so intoxicated and sound asleep that he will never know I'm not here.*

After all the years Anna had been out with Charles, she had always been right there when he awoke. She had never done anything to make him think she had the slightest desire to escape, so he trusted her to remain in the room.

She got dressed and tucked the passports back in her underwear. Grabbed the hotel key from the bedside table and headed to the door. Then it occurred to her that she might need money, so she took several colóns from Charles's wallet.

*He's so rich, he'll never notice the money is missing. He wouldn't want it, anyway. He always laughs about this* play money, *and how he has to spend all the* useless *Costa Rican money before he leaves town.*

As Anna headed for the door, she looked down at herself and paused again. The success of her mission depended on her ability to steal through the night. But the red T-shirt she had changed into would keep her from blending with the darkness. It was the only T-shirt she had with her, so out of Charles' suitcase she grabbed the dark-blue T-shirt and baseball cap he had picked up at the airport for his niece. She slipped his T-shirt over her own, pulled her hair back in a ponytail, and put on the cap.

She opened the door and looked left and right to make sure no one would see her slipping out. Despite her attempt at disguise, the attendants at the front desk might still recognize her as one of Jose's escorts and alert him. So instead of taking the elevator to the lobby, she decided it would be safer to take the stairs and leave through a side door. Just in case cameras were monitoring the hallway, she strode to the stairwell that accessed the parking area behind the hotel.

Anna pushed open the exit door and stepped into the fresh night air. She stood, momentarily savoring the starlit night and the cool ocean breeze. The feeling of freedom excited all her senses. After nearly ten years of captivity and abuse, this moment was exhilarating.

*I'm free! There's no one around. Nothing is restraining me. I can run. And I can find my way back home.*

But Anna's feet didn't move. Like an animal released after years of confinement, she stood paralyzed. Two things kept her from running: her love for the children, and her refusal to leave without Rosa.

*No, I cannot do this. I will not do this. God didn't tell me to run. I believe he has directed me to find the missionaries. But how can I find them? Which way should I go?*

Anna remembered that Jose and the guards had talked about the missionaries handing out religious literature down at the park. But there was more than one park in town. Which park would they choose?

The closest one to the hotel was about two miles away. She could probably get to that park, though she still feared Charles would wake up before she could get back.

After a few minutes of considering who she feared most, Charles or Jose, Anna decided she had no choice but to go forward with her plan to find the missionaries.

Anna started sprinting toward the park. To be even less conspicuous, she stuck to back streets, darting from one dark area to another, and stopped every few blocks to catch her breath.

At this time of night, taxi cabs were everywhere, but she was afraid to flag one down. Jose had sometimes boasted about his *business relationship* with the cab drivers, police officers, and shop owners. So she knew she had to be careful and trust no one.

At some point, Anna went down an alley and came out by a house that had chickens in the yard. Her sudden appearance startled them, and they began cackling hysterically. A man ran out on the porch, ranting and waving his fists.

"Who are you?" he yelled. "And what do you think you're doing? You're trying to steal one of my chickens, aren't you? If you don't get out of my yard, I'm calling the police."

Knowing the noise would draw attention, Anna bolted. Within a couple blocks, she came near the area where the bars and restaurants line the beach. Jose always had guards there watching out for his escorts, so she had to avoid that strip. Charles usually walked her down the coastline and then to the park, so she left the streets and took that route.

Though this route would take more of her precious time, it was darker and safer. Still, danger lurked. Jose's friends included other guards who often patrolled the beach. Anna prayed that no one would recognize her. To make herself look less suspicious, she slowed her pace to a stroll.

It wasn't long before she heard something a short distance behind her. It seemed to advance and stop in sync with her steps.

A cold shiver shot down her spine.

*What was that? Even worse, who was that?*

"Hey, you. Stop!" a man called out.

Anna stopped in her tracks and waited a moment before turning around. Her heart was pounding so hard that she was sure the man must have heard it.

After taking a deep breath to calm herself, she turned to face her enemy.

"Who are you?" she said. "What do you want?"

A face appeared out of the darkness.

"I want you and me to have some fun tonight," the man replied.

Could this be one of Jose's friends trying to find out who she was? Had he recognized her after all her efforts to disguise herself and get away unnoticed?

"What do you mean?" Anna said in a calm tone.

"You think I don't know a hooker when I see one." He let out a sinister laugh.

"Sorry, mister. I'm already busy for the night." She turned and sprinted down the beach.

Finally, Anna saw the park lights in the distance.

# CHAPTER 43

## ANNA MEETS THE MISSIONARIES

As Anna approached the park, she could see two fawn-colored Great Danes in the distance, frolicking under the streetlights. The sight of these stray dogs, which frequented the park looking for food, intensified her sense of urgency. She had seen the dogs before when she and Charles walked through the park, but the sight of them now renewed her fears of him awakening and finding her gone.

Stepping up from the beach's secluded darkness, and into the light of the park, was a dangerous moment for Anna. Jose always had one of his guards there whenever one of his escorts was in the area. So she pulled her cap down close to her face, casting a shadow over her eyes.

Surprisingly, more than the usual number of people strolled through the park at this late hour, enjoying the soft ocean breeze. How could she possibly know who, if any, were missionaries?

She dared not look anyone in the eye. Getting that close could mean looking into the face of one of Jose's guards.

For a brief moment, Anna closed her eyes and whispered a prayer.

"Dear God, please, please help me find the missionaries."

Once again, she surveyed the park, looking for someone unusual, and spotted two men and two ladies standing at the street entrance on the other side of the park. They were handing out literature.

Anna edged closer. At about thirty feet away, she could see their faces had a look of tenderness and care, much different than the harsh, desperate faces of most people. As she stared at them, she glanced down at the materials they were handing out. The men handed out small pamphlets, while the women handed out full sheets of paper with an enlarged picture. After stepping in another few feet, she saw the picture was of Marcos. Underneath was one word in big, bold letters: MISSING.

Praise God! She had found the missionaries.

Anna wanted to run to them, but she had to be careful.

First, she looked to see if Jose's men were there. Sure enough, two of his guards stood across the street, observing all activity in the park. Despite her disguise, they would certainly recognize her if she moved closer into the light. So she drew back into the darkness.

*How can I possibly get the passports to them? My only option is to wait until they leave, and then follow them.*

For almost an hour, Anna watched the missionaries as they continued to hand out literature. They tried to talk with everyone, but they especially desired to help the escorts.

The minutes ticked by painfully slow. Finally, they got their materials together and prepared to leave. Still wondering how she could approach them without the guards seeing her, Anna watched as they headed toward a parking lot.

*No! They can't just get into a car and drive away. They are my only chance to get help.*

Anna continued to watch in disbelief as the missionaries unlocked the car, opened the doors and trunk, and packed everything inside.

*Do I have time to go around the park to get to the parking lot? It's so far away.*

She sprinted after them, begging God to help. Her heart was about to explode. She couldn't take another step. Only a block away, she heard the car engine start and saw the headlights come on.

Anna dropped to her knees. *Noooo! Have I come so close, only to miss them? Dear God, why? Why would you let this happen?*

The car pulled out of the parking lot. But instead of turning right to go into town, it turned left. The missionaries were heading straight toward her.

The headlights shined directly on her as though she were in the spotlight. She sprang to her feet and began waving her arms frantically. Once they got near her, the car slowed to a stop.

The man driving rolled down the window. "Are you okay? Do you need help?"

"Yes...yes...I do," Anna said, between breaths. "I have some important news. Please...let me get into your car."

The man in the back seat got out and helped Anna get in and sit between him and his wife. The lady put her arm around her shoulder and looked into her eyes.

"Honey, what's wrong? We're here, and we'll try to help you."

Still out of breath, Anna gasped. "I watched you hand out literature in the park. Where is the sheet of paper that had a picture on it?"

The lady reached into her purse and pulled out a folded copy of the paper.

"What do you know about this boy?" Anna said.

"He's the son of our dear friends."

Tears filled the lady's eyes as Anna said, "I know where Marcos is. And with your help, I think we can rescue him and a few others held against their will."

The missionaries drove to a safer location, where they talked for more than an hour. Anna shared everything while the lady in the front seat took notes. She told them how Jose had kidnapped the children and forced them into sexual slavery, and the urgency to get Isabella out of danger. Finally, Anna told them how she had managed to get the passports from Jose and smuggle them out. She then handed them over to the missionaries for safekeeping.

"Praise God for allowing us to find Marcos!" the missionary lady said, through tears of joy.

"Yes," said her husband. "We will meet with the other missionaries and try to come up with a plan to rescue you, Marcos, and the children. But it's going to take God's guidance."

# CHAPTER 44

## ANNA RETURNS TO CHARLES

THE WHOLE TIME ANNA WAS AWAY FROM THE HOTEL, the thought of Charles waking up and finding her gone never left her mind.

The missionaries wanted to get her back safely, so they drove as close as possible without arousing any attention. Anna slipped out of the car and entered the back door of the hotel with her room key. As tired and sleepy as she was, she climbed the flight of stairs to their room, but paused at the door.

*Just in case Charles is awake, I need to go back down to the lobby and purchase something as an excuse for my absence.*

She took the elevator this time, making sure the attendants at the desk knew she was coming to the lobby from her room. On her way to the desk, she passed the hotel boutique, which remained closed at that early hour. Nevertheless, Anna took a minute to gaze at the clothes and gift items displayed in the window. Her evening on the run had given her a taste of freedom, and she yearned to be able to go shopping and do other ordinary things on her own.

Anna purchased a bottle of aspirin from the desk and took the elevator up to their room. Hoping not to awaken Charles, she inched the door open and poked her head inside.

Doom swept over her. The bathroom light was on.

*Oh no! Charles is awake. How long has he been waiting for me?*

Her knees went weak. Anna knew she had to hide the cap and T-shirt she had taken out of his luggage, so she stripped them off and stuffed them under her shirt before entering the room.

"Where have you been!" Charles shouted, as he came out of the bathroom.

"I went and purchased this." She held up the bottle of aspirin. "I have a headache."

"It took you thirty minutes to get aspirin!"

She was relieved to know he thought she was gone only thirty minutes.

"Charles, I never have the chance to shop for anything. Jose keeps me shut up like an animal. Please have mercy. I wasn't gone long."

Anna ran into the bathroom and closed the door, crying and pretending she was upset that he didn't trust her. She thought about tossing the cap and T-shirt in the tub behind the shower curtain, thinking she could somehow get them back into his luggage later. But when he followed her into the bathroom, she had to change her strategy. So she pulled the cap and T-shirt out from under her shirt and confessed.

"I wanted these, so I tried them on. I was hoping to go down to the gift shop and buy some just like them with your money. The gift shop was closed, so I only purchased this one bottle of aspirin from the desk."

"I can't believe this! You should never have gone into my luggage or my wallet. And under no circumstance should you have left this room! What made you think you could do this?"

Anna fell to the floor. "Charles, I could have run away, but I didn't. I'm here. I need you to understand that I would never leave you. I just wanted to feel like a normal person. I'm so sorry. Here's all your money back, except for what I bought with the aspirin."

"You know I'm going to have to take you back to Jose and tell him!"

"Noooo! Charles, he will kill me. Please don't. I beg you. I will never do it again. Please give me another chance."

When he heard how scared she was, his anger subsided.

"Anna, you scared me. I didn't know where you were, and I didn't know what to do. Jose makes it very clear to his customers that if they don't bring his escorts back, he will seek revenge. And you know, in my position as a businessman and a politician, I cannot afford to have my reputation come into question."

"You're right," Anna said. "That's why I would never do anything that would hurt your reputation because you have always spoiled me with kindness. Please, please forgive me. I will never again take advantage of our special relationship."

Charles paced the room, running his fingers through his hair.

Finally, he turned and said, "Okay. I will give you this one chance. But if you want to buy something, you must ask me first. We will go shopping to get you a T-shirt and a cap."

"Thank you. Thank you, Charles. I promise I will never, ever disappoint you again."

Anna's heart was more confident than ever that God had designed all the events of the last twelve hours. Now that Charles had forgiven her, her heart continued to leap with joy.

The missionaries knew what had happened to Marcos, and were working on a rescue plan. She had to keep praying that God would deliver him and the rest of them. But for now, she needed to make the rest of her time with Charles as pleasant as possible.

He only had two days to spend in Costa Rica on this trip. For the remainder of that morning, they walked to Jaco's gift shops, where Anna chose a cap and T-shirt. She showed them off as though she were some gorgeous model, and Charles's attitude transitioned from fear and anger to confidence and pride. The thought of Anna choosing to stay with him instead of running away made him proud.

After lunch, they walked on the beach, and then in the park. The Great Danes were still there, running around, scavenging for morsels of food. This time, though, the sight of them brought a smile to Anna's face as her mind replayed the events of the previous evening.

As the couple strolled in the park, they walked by the missionaries who were again handing out gospel tracts and flyers with Marcos's picture. The guards were also there watching. To their approval, Charles and Anna shook their heads and refused the literature. And the missionaries pretended not to know Anna, keeping their secret.

Anna's day with Charles came to an end just as the sun slipped out of sight. They returned to the motel, but Jose was not in his office when they arrived. He was tending to a problem, so they had to wait about fifteen minutes for him to return. They continued to chat warmly, but in her heart, Anna still feared that Charles would tell Jose about her leaving him. The clock on the wall clicked louder and louder as her anxiety mounted.

*Today, I'll live—or I'll die.*

Jose finally returned to the office. "Well, my friend, how did things go?"

Anna sat motionless, afraid even to breathe or look at either of them. After a long pause, Charles stood and looked down on her.

"She is as good as ever, even after five years. A good businessman is willing to pay top dollar for the best merchandise."

Jose looked at Anna with a nod of approval.

"She's my most desired merchandise, and I save her for my most valued clients. I'll make sure she is always available for you."

Anna's heart pounded as she held her breath, waiting for Charles to respond. He now had another opportunity to tell Jose that she had left him.

"Indeed," he replied, with a smile. "I am sure she is your most beautiful *and* trusted employee."

# CHAPTER 45

## CARMEN LEAVES AGAIN

As soon as Charles left, Jose's attitude took an abrupt change. He sat behind his desk, glaring at Anna. A flush of heat swept over her. She cringed, thinking the guards had reported her trip to the park without Charles.

*Oh no! But if that were the case, Jose would have gotten physical with me the moment Charles left.*

Anna concluded that Jose acted peeved because Charles liked her *too* much. Sometimes he took spells where he wanted her all to himself. At other times, he would flip and say she was the reason his business was slow, and that clients weren't asking for her as much anymore. It wasn't unusual for him to accuse any of his escorts whenever something went wrong.

With a swoop of his hand, Jose ordered the guard to take her back to Room 120.

"If I weren't so busy," he said, as she walked out the door, "I would ask for you myself."

Although Anna was away less than forty-eight hours, it seemed like forever. She couldn't wait to see her children.

Before the guard could get the door halfway open, Anna caught a glimpse of Isabella. She was standing, leaning sideways, peeping to see who was coming in the door. Anna's heart leaped with joy at the sight of her. Isabella started to run to her, but then she remembered the rule about not showing affection in front of Jose's people.

Once the guard locked the door, Anna picked Isabella up, gave her a big hug, and swung her around in the air.

"I missed you so much! But guess what. I didn't forget about you and Carmen. I bought something for you."

Anna then gave Carmen the T-shirt, and Isabella the baseball cap. They were thrilled with their gifts, and eager to hear about her outing. But Anna could only share the highlights of sightseeing, shopping, and eating. She wanted to tell Carmen about meeting with the missionaries and the plan to escape, but that wasn't possible right now. The success of the escape plan depended on secrecy between her and the missionaries. This way, if Jose found out about it, they wouldn't suffer because they had not participated in the plan.

Anna's return wasn't all joyful because there was still no sign of Marcos. She felt helpless, and didn't know how to help him.

"Carmen, do you know anything about Marcos?"

"No. I haven't seen him in the dining room, or heard anything about him. It's like he just disappeared."

Anna didn't ask any more questions because she could see by the look on Isabella's face that she was upset that Marcos was gone.

That evening, when they turned off the lamp to go to bed, Isabella asked to sleep with her, which she allowed because she had left her for two days. Isabella soon fell asleep—safe for another night.

The following day at breakfast, Jose was eating at his usual table, so Anna got up the nerve to approach him and ask about Marcos.

"Haven't I told you to mind your own business," he snapped.

"Jose, where is he? You know that if anything happens to him, we'll all be in trouble. He is an American kid."

Jose jumped up, overturning his chair with a *bang!* He grabbed Anna by the hair with one hand, and clenched her face with the other. He punctuated every few words with profanity.

"Are you trying to tell me what to do? Do you think I'm some stupid kid who needs your advice? I told Javier not to bring that kid here. Now I have to get him off the junk he's hooked on. But for your information, Miss Must-Know-It-All, he's in a separate room, drying out. Do you want that crazy kid in your room? From now on, just shut up about him and mind your own business."

Still cursing under his breath, he walked away.

Then he turned around. "Forget him. I know how to make him disappear if he doesn't straighten up."

Anna didn't know what Jose meant by making Marcos disappear, but she'd heard of people disappearing in the Tarcoles River. The locals call it Crocodile River due to the massive crocs that live in it, and the dozens that hang out under the river bridge, eager to eat. To make matters worse, she had no idea where Jose could have Marcos locked up. It could be in another room at the motel, or at another one of his properties.

The one thing Anna did know was that Jose's escalating anger meant she could not jeopardize the rescue of Isabella and Carmen to save Marcos. For now, she felt some consolation knowing she had done everything she could do for the boy. At least the missionaries knew what had happened to him.

Sadly, Anna had no way to let them know how much danger he was in, or that he may no longer even be at the motel.

After returning from breakfast, the guard told Carmen that her client would be coming to pick her up, and she needed to get ready for an all-day escort service. Carmen got prepared, as usual. But this time, she came over and sat on Anna's bed.

"Anna, I never thought I would become attached to anyone, as I have to you. Thank you for everything you have done for us."

Anna's face must have revealed her puzzlement at Carmen's unexpected words of endearment, but she didn't ask any questions.

Carmen's eyes filled with tears as she said goodbye, hugging Isabella and Anna tight.

The sound of the padlock opening interrupted the long embrace. Carmen jumped to her feet, trying to hide her emotions.

The guards seldom interacted with any of the girls because Jose was extremely strict about making sure they left them alone. He was a no-nonsense boss, and he believed he was a good manager. But Goliath, for whatever reason, started to flirt with Carmen.

"You got yourself a real fan." He looked her over. "This blond-haired, blue-eyed American has certainly taken a liking to you. I don't know what you got going for yourself, but you must be really fine."

Who was this American? Anna wished she had talked with Carmen about him before she left. Even if she had thought to ask, they couldn't have spoken with Isabella in the room. Nothing seemed to escape those little ears of hers.

# CHAPTER 46

## JOSE TAKES ISABELLA

THE NEXT DAY, ANNA DECIDED to play school with Isabella instead of playing paper dolls. As the child of farmworkers, Anna didn't have the opportunity to attend school regularly, but her parents made sure she received as much education as possible. The missionaries who frequently passed through their village supplemented primary education, teaching her how to read and write in Spanish and English. Anna loved to read, so her father brought home books from the little library every time he went to the village.

Isabella was at the age of learning, and Anna wanted to provide that opportunity. So she started her class by teaching Isabella how to read. Since the Bible was the only book available, Isabella's first lesson began by learning to read from God's Word. After reading, they worked on mathematics, followed by frolicking and silliness. At the close of the day, they climbed into bed, told secrets, giggled, and snuggled up.

That night, as Isabella struggled to keep her eyes open, she looked up and said, "Anna, I like being your little girl. I want you to be my mom forever."

Anna couldn't have loved her one ounce more if she were her birth mother. Perhaps she loved her even more because she was a special gift from God—a child born in her heart, supernaturally.

"Isabella, in my heart, you already are my child. But we must keep this as our secret for the time being."

Isabella held out her pinky finger and asked Anna to pinky swear their promise to keep the secret.

Isabella soon fell into a peaceful sleep. That is, until the clanking of the padlock broke the silence.

Jose barged into the room, startling Isabella to the point that she shrieked. He then yanked Anna out of bed and put his hands around her neck.

"Where is she!" he yelled, with his nose in her face. "Why didn't you tell me? You knew she was planning this, didn't you? You have become too attached to these children. Well, I can make sure you never have that opportunity again."

"Jose, please stop," Anna choked out the words. "What do you mean? I haven't done anything."

Jose turned Anna loose, snatched Isabella up with the swoop of his arm, and headed out the door with the child kicking and screaming in the clutch of his strong arms. He may as well have ripped Anna's heart right out of her chest.

It all made sense now. Carmen must have escaped. Anna was happy for her, if she had managed to get away—but not at Isabella's expense. That wasn't fair.

Where had Jose taken her little one? Anna began to scream and bang on the padlocked door.

Eventually, she slumped to the floor and called out to God.

"Why did you let this happen? When will you ever deliver us? I don't understand any of this. Please have mercy. Please, please, protect my little Isabella."

Still on the floor in front of the door, Anna noticed Isabella's backpack beside her bed. With sparked interest, she rummaged through it until she found Isabella's cross necklace. In the clutch of her hand, she held the cross tight against her chest and wept. Thoughts of how sweetly Isabella lay sleeping in her arms until Jose snatched her away grieved Anna down deep in her soul.

# CHAPTER 47

## ISABELLA RETURNS

THERE WAS NO SUNSHINE the next morning, just lingering rain and the occasional roll of thunder. It had stormed all night, and the weather matched the dark, turbulent mood of Anna's heart.

Upon awakening, she turned her face to the wall, feeling like God had forsaken her again. As she lay there, sulking, she heard a rooster crow. A familiar sound in these parts of the world, even when it rained. But this time, the rooster crowed three times and stopped. That nudged Anna's conscience.

*I know the Apostle Peter was afraid the night Jesus was on trial before his crucifixion. But the sudden crowing of a rooster in the night brought conviction to his heart about his needless fear and lack of faith. Peter immediately repented, and so must I. Lord, forgive me.*

Later that morning, the guard removed the padlock, and in walked Isabella. Anna didn't know why she was so shocked that the child had returned. God had already answered many of her prayers.

When the guard relocked the door, they held each other tight without saying a word. Anna didn't want to talk about what had happened until Isabella was ready. It was evident that what she needed most was rest, so they lay on her bed and slept until it was time for lunch.

Isabella usually enjoyed going to the dining room, but this

day she dreaded leaving their room, even for food. She was afraid, and she inched down the hall beside Anna, with her head hung down.

As soon as they entered the dining room, Anna saw Marcos sitting with the guards.

"Do you see Marcos?" Isabella whispered.

"Yes, I do see him."

*So happy to see him. Thank you, Father, for answering another prayer. Just knowing Marcos is alive is further proof that you are still at work.*

Anna watched Marcos, hoping he would glance at her, but he never looked around at any time. His eyes were dark and hollow, and he had lost weight. He was clean now, but she couldn't imagine him being of any value to Jose with his spirit so broken. She just hoped he wouldn't continue fighting. Otherwise, Jose would get rid of him.

"Where is Carmen?" Isabella said, when they returned to their room.

Anna was reluctant to answer the child, just in case Jose questioned her again. And she didn't want her to worry either. Jose had already put her through enough trauma.

"I'm not sure where Carmen is," Anna replied. "The only thing I am sure about is that God is answering prayers, and he will take care of her."

Anna didn't know where Carmen was, but she had a pretty good idea that her last client was Andrew. The guard's remarks about him certainly fit Carmen's earlier description of him. He must have returned for her, as he had promised he would, and helped her escape. That would explain Carmen's loving remarks when she left.

The probability that Carmen had gotten free from a life of slavery filled Anna's heart with joy. But she still feared that Jose would catch her, and that her life was still in jeopardy. If Carmen didn't make it out of town, and out of Costa Rica altogether, Jose would indeed find her—and kill her.

"Would you like to play dolls some more?" Anna asked

Isabella, hoping she would relax and tell her about what happened after Jose took her away.

When Anna was young, she and her sister would count down the days until their birthdays. Now, strangely, she was counting down the days before Isabella's client would come for her. If Isabella had heard something while she was with Jose—something that might help them escape before that happened—Anna needed to know about it.

As soon as Isabella spread the dolls out on the floor, she began to talk.

"I sure hope the guards don't find Carmen."

"Oh, did you hear something about it when you were with Jose?" said Anna.

Without looking up, Isabella wrinkled her nose and squinted as she recalled something dreadful.

"Yes. Jose was mad. He said he would kill somebody."

"Hmm. Is that right? Who was he talking about?"

"I don't know. He was mad at some man." She sat close to Anna. "I was so scared. I cried and begged Jose to bring me back here. He yelled and told me to shut up and stop crying. But I couldn't stop crying. He was throwing stuff around and saying bad words. I was so scared."

Anna didn't want to upset Isabella, but she needed the little girl to tell every detail she had heard or seen.

She wasn't worried that Jose had sexually abused Isabella because the client coming for her had explicitly requested a virgin child.

Anna said, "Did Jose know you were listening?"

"No! I acted like I was sleeping. Jose is always mean. And he yells bad words all the time. I was afraid to say or do anything except close my eyes after he told me to stop crying and go to sleep."

"You are a brave and smart girl. Why don't you tell me everything you heard in the office? It will be our secret forever."

After a long pause, Isabella said, "W-when Jose picked me up, h-he took me down to his office, where he keeps all of those papers. He said he wanted me to tell him where Carmen was. I-I told him I didn't know. He screamed at me. But I really didn't know what he was talking about."

Isabella began to cry, so she paused again to play with the dolls. In a few minutes, she took a deep breath and continued. This time, she rattled off the rest of her story without stopping.

"When Jose took me to his office, he told me to get on the bed and not to move. So I did. I put my head under the sheet and didn't come out. Two guards came in and told him they had looked everywhere for Carmen and her client. They thought the American had planned for a long time to take her away someplace. Jose yelled so loud that I put my hands over my ears. He even yelled at the guards to get out."

"And then what," Anna said.

"Then I was so afraid, I started crying out loud. Jose came over and yanked the sheet off me. I begged him to please, please, not hurt me. And he didn't. He just opened his desk drawer and drank out of a bottle."

"Go on," Anna said. "What happened next?"

"Then a guard came in and said someone saw Carmen leave Jaco with a man that had blond hair. He said he thought they went to the airport. Jose then laughed and laughed. He said he had people everywhere."

"Then what?" Anna said.

"Then he called somebody on the phone and asked what cab driver had picked Carmen up. Jose yelled more bad words and slammed the phone down. He told the guard to go to the airport and bring Carmen back."

"Wow, Isabella! You are a smart girl to remember all that."

"Yeah. That's not all. In a little while, Jose drank more of that stuff. And when he tried to stand up, he fell over his chair and landed on the floor. He didn't get up all night. I had to go to the bathroom, so I tiptoed right past him. He never knew I even got up."

Isabella paused long enough for Anna to praise her bravery.

"Next thing I remember, there was a loud knock on the

door, and it wasn't night anymore. Jose got up and brought me back here. That's all I know."

When Isabella finally got the whole story out, Anna started to laugh.

"What's so funny?"

Through bursts of laughter, Anna said, "Isabella, I think Carmen outsmarted Jose. If this client is who I think he is, I think they went to the airport to throw Jose off the trail. This client won't be taking Carmen to America—at least not right now. I think he'll be taking her to see their baby. I'm not quite sure about all that's going on, but I know God does."

# CHAPTER 48

## ROLEPLAY

For Isabella's sake, Anna knew she couldn't tell her about the missionaries. Still, she needed to convey to the child some idea about what might happen if there was a rescue attempt. So Anna started a new game with the paper dolls. This time, she chose two men and two women, and told Isabella they were missionaries.

"What are missionaries?"

"They are men and women who give their lives to help others learn about Jesus and the cross. Also, they help people because of their love for God."

"Oh, I bet that's why the lady at the airport was so nice to me. She had that cross necklace. Do you think she was a missionary?"

Anna couldn't help but smile. "She may have been. If not, her heart appeared to be the same as a missionary's."

Next, Anna chose a man doll to represent Jose, and a woman doll to be herself.

"Which doll do you want to be?"

Isabella chose the youngest girl doll.

"Well, which doll is Marcos?" Anna said.

Isabella took a minute to look at each of the male dolls, before selecting the youngest one that showed the most fraying.

"What about Carmen?" Isabella said.

Anna smiled. “Oh, I don’t think we need a Carmen doll. Remember, she’s with her American friend.”

Isabella giggled. “Oh, that’s right. I forgot. But I sure do miss her.”

While Isabella put up the other dolls, Anna folded her bedsheet into a square and placed it on the floor, telling her that they would put on a puppet show. She explained that they would pretend the sheet was the motel. Anna then placed the dolls in separate areas in the *motel.* Isabella and Anna were in Room 120. Jose was in his office. Marcos was in his new room, and the missionaries were outside the motel.

Using the dolls that represented themselves, Isabella and Anna talked back and forth like puppets, laughing and having fun. After a bit, Anna told Isabella they needed to include some of the other dolls.

“You can pretend to be Marcos,” Anna said, “and I’ll be the missionaries.”

“I don’t want to be Marcos,” said Isabella. “I want to be a missionary. Marcos gets beat up all the time.”

“Well, I’ll let you be one of the missionaries the second time we play. Right now, I would like to see how you can make Marcos be a good boy.”

Isabella beamed. “Oh, I can do that. I’ll make Marcos behave.”

She picked up the Marcos doll and held both paper dolls up, ready to pretend. Anna picked up two of the missionaries and began a conversation with them. Isabella looked puzzled because Anna wasn’t interacting with her.

“Why are you playing over there by yourself, and not with me?”

“Because I want you to watch me so you can learn about missionaries. See, I know about them. You don’t. After you watch me play like a missionary, you’ll know what they do.”

Anna began to speak as the missionaries who were saying that they wanted to help the children at the motel. They needed to get them to a better place to attend school and play with other children. Anna hoped that if the missionaries did come to rescue them, Isabella would recall this game and understand why they wanted to take them away from the motel. The success of the escape plan could hinge on Isabella's understanding and cooperation.

After a bit, Anna had the lady missionary say to her, "We want to help the children. How many do you have?"

The Anna doll responded, "There are two children in my room. I would like for you to help them first."

"Yes. I see the two children. How can we help them? Jose doesn't like sharing. He doesn't allow them to play outside of the motel."

The male missionary replied, "We will have to buy them. Jose likes money."

"How many will we be able to buy?" the lady said.

"We will get as many as we can. But we may have to make separate attempts to get them."

"That makes sense. I just hope Jose doesn't find out."

"That's why we must keep this top secret and act this out very well," the man whispered.

"Oh, happy day!" said the lady. "We will be able to bring all the children to our place, where they will be able to play and pet the animals. And I will cook all kinds of good food for them. I want to make sure they enjoy three healthy meals a day."

Anna then asked Isabella if she would like to play the missionaries this time. She had to get this part down before they could add any new information.

Isabella took the missionary paper dolls and began playing. Anna could hardly believe it. Isabella repeated nearly everything she had said. Before putting the dolls down, she added a little more.

The missionary man said, "That Jose is a mean man. He is not good to people, but I will take care of him one of these days."

The missionary lady replied, "We must pray that Jesus will save him."

It blessed Anna's soul to see that Isabella knew they should pray for the salvation of those who hated and abused them.

They continued to play for the rest of the afternoon, and Anna kept reminding her that they must keep this game a secret.

"Isabella, we have been playing in our dream world, but I want you to know that sometimes dreams do come true. And I want you also to understand that some dreams come true, only if you keep them secret. Promise me that you will keep our dreams a secret, so maybe one day we can be in a new place with the missionaries."

"I promise." Isabella held up her pinky finger to link with Anna's to seal the deal.

# CHAPTER 49

## MORE ROLEPLAY

Marcos wasn't at lunch that day. And as dinnertime approached, Anna longed to see him again. Doing so would give her peace of mind, knowing that whatever shape he was in, at least there was still hope.

Within minutes, the guard came to get Isabella and Anna. As soon as they entered the dining room, Anna saw Marcos sitting alone at one of the cold metal tables in the corner of the room. Tears of delight welled up in her eyes. Though he looked thin and frail, he still appeared to be clean.

*I hate for his parents to find him looking so bad. I don't even know how the missionaries could rescue him because Jose locked him up in isolation. And I don't think he will allow Marcos to go out with a client until he is sure the boy is totally off drugs.*

Isabella and Anna went to their assigned table and sat across from the two vacant chairs. Looking at Carmen's empty chair gave Anna a sense of hope that one day someone would free them as well.

On the other hand, looking at the chair where Marcos used to sit brought sorrow. Though problems always surrounded the boy, she still loved and missed not having him in Room 120. As bad as things were for him now, he was still a part of her little family.

Even at a distance, seeing Marcos free of drugs was God's

blessing. Perhaps even a token of what would soon be a reality.

At one point, he lifted his eyes to meet Anna's. What she saw in him was deep despair and hopelessness. She smiled at him with as much love as she could give him through facial expression without being noticed. He looked back down, pretending he hadn't noticed.

Jose walked up to Anna's table and stood with his hands on his hips, looming over her as though she had done something wrong. She feared he had noticed her smiling at Marcos.

He led her to the door where the guard was standing, and stared at her with his face just inches from hers.

He said, "You just need to remember that my client is paying a high price for Isabella, and she better be ready and willing."

"I'm training her, and she will be ready."

*Yes, she will be ready—but not the way you think.*

When Anna walked back to the table, Isabella looked up with fear on her face.

"Don't' worry, little one. Everything is fine."

As they walked back to their room, Anna remembered her father saying that many of God's people have suffered persecution and imprisonment at the hands of their enemies. Those who hate God will, by nature, hate and hurt those who love and obey him.

This recollection brought consolation. Anna realized that this evil they were experiencing was not from God. They cannot blame him when people break his moral laws, and innocent people get hurt.

*Still, I can't understand why this evil came upon me, especially when Father and Mother trusted God and committed me into his hands when I left home. Why, God? Will I ever know why?*

When Anna's parents struggled with hardships, they gained strength and encouragement from reading the old Bible that missionaries had distributed when they visited their little village over thirty years ago. Just holding that sacred, God-inspired book in their hands brought peace and comfort to their hearts.

Before Anna left home, they took some of their hard-earned

savings to buy her a Bible of her own. These past years, she tried not to think much about the Bible or home. She couldn't—it hurt too much. She couldn't bear to think of what may have happened to her parents and little sister. Were they still alive? Would she ever be able to see them again?

Only God knew.

That evening, back in their room, Anna and Isabella played the puppet game again. This time, they practiced keeping their plan a secret from Jose and the guards.

"Isabella, I want you to pick out two more male dolls from the collection. One will be a guard, and the other will be Jose."

Isabella selected the largest doll to represent Goliath, and the only doll without a smile to represent Jose.

"This time around," Anna said, "you will use the doll that represents you in one hand and the doll that represents me in the other hand. You will pretend that you and I are playing dolls on the floor. I will use the Jose doll, and I will pretend to come into the room and catch you playing dolls. But remember, you must keep our secret about the missionaries coming, okay?"

"Okay. I can pretend that." Isabella got down on the floor and played like she and Anna were talking about the missionaries coming.

Anna appeared, holding the Jose and the guard dolls, who acted mad and wanted to know what they were pretending.

"We're playing paper dolls," Isabella said. "We're pretending guests are coming. They're going to take us someplace to have fun and play games. Anna says I must get ready to go with the guests. That's what we're pretending."

"That's a good game," Anna said, as she pretended to be Jose. "Anna is doing a good job of getting you ready."

The next time around, Anna pretended to be one of the guards who came in and wanted to know what they are playing. Again, Isabella kept their secret, never once mentioning that the guests were missionaries. She did so well that Anna was shocked and proud of her at the same time.

After they played dolls for a while longer, they went to bed.

Isabella quickly fell asleep, but Anna continued looking through the barred window at the full moon, wondering where the missionaries were and when they would act on their plan. She always dreaded the nighttime, when her mind played out the events of the day. This night, it refused to shut down and let her sleep. As she lay awake, listening to Isabella's breathing, Anna began to worry.

*What will happen if Jose goes into the safe for something and discovers the passports are missing? What if one of the guards recognizes the missionaries when they come to the motel? Or worse, what if Isabella's client gets here before the missionaries? Isabella will happily go with the client, thinking he's her* angel.

Thoughts of imminent danger for the little girl horrified Anna. The idea of a man forcing himself on sweet, innocent Isabella was unbearable.

Unable to sleep, Anna got up and stood over Isabella for a good while, watching her sleep peacefully. At last, she crawled back into bed, begging God to keep the child safe and to give herself childlike peace.

The following day, after breakfast, Isabella and Anna played paper dolls again. To Isabella, it was just a game. But it was a matter of survival to Anna. Not knowing what would happen, she wanted Isabella to be ready for different situations. This time, she had only one male missionary to arrive at the motel to request a six-year-old girl.

With eyebrows drawn together and lips pursed, Isabella expressed her disapproval of that idea. "I don't want the man to come for me. I want the lady to come for me!"

"It's okay," Anna said. "The lady is scared to come here, so the male missionary is the best choice. He will protect you with his big arms and muscles."

A mischievous smile spread across Isabella's face.

"Oh well, in that case, I want that one." She pointed to a large male doll.

Anna picked up the doll that represented Isabella. "This time, I'm going to pretend that I am both you and Jose, and you will be the big missionary. We will play like he has come to take you away with him."

The missionary said, in a man's voice, "Hi, Jose. I'm the missionary man, and I want to buy a pretty little six-year-old to come and live at the school. We have lots of toys."

Fear gripped Anna. "Isabella, don't forget that we don't want Jose to know that these men and women are missionaries. They are good people, like angels, who go about doing good things. Jose would not like these missionaries if he knew who they were, so never act like you know who they are." She set the doll down. "I have an idea. Since you and I are good at keeping secrets, we will make up a secret sign that stands for angels. What kind of sign do you think we should make up?"

Isabella put her hand to her chin and rolled her eyes in deep thought.

"Wings," she said. "Angel wings!"

"That's a great sign," Anna said. "All angels have two wings. If we want to signal the presence of an angel, or a missionary acting like an angel, we will hold two fingers down by our side. That way, no one will notice the signal. Just remember two super-important things. First, remember that the secret signal means you are safe and with an angel. Second, remember that if an angel comes to you, pretend he is a client who has come to buy you."

"Okay," Isabella replied. "I will pretend they are bad people, and not good missionaries."

Next time around, when the missionary came to the motel, she said, in the man's voice, "I have come to buy a pretty six-year-old girl. Do you have one?"

Anna replied to her request, imitating Jose's voice. "Yes, but she costs a lot of money."

Isabella pretended to give Jose money for the girl. Then the missionary and the girl walked away. Suddenly great sadness came over her. Tears welled up in her eyes as she dropped her chin onto her chest.

"I don't want to leave you," Isabella said.

"It's okay. You will be safe with the missionaries. They will take you to a beautiful place to play games with other children. They'll give you lots of good food, and they will take good care of you until I get there. It's part of a game. You'll see."

Isabella said, "Do you promise?"

Anna held up her pinky finger. "Yes. If God permits."

That evening, Anna lay on her bed, thinking about how the time for success or failure drew closer to the end.

*Where are the missionaries? If they don't show up in time, I will have failed Isabella by not preparing her for the terror she will experience. So many things can still go wrong. What if Jose decides he wants me to stay with him when I need to spend these last days with Isabella? Dear God, this thing called trust is so hard. Please have mercy. I beg of you.*

# CHAPTER 50

## ANNA GETS BAD NEWS

JOSE CAME OVER TO ANNA'S TABLE at breakfast the following day and ordered her to go with him to the office. Every time he summoned her to his office, he gave her bad news. This time was no different.

"Isabella's client is coming a week early. His assistant called and said they should arrive this morning. I will come for her as soon as he gets here. I have told you repeatedly to prepare her. She better not give me any trouble. The client strongly insisted that she should not make a scene. So you better make sure of it."

Jose's words hit her like a deathblow. Her worst fear had come true. The blood drained from her face as she struggled for breath. Feeling week, she leaned against Jose's desk to steady herself.

*The missionaries are too late. Where is God? Why did he leave me again when I was doing my very best to trust him? In what way have I failed him?*

Jose slammed his fist on his desk and lunged toward her.

"Did you not hear what I've been telling you for the past weeks!"

"Y-yes. I have been preparing Isabella." Anna wrung her trembling hands. "I have roleplayed with her. M-make-believe will help her deal with her job."

He snorted and glared at her. "Well, we will see if you have done something to prepare her."

"Jose, may I at least bring her to your office and stay with her until she leaves with the client? Isabella is calm when I'm with her. She will perform better."

"Okay, but you better not shed a tear or cause any trouble. If you do, it will be bad for both of you."

Anna returned to the dining room, and there sat her innocent little girl, staring at her. Isabella could sense Anna was upset, but she didn't say anything. She had learned that Jose always upset Anna.

*Why didn't I prepare Isabella for the what-if situation? All this preparation for the missionaries to rescue us was a total waste of time—a disaster. Right now, nothing but divine intervention can save my little girl.*

The thought of God saving Isabella brought to her mind the Bible story of Moses, the leader of the nation of Israel. When Pharaoh, king of Egypt, issued an order for his guards to kill all Israelite male babies, the infant Moses's mother took a drastic step of faith to save his life. She put him in a basket and floated it on the water, hidden by the bulrushes growing along the riverbank. She must have worried that her son could starve or drown, yet she trusted God. And as God would have it, Pharaoh's very own daughter rescued and raised Moses in the king's palace.

Remembrance of this instance of God going beyond logical expectations to accomplish his will brought Anna peace of mind. She believed she had done all she could do. Now, she just had to *put her baby in the bulrushes* and trust in God to keep Isabella safe.

*I have to keep trusting God. Maybe, just maybe, this client is one of the missionaries. But Jose seemed confident that he was the client who had arrived early. I'm sure Jose has already confirmed the man's identity. He is a shrewd businessman, one not easily fooled. There is no way the missionaries could come up with this ruse on their own. I didn't have enough time to give them much detail, but I did tell them that a man was coming for her in two weeks. Could they have fooled Jose? Maybe I'm worrying when God is working.*

Back in Room 120, after breakfast, Anna grabbed hold of Isabella's hands.

"My dear, today we are not going to roleplay using paper dolls. Instead, we are going to act out our play with real people."

Isabella wrinkled her brow. "What do you mean?"

"We will use Jose's office as our stage, and we will perform the play just as we have practiced it. You must remember, though, that missionaries serve God, as angels do. You must play like you don't know who they are. That's their secret, and you must keep it. If you act happy to see them, you will give that secret away."

"I know." Isabella gave a vigorous nod. "We have gone over this many times. I'll pretend like we've been playing."

Soon, the guard came and unlocked the door. Jose stepped into the room with his chest puffed out and chin high in the air.

In a buoyant tone, he said, "It's time, girls. Come with me."

Isabella picked up her backpack and stood by Anna's side. Hand-in-hand, they followed Jose to his office. When they arrived, Anna realized the man waiting for them was not one of the missionaries. Her heart plummeted to the depths of Hell. She was sure she was looking at the devil square in the face.

There was nothing she could do now to save Isabella from sexual abuse. And like a little angel herself, Isabella stood fearless, acting out her make-believe role.

# CHAPTER 51

## ISABELLA'S CLIENT

"Girls, I want you to meet Juan. He will be taking Isabella out for several days of fun and good food."

Anna kept looking at the man, and he stared back at her.

"What is *your* name?" he said.

"She's not for sale," Jose snapped.

"I didn't ask to purchase her. I asked her name."

Jose was getting more contentious by the minute. A scowl now replaced his happy face.

"Why are you asking?" he said. "You said you wanted the little one."

The man grinned. "Ahhh, this woman is a nice product for another time."

"She is *not* for sale."

The man laughed. "Am I not allowed even to admire your merchandise?"

"You can have any of my escorts except her. She is mine."

"The old saying is, *Everything has a price*. So are you sure about that?"

"I'm sure she's not for sale today."

"One more thing," the man said. "Do you have any boys to go along for my partner?"

Jose was puzzled at all the questions about his other merchandise. But seeing a possible opportunity to market the problematic Marcos, he tempered his tone.

"How old?"

The man grinned and leaned forward. "Young is preferred."

"I do have a young boy, but he isn't available today. If you call in advance, we'll reserve whatever you want. But we stay busy around here. The next time he is available is next week."

The man said, "Maybe I don't want to wait till next week. Maybe I don't want him at all. I'm picky. Do you have a picture of him?"

Anna knew the missionaries wanted to get Marcos and Isabella out together, which made her wonder if this man might be one of them, after all. Then the man asked an odd question.

"Is this little girl an angel? You do remember that I specifically requested a pure little angel."

That comment was a confirmation. This man was indeed a missionary, and not a client.

A cold wave of goosebumps swept over Anna as joy filled her heart. She could barely keep her face from showing it. At the same time, though, the man continued talking too much about the boy. She began to worry that he was asking too many questions, and it looked like Jose was getting suspicious.

"Okay, I will be back to get the boy," he said, picking up on Jose's temperament.

Jose looked even more puzzled. "I thought you wanted the girl for a week."

"I do want her for a week. What is the amount you will take for her?"

Anna knew then that they might be in trouble because Jose would have already given the real client the price. Worse than that, what would happen if the missionary didn't have enough money for Isabella for the week?

"Where's the money?" Jose held out his hand. "You know what we agreed on. Hand it over."

"Look, how much will you charge if I go ahead and pay for the boy upfront as well? I'm all about deals."

Jose cocked his head to the side, as he always did when he

was wheeling and dealing.

"How long do you want the boy?"

"One week for each of them. That's two sales." The man held up two fingers right in Jose's face.

"Well, just double the amount we agreed on," Jose said.

Because the client didn't respond immediately, Jose narrowed his eyes as he stared at him. The man needed to name the price quoted earlier, but he had no way of knowing that price.

Anna had to do something fast. She knew that little American girls ran $150 a night, but Jose would have quoted more since Isabella was also a virgin. Anna also knew that Jose would gladly accept the higher price without further discourse if the man offered more than the original amount. It may not be the right amount, but Anna discretely moved her right hand a bit to get the man's attention. Then she flashed two fingers, hoping he would notice them.

The man glanced at her fingers. "Yes, I know you wanted two hundred."

"Don't try to cheat me," Jose said. "You know it's two hundred a night for each of them."

"Yes, I know. But since I'm purchasing two escorts, you should give me a better price."

Jose got in the man's face. "This is the price. Take it or get out."

"Okay, I'll take it." The man shrugged. "You win some, you lose some. Here's three thousand for both, for one week each, including your tip."

Jose snatched the cash from the man. "You better have her back by sundown, in seven days."

Isabella turned and looked at Anna with obvious confusion. Anna had known this moment would come when Isabella would struggle and need a nonverbal sign to give her courage, so she gave her the angel wing sign they had practiced. Isabella gave a slight smile, and slowly released two fingers, holding them close to her side. Though she understood this man was an *angel*, it was still hard for her to leave.

She stood silently with her gaze fixed on Anna's. The man took Isabella's hand to lead her away. She turned to follow, but continued to look back at Anna over her shoulder. It was every bit as painful for Anna to see Isabella walk away, yet her heart leaped with joy, knowing this child was only a few steps from freedom. She had to let this precious little bird fly, even if she never saw her again.

"I have my suspicions about that man," Jose said, after they left. "I'll have the guards keep a careful watch on them. For a few minutes there, I had my doubts that the deal was even going to go down. But I must say, Anna, you surprised me. You trained her well."

He followed his praise with a slap on her backside, which he did on those rare occasions when she pleased him.

"Yes. Yes, I did," Anna replied. *He has no idea just how well.*

"Now, let's see if you can help Marcos to have a little more cooperative attitude." Jose wore a smirky smile. "If not, I will personally train him."

"Oh, I'm sure I can help Marcos," Anna said. "Just give him back to me."

The guard walked her back to Room 120, where the concrete walls were darker and more dismal than ever before. It had been a long time since none of the children were in the room, and loneliness crept over her. Looking around, she noticed Isabella's paper dolls staring back at her with the same emptiness that she felt.

Isabella's rescue was bittersweet.

# CHAPTER 52

## THE REAL MARCOS

THE SUN CAME UP LATE THE NEXT DAY—or so it seemed. Anna had slept long and hard for the first time in years. When she finally opened her eyes, her heart filled with happy thoughts. Two of her children had escaped Jose's prison. Now, there was only one child left. That one was Marcos, and that rescue would be difficult and dangerous. She didn't even know where he was.

As soon as Anna thought of Marcos, the guard removed the padlock and opened the door. There, in the doorway, the boy stood straight and tall, which was not typical. Neither was his mode of entry into the room usual. A guard usually pitched, pushed, kicked, or shoved him in. This time, Marcos walked in without a hand laid on him. Anna could hardly believe her eyes.

Once the door closed, she jumped up and gave him a big hug. Typically, he would have pulled away. But again, he wasn't acting like his usual self. This time, he wrapped his arms around her and hugged her back.

"Anna, I'm sorry for everything I've said and done to hurt you. I-I almost killed you. In confinement, I thought a lot. And I see now that you only wanted to help me."

"It's all right, Marcos. I understand that you were angry. And you had every right to feel that way. These people kidnapped, imprisoned, and abused you in every possible way. I can see why you wouldn't trust me or anyone else. But no matter what happens, you must know that I will always love you. You, me, and the girls, we are family."

Marcos sat down on his bed, shaking his head. "Anna, I've got to get out of here. Sometimes I just want to kill myself. But inside, I know I should not do that. Anna, how do you take this?"

"For years, I only survived by using drugs and alcohol. I would have taken anything to numb my pain. But after you all came, something in me came alive. I wanted to find a way to get us out of here. God used you, Isabella, and Carmen to give me purpose. And I believe he will free us."

"He hasn't freed us yet, so why do you still believe?" Marcos said.

Anna paused, wondering if she should tell him about the missionaries and the rescue plot.

"He's working on it," she said.

Marcos looked around the room. "What happened to Carmen and Isabella?"

Anna realized she had no choice but to tell him what had happened. Right now, he needed hope. Besides, Anna knew the secret would be safe with him. So she sat beside him and explained everything. She even relayed how she had found some missionaries in the park who were looking for him.

"They were looking for *me*?"

"Yes, and that's not the best part. The missionaries said your parents are also here looking for you."

"What! My parents are here in Jaco?"

"Yes, your mother and father are here, but I didn't see them. They're working with other missionaries, and I know they must be praising God that they have finally found you."

For the first time since his imprisonment, Marcos started to cry.

"Why did it take so long?" he said. "Why didn't they search every place before now? Why didn't the missionaries in this area know that we might be at Jose's motel?"

"Marcos, there's just so much you don't know about life. That's because you are young. And your parents were probably unaware that you could be in this kind of danger. But I want to share with you even more about Jose's operation, which may help you understand why it has taken so long for your parents to find you."

The boy nodded.

"You see, Marcos, even in this town, Jose has several rental properties where men come for vacation and legal prostitution. I've been here for years, and from what my clients say, it appears this place is the only property where he sells children. This activity is not well-known because Jose is careful, only selling the younger ones out of the motel's back building. Plus, he's so careful that he only sells the children to foreigners. To keep clients from leaving the country with his *merchandise*, he requires them to leave their passports with him until they return his property. Some of the local shop and restaurant owners know this is going on, but they don't care because Jose's operation draws much-needed income for them as well."

Marcos balled his right hand into a fist and punched his mattress as hard as he could. "One day I'm going to give that man what he deserves!"

"You need to be thankful that your father and mother never gave up looking for you. I found out that they even asked missionaries from all over the country to join in the search to help find you."

"They did!" he shouted. "How do you know all this?"

"It's a long story, so I'll leave out the details for now," Anna whispered, as she scooted closer to make sure no one in the hallway could overhear. "But one day, when I was in Jose's office, a guard came in and told him that missionaries were in the park, handing out gospel literature. Then he broke the news that they were also passing out a sheet of paper that had your picture on it and said you were missing. Jose was furious, claiming these people were ruining his business."

"They were in the park, showing my picture!" Marcos shouted again, forgetting that they were supposed to be speaking in secrecy.

"Yes, but listen to this," Anna said. "One evening, not long after that, I slipped away from my client at a hotel near the park, and met up with the missionaries. I told them all about you and the other children, and they assured me they would come up with a plan to rescue all of us. Carmen has already escaped. The father of her child, who pretended to be a client, rescued her. Marcos, I already see the hand of God working miraculously."

The boy sat on the edge of the bed, shaking his head.

"But Marcos, listen to this. The man who came for Isabella also wanted to take a young male with him. He was so insistent that I have a suspicion he may have been your father.

"What! You think he was my father. What did he look like?"

"He was tall and slender, with dark-brown eyes and dark hair that was nearly black, except for a little gray at the temples."

Marcos gasped. "Did you notice his hands or fingers?"

"Now that you mention it, I do recall that when he counted out his money, half of his right pinky was missing."

Marcos jumped up. "That *was* my father!"

Anna's first instinct was to tell him he had to be quiet so the guards wouldn't hear him, but he immediately dropped to his knees, sobbing. He was not the God-hating, tough kid he pretended to be. It was all a front to help him survive. Inside, he was only a boy missing his family, trying to survive the unspeakable, horrible sexual abuse he experienced nearly every day.

# CHAPTER 53

## MARCOS'S LETTER

After breakfast, Marcos came over and sat beside Anna as she read her Bible. In a meek spirit, he again offered an apology.

"Anna," he said, ashamed to even look her in the eyes. "Thank you for risking your life to help us. I know I'm only a boy, but one day I hope I can pay you back."

"We're in this thing together," she replied.

"I also hope I have the chance to apologize to my parents," he said. "I have never been the perfect kid, but I want them to know that I didn't run away. I wish I could tell them how much I miss them, and how I wish I hadn't been so much trouble. They tried hard to raise me right, but I wanted to do stuff my way."

"Marcos, there is no perfect kid. No one is perfect. Everyone can look back and say they wish they had done things differently. I can tell you are strong-willed, and that's a good thing if you stay on the right track."

He shook his head. "Anna, I'm in this place because I *am* strong-willed *and* disobedient. The day Jose's men kidnapped me, Mom had told me not to ride my bike outside the mission camp. She said it was dangerous. But I did it anyway because it was a shortcut to my buddy's house. It's been more like a shortcut to Hell. When are they coming to get us?"

"I've had no communication with them since that one night in the park," she said. "I don't know the details of their plan.

But when the missionary took Isabella out, he did pay for your services ahead of time to make sure you would be available and ready to go. I don't know who will come for you because your father told Jose that another man wanted the young boy. Jose didn't seem to like your father because he insisted on taking you with him. But Marcos, don't worry. I believe we're going to get out of here."

"I guess I never realized how much my parents loved me back then," he said. "B-but I don't see how they can love me at all now. I disobeyed and caused all this trouble. And now I-I'm dirty. They'll be embarrassed and ashamed to call me their son. My life is ruined. I have no future."

"Not at all, Marcos. Not at all! You are not responsible for what Jose did to you." Anna rubbed his back. "What happened to you—what happened to us—could happen to anyone."

"I only wish I could redo everything," he said. "I wish I could tell them that I'm sorry. Anna, if someone rescues you first, would you at least try to give a note to my parents for me?"

"Of course. I will do anything."

After she said that, Anna wondered how she could keep that promise. For one thing, they had no pencil or paper.

*Pencil...pencil. Where can I find a pencil? Humm. I do have an eyebrow pencil. No. That won't work. It's too thick, and it won't stay sharp. I've got to find some paper and a pencil.*

With her arms crossed, Anna searched around the room, trying to find something useful. After looking around a bit, she spotted Isabella's backpack. From it, she retrieved the sack of goodies that Carmen had smuggled in for the child. It contained Isabella's treasured coloring book and a box of colored pencils.

"Yay!" Anna turned around and held the pencils up for Marcos to see. "We have something to write with. Now we just have to find something to write on."

Unfortunately, Isabella had already used up her pad of paper and hadn't left a scrap.

Looking around further, Anna spied the edge of her Bible poking out from underneath her mattress, where she kept it hidden from the guards. It was a miracle the guards had never thought to search there, but this morning she had carelessly left it partially exposed. She smiled to herself, believing God was also smiling. That little *accident* now served a purpose.

With reverence to the Bible, she reluctantly tore out the blank pages in the front and back of the book.

"Here, Marcos." Anna handed him the two pages with ragged edges. "These are thick, and will last a long time. And if the missionaries come for me before they come for you, I want you to have my Bible. You can try to smuggle it out when you leave, but just know that Jose will destroy it if he finds it."

After a few thoughtful moments, Marcos looked up at Anna.

"I already have several Bibles—gifts from other people. But your Bible would mean more to me than any of the others. Thank you for wanting me to have it."

For almost a half-hour, the boy sat propped up on his bed, pencil in hand, thinking about what he wanted to say to his parents. So much had happened, and he had so little space to recap the events.

Marcos told Anna that he wanted to apologize for every wrong thing he had done. There certainly wasn't enough space for all that, so they prayed together that God would guide him in saying the things they needed to hear the most.

Filling both sides of one page, he scribbled:

> Dear Mom and Dad,
>
> Thank you for looking for me. If I never see you again, I want you to know what happened to me. The day I went missing, I was riding my bike. I disobeyed and went outside the camp to go to Pedro's house. A van pulled up, and a man suddenly jumped out. He grabbed me and threw me and my bike in the back. They beat me over and over, but I fought them the whole way. They took me to a camp where kids from all different places had to work hard. We had to pick coffee

> beans, and they treated us like animals. Then they sold me for sex. They forced me to do bad things that I knew you would hate. Please don't hate me. I hated it too. And I hate them. In case I never see you again, I want you to have this letter to know I'm sorry for all the bad stuff I've ever done. I've asked God to forgive me.
>
> I love you,
>
> Marcos

With the colored pencils, Marcos artistically embellished the borders of the letter. He said he knew his mother would especially like the border. She always encouraged him to develop what she called his God-given talent.

Marcos took the second page. For the rest of the day, he worked on a portrait of his mother, father, and himself. On the back, he wrote, *Together*.

All the time Anna watched Marcos draw, she savored the sight of this boy, now functioning in his right mind, doing something that evidently brought great satisfaction. And why not? God had given him a great talent.

Marcos finished working on the papers, and brought them over to her to deliver to his parents. She read the letter first, and then looked closely at the picture. Anna could hardly believe the talent this boy had at such a young age.

"Marcos! This is, without a doubt, the man who came for Isabella. Your father came here to this very place, looking for you."

# CHAPTER 54

## ISABELLA'S ANGEL

JUAN, MARCOS'S FATHER, had successfully taken Isabella from the motel the day before. As paramount as that was, it was only the first stage of her rescue attempt. They now had to hole up at a condo until Marcos and Anna were also out of the motel. Everyone had to make their attempts to leave town at the same time. Otherwise, Jose would kill anyone left behind.

Of course, at the age of six, Isabella had no understanding of the escape plan. But she did have a lot of curiosity. When her *angel* drove away from the motel, she was riding in the front passenger seat. Sitting low in Juan's car and unable to see much of the scenery, the child entertained herself with conversation.

"Are you a *real* angel? Anna told me all about how angels protect us all the time. Ever since she told me that I had a guardian angel, I've wanted to meet mine. Are you my guardian angel? If so, I must say, you are doing a good job. Anna always tells me I do a good job when I play paper dolls or clean up after myself."

Juan chuckled. "Well, I do know that angels are God's messengers and his servants, doing his will. So I guess today, you can call me your angel. We know the name of some of God's angels. Would you like to know my full name?"

"Yeesss! What is it?"

"My name is Juan Marcos Ramirez. You can call me Juan."

"Oh." Isabella sat up and leaned in toward him as though she had a secret. "I know a boy named Marcos," she whispered. "He's still back at Jose's motel."

Juan leaned over and whispered back, "I know. He's my son."

"Your son! I didn't know angels had children."

"Well, angels in Heaven don't have children. But people on earth acting as angels *can* have children."

"Anna was right. You sure are nice. When will the angels come to get Anna and Marcos?"

Her words struck the chords of Juan's soul, for he had asked God that same question many times.

He choked back his emotions. "I think they're planning on doing that soon."

"I sure will be glad. I'm tired of seeing Marcos get beat up."

Juan took a deep breath and swallowed hard. "Is that so?"

"Yes. Maybe you should tell Marcos's angel so he can get a rush on getting him out of that place."

Juan couldn't help but smile. "My, you are a precocious little girl."

Isabella wrinkled her forehead. "What does that mean?"

"It means, little one, that you are smarter than the average bear."

She perked up. "Are bears smart? I have never seen a bear."

Holding back laughter, he nodded. "Yes, bears are supersmart. Maybe you will see one someday, and then you'll see for yourself just how smart they are."

As they traveled, Isabella continued to talk about the hotel and how mean Jose was to Marcos. This information overwhelmed Juan. He felt like he had failed as a father. Though he had sought help from the authorities, they had also failed him. Perhaps they had done their best, and perhaps they were unaware of Jose's covert business. But some of the locals must have known. Most likely, they turned their heads out of fear.

Juan hadn't realized it, but Isabella had been watching him while he was deep in thought.

She said, "You are not smiling anymore. Are you sad?"

"Yes, Isabella, I am. I am sad about what Jose has done. We must always love people, but sometimes what they do can make us very sad."

# CHAPTER 55

## THE WAIT BEGINS

JUAN AND ISABELLA ARRIVED at the gated resort without incident, but the knowledge that they still weren't out of Jose's grasp put a damper on Juan's sense of success.

Jose owned some of the units at this facility, as he did at other properties around Jaco. The missionaries and rescuers needed to stay close to Jaco to coordinate the escape plan, but they didn't want to stay in units where Jose could have hidden surveillance devices.

The missionaries had spent many hours researching the ownership of the area's condos to avoid this situation. And to their amazement, God allowed them to find a resort where they could rent a private unit for themselves, and one for Juan and Isabella. Still, they weren't entirely safe. Anna had warned the missionaries that Jose's guards watched all clients, noting where they went and what they did. This meant they couldn't meet anywhere to discuss plans.

Once Juan and Isabella got inside their condo unit, Isabella couldn't believe how beautiful it was. She had never seen such a big and beautiful living area. She twirled around like a princess, and then inspected every room.

"Wow!" she said, with big eyes. "Angels sure do live in nice places."

Juan's heart melted as he observed her intense curiosity. She didn't know it, but she was an angel to him, sent from God to help him deal with the anger he felt about the evil things this Jose had done.

"Do angels have good food, too?" Isabella rubbed her belly and licked her lips.

Juan opened the refrigerator. "Well, what do you think?"

The refrigerator was full of food—everything that she could want—and she ate and ate. It was evident that Jose didn't adequately feed his sex slaves.

Juan also noted that Isabella's shorts and T-shirt were too small, and her hair and nails needed a trim. Overall, she looked frail and neglected.

"Would you like to watch television while you eat?" he said.

"Oh, yes. I haven't had a chance to watch TV for a long time."

Juan needed to phone the other missionaries to let them know that he and Isabella had arrived safely. But just in case Jose had bugged the condo, he only told them that he had arrived safely and was expecting to enjoy his vacation.

Isabella continued watching TV and eating her favorite foods.

After he finished his call, Juan watched Isabella as she sat cross-legged on the floor, watching a cartoon. He was beginning to regret that Marcos was an only child. Had he known little girls were so delightful, he would have loved a little Isabella around the house.

Juan could hardly believe that any man could go so low as to violate a precious child. Silently, he thanked God for allowing him to have a part in rescuing Isabella, and hopefully, Marcos and Anna as well.

The events of the day had taken their toll on Isabella. She stretched out on her tummy and fell asleep on the floor. While she slept, Juan placed bags containing gifts next to her. The missionaries had bought new clothes and toys to keep her occupied at the condo for a week. That would be extremely difficult since Isabella and Anna had grown so close.

When Isabella awakened and saw all the gift bags, she

rubbed her eyes as though she thought she was dreaming.

"Would you like to open some birthday gifts?"

"Is today my birthday? Is it November eighteenth?"

He winked. "Since we missed your birthday, we'll make believe it is. That is, if you want to."

"Oh, yes, yes! I have never had a real birthday party. It will be my first. But sometimes I pretended I had a party, using my dolls as friends."

Meticulously, Isabella opened the first gift: two Barbie Dolls—the most prized Ken and Barbie. She opened the second gift, which was the house for her Barbies. The next one had the Sunshine Family and a GI Joe, all of which were old donations left at the mission house.

"Oh, I love playing with dolls. Do angels like to play dolls?"

Juan said, "Well, you will have to show me how to play dolls because I've never had that opportunity. You can teach me after you finish opening your gifts."

Isabella took a deep breath. "Anna was right. Guardian angels are wonderful."

The last gift was a box filled with clothes—shirts, shorts, shoes. And of course, a princess dress. Isabella had never owned new clothes, so she examined each garment, tracing each detail with her finger and inhaling that new-fabric scent. With pride, she held each piece of clothing up to her body to see if it would fit. Then she tried on a pair of her new shoes.

Looking down at her feet, Isabella said, "How did you know my shoe size?"

"Remember, God knows everything about us, even our shoe size," Juan said with a shrug. "And he tells both his heavenly and human angels what we need to know and do."

Isabella ripped off the store tags to try on the clothes. Juan pointed to the bedroom.

"Why don't you act like a princess and change clothes in there? Then come out and let me see what I think looks the best."

She returned to the living room with every outfit she put on, modeling in her childlike manner. Each time, Juan would applaud and praise her, telling her how beautiful the clothes looked on her.

She especially liked the princess dress, just as Anna said she would.

That was the last outfit Isabella tried on, and she wore it for the remainder of the day, twirling and bouncing whenever the notion struck her fancy.

After eating lunch, Isabella hopped down from her seat at the counter and announced that it was time to play dolls. She unpacked the dolls and spread them on the floor in front of her. Then her happy face turned upside down.

"Isabella, what's wrong? I thought you liked playing dolls."

"GI Joe is not nice. He looks like Jose. Would you like to be GI Joe? I don't want to be him. Anna has always played dolls with me. Do you know Anna?"

Isabella's rambling response puzzled Juan. He didn't know how to answer that last question.

"Was Anna the lady who brought you down to meet me?"

"Yes, of course, you know Anna." She giggled.

Juan had many questions he wanted to ask Isabella about her and the other occupants in Room 120. He wanted to learn how each of them got there, and how Jose had treated them. But the child's mind moved on before he could get the first question out.

Isabella reached out and grabbed the young boy doll from the Sunshine Family, announcing they would pretend he was Marcos. She then picked up Barbie.

"This is Anna, and you can be Ken."

Juan laughed as he reached out to take the Ken doll. "I sure am glad you didn't make me that old man. I would much rather be the young and handsome Ken."

Isabella acted out how mean Jose was, and how he had treated her at the motel. Still in her make-believe world, she continued playing with the dolls, acting out all the scenarios she and Anna had practiced with the paper dolls. Finally, she acted out all the ways Anna had loved her and mothered her. She never asked Juan to do anything except watch her play with all the dolls.

Juan remained Ken, the guardian angel, learning the heartbreaking story of these victims.

Eventually, Isabella looked up at Juan. "I didn't know God had angels watching over me. I wouldn't have been so scared if I had known."

"Little One, just remember that angels are not the ones who should get credit for anything. because it is God who has the knowledge and power to help us. Angels work for God, just carrying out his missions."

Isabella became sad after playing with dolls because it reminded her of Anna and how much she missed her. So Juan asked her if she would like to go out on the balcony to see the ocean and look for the beautiful parrots that sometimes fly overhead and perch in nearby trees.

"Have you ever seen these beautiful birds?" he said.

"No, but I would like to see them. Do they talk?"

"Some parrots talk, but these birds just squawk loudly. If you want to watch them, we must be quiet. Let's go out and see if we can see some."

A couple from the mission camp, Cruz and his wife, Maya, were the missionaries who had rented the unit just across the common area from Isabella and Juan. They were one of the two couples Anna had met in the park the night she slipped away from her client. The third person in the unit was Lola, Marcos's mother and Juan's wife. From their balconies, everyone had a clear view of each other.

When Isabella and Juan went out to look for the parrots, he saw the other missionaries watching them. They all longed to get together and rejoice, but they couldn't risk blowing their cover. Nevertheless, seeing this precious child encouraged the missionaries to move forward.

Juan had succeeded in getting Isabella away from Jose a week before the real client was to come, but they now had to get Marcos and Anna out before Jose realized someone had rescued Isabella.

In only one week, the escape plan had to be fully executed.

# CHAPTER 56

## WHERE ARE THE CHILDREN

A COUPLE DAYS AFTER JUAN TOOK ISABELLA, the guard came to take Marcos and Anna to breakfast. Even though things were always quiet in the dining room, the place was strangely quiet this day because no other children were present.

*What happened to all the children? Has Jose sold them?*

Anna didn't say anything to Marcos, but she could see that he also was concerned. Jose was at his usual table, so she went over to him.

"Jose, where are all the children this morning?"

"I don't think that is your concern, is it? Sometimes you just have to change the scope of your operation when you know there are spies out there."

"Spies?" Anna replied.

"Yes, spies. Government spies. They want to take down my business."

"Jose, in all the years I've been here, no government agency has sent inspectors to look at your business."

"What do you know," he snapped. "You don't know anything about government authorities. They are getting stricter about underage girls."

"You're probably right, Jose. Maybe you should not have started selling underage girls." She turned to go back to her table.

After breakfast, Anna sat on her bed, thinking about Jose's state of mind and the children's safety.

"Marcos, I think I know where the children are. I think Jose sent them to the coffee bean field to get them off the premises. He thinks government authorities are coming to inspect his hotel."

"Well, that's a good thing, isn't it?" Marcos said.

"Maybe. Maybe not."

"Why not. At least they're out of this place."

"For one thing, Jose didn't send you away with the other children. He must have something up his sleeve for you. I also fear that this will jeopardize everything."

Nevertheless, Anna and Marcos began to discuss the escape plan, wondering which one of them the missionaries would come for next. She didn't want to leave before Marcos. Even if both of them made it out, she was concerned about his emotional state if she went first.

In silence, Anna kept praying that God would allow Marcos to get out first.

Just in case she left first, she needed to figure out how she could get Marcos's letter to his parents. Smuggling was risky and nearly impossible. The guards searched their bags before they left with a client, and after they returned, unless they got distracted.

Anna paced, thinking.

An idea flashed into her mind. She would use her sewing needle, one of the few things Jose allowed them to have in their possession.

With the needle, she pulled a thread and opened a seam in the lining of her bag. Then she tucked the papers in the bottom and carefully stitched the seam back together. With her clothes packed in the bag, she hoped the guards wouldn't detect the letter.

About midmorning, the padlock opened, and the guard said a client had requested Anna. She always complained if Jose didn't give her prior notice to prepare herself for a client, but she wasn't about to do anything that might draw his attention to this request. After all, this client could be a missionary.

Leaving Room 120 was one of the hardest and saddest things she had ever done. Marcos was now sitting on the side of his bed, all alone. Anna fought back the tears. But before she left, she dared to go over and hug him.

"I promise you," she whispered in his ear.

Marcos flashed a little smile because he knew she was saying that she would give his letter and drawing to his parents. Although smuggling these pages out was a high risk, Anna wasn't worried about her safety. She was worried that Marcos would also suffer the consequences. Jose could make him completely *disappear*. And that wasn't the worst of it. The whole escape plan could be in jeopardy—other lives were also at stake.

# CHAPTER 57

## GOOD COMES OUT OF BAD

WHEN ANNA ARRIVED AT JOSE'S OFFICE, he introduced her to the new client.

"Señor Diego, I want you to meet Anna, the maid for the day. We are happy to offer full *service* at this hotel."

The smug comment prompted a flash of Jose's fancy gold tooth, which was always a sign of his pride and power. For Anna, it was always a painful flashback to her first night at the motel.

Anna was expecting this client to be her rescuer, but she was concerned. The man was not one of the missionaries she had met earlier. Neither did he have the look of a missionary. He had a ne'er-do-well look about him. His appearance was so rough that she was surprised Jose would even consider letting any of his girls go with him.

Whenever a client injured one of his escorts to the point where they couldn't work, he ended up losing money. And that was the bottom line. It was always about the money with him.

Jose's only warning to the man was that he had to have her back by noon the next day.

*It appears to me that the missionaries went overboard trying to disguise this man. But they've obviously done an excellent job. Jose is not suspicious at all.*

Anna's puzzlement didn't go unnoticed. Jose knew her well enough to read her face.

"Big money sales," he whispered.

Jose had pictures of all his escorts, with prices on them, so Anna already knew her price was higher than any other girl until the children came. Her body had more curves than anyone else, and she was in high demand. Jose must be losing a lot of money these days, or he would never send her out with such an unprofessional-looking man.

She still had doubts, but she wanted to believe he was her rescuer.

Diego pulled out a wad of money and paid Jose. Then he hustled Anna out to his car and drove off without saying a word to her. They traveled several blocks in silence, with him staring ahead.

*Is he ever going to reveal that he's a missionary? Why is he still acting out the part in the car? Maybe he's afraid Jose has sold him the wrong person. Maybe he's waiting for me to say something first, but I dare not mention anything about missionaries yet.*

The daunting silence broke when another car pulled out in front of them, almost causing a wreck. The man started banging on the steering wheel with his fists, and shouting threats to the other driver. Whoever this Diego was, Anna was even more suspicious of him now. His language didn't shock her, but she doubted such words would ever come out of a missionary's mouth, even if he were in disguise. A cold wave of breathtaking fear rolled over her.

*This man has to be one of the missionaries. He just has to be. The timing is exactly right.*

Diego took her across town to the same hotel where she had stayed with Charles. The place appealed to men with lots of money, but it was not likely a missionary could afford to stay here.

Once they were in the hotel room, the man's actions confirmed Anna's suspicions—he was not a missionary.

As soon as they got to their room, Diego began drinking and taking drugs. When Anna refused to get drunk with him, he punched her several times. Fearing for her life, Anna fought back.

"So you like it rough, do you." He roared with laughter. "Well, so do I!"

Diego tied her hands together, threw her on the bed, and straddled her.

"Please, please untie me. Don't hold me down. I can't breathe. I can't breathe!"

"Shut up, you little whore." He held her mouth shut with one hand. "I'm getting what I paid for."

Anna struggled until she fainted due to intense fear. While in that state, Diego removed her clothes and tied her hands. She came to with the realization that the man was about to rape her. She wasn't sure she could bear the burden of life another minute. Then the mental image of Marcos sitting on his bed, waiting to get out brought a surge of courage.

*What can I do? I'm afraid to leave this man like I left Charles. If he catches me leaving, I'll be the object of his uncontrollable temper again. Then Jose will take his turn at punishing me. Yet I promised Marcos I would get the papers to his parents. I cannot—I will not—throw them away Dear God, please show me the way.*

Never had Anna gotten an answer to prayer so quickly. She heard the rumble of the maid's cart in the hallway. There was a sign on their door, alerting the cleaning service not to disturb the occupants in the room until later, so Anna slipped from the bed, put on her clothes, and retrieved her bag. She opened the door gently and closed it behind her. Approaching the maid, she continued to look over her shoulder, making sure Diego had not awakened and discovered she was missing.

Anna's beat-up appearance shocked the maid. "Is everything all right, madam? Can I help you?"

"Yes. Please, please help me," Anna whispered.

She explained her situation, continuing to look over her shoulder as she fumbled with the lining of her bag, pulling apart the stitches.

"I'm with a client and cannot leave the hotel, but I desperately need to get these papers to some friends." She pulled the pages from her bag. "Can you please take them to the missionaries at the nearby park? It's a matter of life or death."

The maid vigorously shook her head and put up her hands, gesturing for Anna to stop.

"Please, listen to me," Anna said, "I work at a motel, and my boss also calls *me* a maid. But the truth is I am a sex slave, held against my will. I can't get away to deliver these papers. I know they don't look important, but they are vital. Please take them and give them to the missionaries in the park. I tell you the truth. There are lives at stake here. Please help me."

The maid paused, studying Anna's beaten face and the desperation in her eyes. Finally, she nodded, took the folded papers and stuffed them in her pocket. As she pushed her cart down the hallway, Anna thanked God for sending her a maid who had a heart.

Back inside the room, she showered and waited for Diego to take her back to the motel.

# CHAPTER 58

## TIME'S UP FOR MARCOS

JUST HOURS BEFORE ANNA ARRIVED BACK AT THE MOTEL, a man stepped inside the lobby of Jose's motel to request an escort. Considering the reputation Jose had for sex trafficking, the man thought the facility would have been much more upscale than it was. Neither was the place bustling with patrons or employees. The only person he saw was a gigantic guard standing behind the check-in counter.

Still looking around, the man approached the counter, and the guard said, "What's your name, and do you have a reservation?"

"My name is Lucas Martin, and I do not have a reservation. I'm here to obtain an escort."

"Do you want a male or a female, and how long will you want to keep the escort?"

"A male. A *young* male. And I want him for a week."

The guard stuck out his hand. "Let me see your passport." After examining it, "Follow me."

They went back through the main lobby to the old adjacent section behind the hotel. The guard handed Jose the man's passport.

"I see, Mister Martin, that you are from Canada. What are you doing in Costa Rica?"

"I'm an international businessman who comes here on

occasion for vacation. You should know that I am a well-traveled man, and I know what I want."

"So tell me what it is that you want."

"Sir, what I want is a young male. The younger, the better."

Jose replied with an air of self-importance. "My inventory is low right now, but I do have one I think you'll like."

Jose opened his desk drawer and pulled out a picture of Marcos. He knew another client had prepaid for Marcos when he paid for Isabella, but he could care less about cheating. This way, he doubled his profit. That boy had been trouble since day one, and he felt justified in getting as much money for him as he could. Besides, he needed extra money, and he knew the other client could do nothing about it. It's not like he could complain to the police.

Still looking at Marcos's picture, Lucas said, "What is the cost? And can you guarantee he will be responsive to my requests? I like challenges, but I will not pay for a fight."

"He was a tough buck to train," Jose said, "but he is one of the best now. He has become a willing partner, if you know what I mean. And the cost is two-fifty a night because boys like this are in great demand. You're a businessman—you should know how the law of supply and demand works."

"How many nights is he available, and what are your rules?"

"First, you are only allowed to take him to certain places. Next, you must remember that my guards are always watching. If you break the rules, I will not return your passport. Remember, if you do not play by my rules, you will regret it."

Lucas hesitated. "You never answered my question. How many nights? I have already given up a lot to come here, so I will play by your rules. But I want him for a week, unless he doesn't perform. If he doesn't perform, what is your return policy."

Jose let out a roaring laugh. "Policy? The only policy I have is this: if you do not follow my rules, I will ruin you with the information I have on you. But to answer your questions, he will perform, guaranteed. And you can have him for a week, under the stipulations I gave you."

The guard opened the padlock on Room 120 and ordered Marcos to come to the office. But when Marcos saw Lucas, his eyes glazed over and his body stiffened. Lucas knew from the other missionaries that the boy had expected his father to be the one who would come back for him. Now, Marcos would think a real client had come for him.

It looked as though Marcos was going to put up a fight, so Jose pulled him outside the office door and threatened him.

"Marcos, this is your last chance. If you mess this one up by fighting, your life is over. Do you hear me?"

"What life? The only life I have is Hell on earth!"

Jose slammed him against the wall. "You better listen to me. Your life is not the only one on the line here. Do you understand what I mean?"

"I understand more than you think." Marcos gave a slight nod.

Lucas wanted to rush out to defend Marcos, but he knew he could not intervene.

When they came back into the room, Marcos still had the look of defiance in his eyes. He stood there, with his chest heaving and his face red with anger. But in a few minutes, he calmed down.

Lucas handed Jose the cash for the week, and the guard ushered them out through the front door. Marcos was frustrated and afraid, but he followed Lucas as they walked to the car parked in the lot across from the hotel.

Marcos paused. He thought about breaking away and running as far as he could. He knew in his heart that he couldn't get away, and that Jose would certainly kill him, but dying on the street was better than living in that hellhole.

The second he was about to act on the idea, he thought about his parents and the risk Anna would take for him.

"Come on, boy," Lucas called out. "I don't have all day. Get into the car before they change their minds."

Marcos got into the car and slumped over with his head on his knees.

*God, you've got to help me. Please help me. Help Anna, and help my father to find me.*

"Buckle up," Lucas said. "We've got a ways to go." Once they were away from the premises, "I know what you were thinking back there. I've been where you are...in a way."

"What?" Marcos said.

"I know you were thinking about making a break for it."

"How do you know that? And what do you mean you've been where I am?"

"I've never been an imprisoned sex slave, but I've rescued many who were. That's why I knew you wanted to take the chance to get away. I haven't been in your shoes, exactly. But I've been close to those who have, and I feel at one with them. Rescuing victims is my life. It is my heart."

"How? How did you know? Are you one of the missionaries?"

"No. No, I'm not a missionary. I'm a different kind of servant, I guess you could say. I'm an ex-cop who now specializes in rescuing sex trafficked victims. I'm an old friend of your father's. When he was unable to get you out, he contacted me, begging for help. Your father has Isabella, and they are staying at a condo unit in a nearby resort."

Marcos shouted, "Are you serious!"

"Yes, but don't act excited. Jose's people may be watching at a distance. So try to contain your emotions."

The realization that the missionaries had rescued him was like heavy chains had finally fallen off. Marcos began to shout and laugh. He could hardly believe it. God had heard and answered his prayers. He was so elated that Lucas reminded him again that Jose's men would continue to watch, and he had to act like an escort unless they were in private places.

"Did you say my father has Isabella at a condo?"

"Yes, but we're not able to see them yet, even though our unit is at the same resort. Your father and Isabella are renting one unit. The other missionaries, including your mother, are renting a separate unit. But unlike them, we had to rent a unit owned by Jose. That means he may have listening devices hidden in our unit, and his guards are always watching from a distance."

"Are you saying I can't see either of my parents now that I'm finally free and so close to them? I really want to see them."

"Not yet, Marcos. We must always be careful in any attempt to communicate with them, especially with your father. Everyone is waiting to see you, but it can only be a distant glimpse."

Marcos forced back tears. "I knew my parents would never give up on finding me."

*I just wonder if they know what Jose did to me. I wonder if they know that I'm not pure like I used to be. In their hearts, they won't love me the way they used to.*

After a few minutes of silence, Marcos said, "Are you really from Canada? How will you get home without your passport?"

"Yes, I am from Canada, but don't worry about my passport. It was a fake one."

It had been a long time since Marcos had laughed, and he made up for the lost time. Both he and Lucas hoped they had the last laugh on Jose—but that was not the case.

# CHAPTER 59

## JOSE ACCUSES ANNA

As soon as Diego took Anna back to the motel, Goliath returned her to Room 120.

She said, "Do you know where Marcos is?"

The guards had strict orders from Jose not to divulge any information about the whereabouts of his escorts. Nevertheless, Anna held her breath, hoping she would get an answer.

Goliath rubbed his chin, thinking.

"A client from Canada came for him right after you left yesterday. He should be back in a week."

*In a week? Marcos's father paid for another missionary to have him for a week. That must have been who came for him.*

Anna believed God was working miracles. Even though the children in Room 120 were now gone, she did not feel the despair that she did before they came into her life. Yes, she was alone, but she was not lonely. She had hope for the future.

When Jose learned that Anna was back, he ordered the guard to bring her to his office. Anna noticed the entire facility showed little activity, and most of the guards seemed to have crawled back into the woodwork.

"Jose, what is going on? Where is everyone?"

"You ought to know!" he said, through clenched teeth. "Those people who are constantly down at the park handing out stuff are trying to ruin me, and you are a part of this whole thing."

"What do you mean?" Her eyes grew wide.

With scowl, Jose opened his desk drawer, pulled out her Bible, and plopped it on top of his desk.

"This is what I mean. While you were away, I had the guards search your room. The missionaries gave this to you. And just like a little missionary, you've been preaching to my children." He reached into the drawer again and threw down the knife comb and manicure kit. "And what about these? What were you planning on doing with this stuff?"

"Jose, I had nothing to do with this. Please let me explain."

"No! You let *me* explain."

He slapped Anna across the face so hard, she stumbled backward against the wall.

She knew her life was on the line here. Since Carmen had already escaped and was no longer in danger, she told Jose the truth, keeping herself beyond his reach.

"Jose, the Bible is mine. I had it when I came here ten years ago. If that was a problem, why didn't the guards bring it to you in their previous searches? And it was Carmen who brought the comb and manicure set here. A client who liked her a lot got them for her. I had nothing to do with that."

"Oh yes! Yes, you did have something to do with this." He stormed back. "You knew these things were here, and you didn't tell me. This shows me you must have planned on using the stuff."

"Jose, look at those silly little things. None of them could take down any of your well-trained, burly men. Any such attempt would be suicide. If you're going to be mad at anyone, it should be the client who bought them in the first place. If I was going to use this stuff, I would have done so already."

Jose stopped his ranting for a minute to consider what she had said. This just added to his mounting paranoia and belief that the authorities would shut him down.

He opened his desk drawer, pulled out his bottle of tequila and guzzled it down.

"You have my Bible," she said. "I wish you would read it."

Jose let out a hideous laugh. "You little whore. Are you going to preach to me?"

"You, Jose, forced this kind of life on me. God knows my heart, and he knows I'm not a willing party in this. And in his time, he will deliver me."

With both hands propped on the desk, he stretched forward and snarled.

"I could do away with you in an instant, but I'm just going to watch and dare your God to deliver you. Until then, I'm going to keep a close eye on you. You'll be staying right here under my nose from now on."

*From now on. From now on.* Those words kept ringing in Anna's head. She couldn't be with him from now on and expect someone to rescue her.

She couldn't bear the thought of staying with Jose. Her only consolation was that at least the children were out of this prison.

# CHAPTER 60

## MYSTERY MAN

THE FIRST DAY ANNA STAYED WITH JOSE, she realized she was the only escort still at the motel. Once again, Jose made her work as the motel maid. If a customer asked for escort service, he offered the *maid for the day*.

From the conversations she overheard in the office, Anna learned what had happened to all the children. Jose had indeed taken them to the coffee bean farm. A few older children were at the resort where Rosa worked...wherever that was.

Thoughts of Rosa saddened her heart even more. Hardly a day went by that she didn't pray that she would see her friend again. Anna was determined to rescue the children *and* Rosa.

She knew it would be difficult for her to escape because Jose no longer allowed a client to take her off-premises. And although he had suspicions about her loyalty, she was not his primary concern. He was becoming increasingly paranoid because he feared the missionaries had told the American embassy that his motel was nothing more than a brothel where pimping and underage sexual activity was going on.

In Jose's circle, however, he never worried much about his illegal activity. But he was smart enough to know that if the missionaries relayed their stories to the embassy or the American news media, the authorities might shut his business down and even arrest him.

Jose knew he could become the prisoner instead of the one holding others as prisoners. This fear fed his irrational behavior, which had reached the point where he was mixing drugs and alcohol to help him make it through the day.

Another day passed as Anna waited for someone to rescue her. Time was running out. It would soon be too late to get out. These days were sad and lonely, and she missed Isabella so much her heart ached. Anna had enjoyed living in a world of make-believe with her. Isabella's childlike innocence and faith encouraged her own soul to have hope. Without her, and in Jose's captivity, Anna fought the temptation to drown out her sorrows. Only by recalling Bible verses and praying did she find courage and strength in those hours of temptation. She desperately wished that Jose had not taken her Bible from her.

While Anna was staying in his office, she learned a lot. She realized that loyalty to him had slowly deteriorated among the few remaining people on staff. She saw how he had become verbally abusive, accusing them of leaking information about his business to the authorities. On several occasions, she saw him abuse the guards by slamming them against the wall and threatening to kill them if spies got into the hotel.

Jose was destroying everyone's trust and loyalty, which worked to Anna's advantage. Now that Jose was on the outs with the guards, they trusted her as though she was one of them.

One day, his two top guards talked with her while Jose was out of the office.

"Everyone here at the hotel is in danger," Goliath said. "Jose has flipped out. He even threatened to kill us. We know his past, and we know what he's capable of doing it. Even if he doesn't kill us, we'll be without jobs if his business goes under. We have families, and we have to work."

"Yeah," said another guard. "He keeps insisting that there's going to be a big raid on all his locations except the one that is upscale and private. That place is for the wealthier clients, and the escorts are more expensive. Large concrete walls and iron gates border it. It has a good reputation, and Jose feels that place is the only safe location."

Goliath said, "Jose also rents these luxury condos with or without escort service. Some guests don't even realize all that's going on there. It's a much more undercover operation. Jose even keeps all the condo bookings and management separate so nobody can trace that business back to him."

*I wonder if this could be the place where Jose took Rosa? If so, how could the missionaries get into such a private place to rescue her, especially now that Jose is more vigilant than ever to keep his business a secret? And how could the missionaries possibly afford to rent such an expensive unit?*

As much as Anna loved her best friend, Rosa was not her immediate concern. All she could think of was the narrow window for her own escape. Four days had now passed since Juan had taken Isabella, and she knew the missionaries had only three more days before Jose expected her back at the motel. If she didn't get out before Jose discovered Isabella had escaped, Jose would kill her in a fit of rage.

Later that day, a guard came to the office and said, "Boss, there's a distinguished man in a suit, wanting to speak with you."

Jose had been taking drugs that day, so he was out of touch with reality. Though he wasn't himself, he knew enough to recognize he was not capable of taking care of business.

"Anna, come with me to the lobby to see what this man wants. And be careful of what you say. He may be a spy."

When they got to the lobby, Jose just stood there, propped against the counter, staring at the man without saying a word.

After a long few minutes, Anna said, "Sir, how can we help you."

"I'm looking for a place to spend a few days, but most resorts have no vacancies due to the sportfishing tournament. I would book a room here, but I'm accustomed to...well...more upscale accommodations. I'm willing to pay a booking fee if you find me a premier facility.

"Upscale?" Jose slurred. "How much are you willing to spend?"

The man squinted and tilted his head. "I'm willing to pay the price others charge for an upscale condo, if you know what I mean. I cannot find any around here, and I have a reputation to protect. So do you have a place or not?"

Jose acted put-off by the man's response. "Where're you from?"

"I'm from the United States."

"Let me see your passport."

The man handed over his passport, and Jose inspected it as though he were a security officer.

"Well, Mister Steven Price, I can't help you. My rooms are full, and I don't know of any *upscale* place that might have a vacancy...if you know what I mean."

Jose slammed the passport down on the counter, turned around, and staggered back to his office.

As soon as he left, one guard whispered to the other, "Jose is losing so much money."

To Anna's surprise, the other guard took a pen and pad from the counter and wrote something.

He said, "Here is contact information where you can find a nicer place. The name of it is The Hideaway."

*The Hideaway! That was the name written on the back of Rosa's picture.*

Anna looked at the man with suspicion. She didn't know whether this mysterious man was just a regular client or a missionary. Whoever he was, he had the contact information on Rosa. Hopefully, that was a good thing.

# CHAPTER 61

## THE HIDEAWAY

AFTER STEVEN LEFT JOSE'S MOTEL, he contacted the missionaries at the resort. Regretfully, he had to report that Jose had refused to book him a reservation at the place where they suspected he had Rosa working.

"Jose didn't want to have anything to do with me or my money," Steven said. "He seemed to be high on something. Also, there was a lady with him who must be Anna. The good news is, from the look on her face when the guard gave me information on another resort, I'm fairly sure that's where Jose is holding Rosa. One of Jose's guards gave me the phone number, so I'm going to see if I can book a unit."

Steven called the number and asked for a room.

The lady who answered the call said, "Sir, how many people are in your party?"

"I am alone."

"Sir, we do have one unit left. It will be two hundred dollars a night for a one-bedroom, with a minimum stay of one week."

"I'll take it. And I'll be paying in cash, so make sure you hold it for me."

The lady gave him directions, and told him that he would have to come at once to secure the unit because they were in high demand.

After hanging up, Steven gave the missionaries the good and the bad news.

"I have snagged the last unit where I think Rosa is working, but I'm going to need a lot more money. I'll have to pay fourteen hundred cash for the week, and that doesn't include the escort service."

The missionaries counted their cash, and altogether there was only $1,000. They would have to come up with the extra money quickly and get Steven on his way. So they started calling every benefactor, asking them to wire money. Hours and many phone calls later, the missionaries rejoiced because they had managed to raise an additional $5,000.

As soon as Steven got word that the money was in the bank, he withdrew it. The transaction went smoothly, but it took him longer than he had expected to get the cash in hand. He then tried to follow the lady's directions, but they were intricate. He made several time-consuming wrong turns. Now he knew why the place was called The Hideaway.

Meanwhile, the missionaries remained prayerful, begging God to keep that one last room and allow them to rescue Rosa.

Steven knew somewhat how Rosa looked because the missionaries had shown him her passport. But that picture was ten years old.

*What if Rosa has changed so much that I don't recognize her? What if I don't have enough money, after all? What if they get suspicious? Is it even possible to get her off-premises once I find her?*

Steven arrived at the beautiful resort and followed the sign to the main entrance. When he stepped into the lobby, he was surprised by the posh decor: marble floors, high-end pieces of art, and enormous fresh floral arrangements everywhere.

An attractive lady standing behind the counter asked if she could help him.

"Yes. My name is Steven Price. I'm the man who called several hours ago, reserving a unit."

"Sir, I never spoke with you. Just one moment while I search for such a reservation. I hope someone didn't book our last unit before you arrived."

The lady turned aside to look for the reservation.

When she returned, "Yes, Mister Price, you are a lucky man."

*No, I'm a blessed man.*

"Sir, your total cost is two thousand dollars."

"I thought it was two hundred a night."

"Well, there are additional fees. Is it a problem? There is a great demand for our units, and our clients are more than happy to pay for their services."

"No, there's no problem." He paid the bill.

The lady at the desk handed Steven the room key and a map to show his unit's location. She then gave him a code that unlocked the security gate, warning him to keep it with him always. She stressed that there is no getting in or out of the facility without the code after business hours.

"By the way," Steven said, as he turned to leave, "what services do you offer here?"

"Our complex has a state-of-the-art gym, an Olympic-size pool, a spa, and fine dining."

Information on the escort service was what Steven wanted, but he felt awkward asking about that. He had never used such a service, and he didn't know if he could even book an escort without a referral.

"Could you tell me more about your escort service?" he whispered.

"First of all, Mister Price," she said with an air of dignity, "we run a strict operation here. We only offer women and men of legal age. We do not offer children. So if that is what you are looking for, it will not be happening here."

"Yes. An escort would be nice. I-I don't like dining alone. What are my choices?"

She handed him a book displaying pictures of all types of women, and instructed him to take a seat in the lounge, have a glass of wine on the house, and find the lady of his dreams.

"Now, I can't promise you that all of them are available at this time because we stay busy around here. And another thing, we do not allow drugs on the premises. Again, you need to understand that our operation is above board, and we are careful because our clients have reputations to protect."

Steven took the book and tried to find someone who looked like the picture of that fifteen-year-old girl on the passport. Page after page, they all looked a lot alike. They wore virtually the same sensual outfits, with so much makeup that it was difficult to distinguish one escort from another.

Then he saw a picture of one who looked like Rosa. Looking closer, he knew for sure because she had a mole on her right cheek, just below the eye. It perfectly matched the picture on the passport. Some people call such a feature a beauty mark, which it was to him that day.

"This is the one." He tapped his finger on the picture of Rosa. "I want this one."

The lady looked puzzled at Steven's enthusiasm, and he realized that he needed to be more careful, or she might become suspicious.

"You seem extremely excited about her. What is it that made you choose her over all the others?"

"She reminds me of a lady I once loved."

"Well, just remember, you can't take her home." The lady winked and grinned. "So don't get too attached."

She tried to enter the booking, then looked up. "Sir, I'm sorry. The escort you chose is out at the moment."

"What do you mean she's out? When will she be available?"

"Sir, we have a lot of other nice escorts to choose from in that book. Please go back and look some more."

"No. I told you that I want this one. She reminds me of someone that I once loved."

"Sir, I am not sure that you should have this escort since you are already attached to her."

He nodded. "No, I just really liked her looks."

"Sir, why don't you go to your unit and think about it. Check back later when you decide that you feel like looking at some other escorts."

Steven knew he didn't have a choice in the matter, so he went back to the Jeep Wrangler that the missionaries had borrowed for him, opened the security gate, and drove through. The unit had a garage, so he pulled his car inside and put the door down. Inside the unit, he dropped his bags on the floor, amazed at the stunning view just outside the balcony. The sandy beach, sparkling aqua water, palm trees, and tropical flowers were a scene right out of Paradise.

*Wow! I've never seen any place so beautiful. No wonder sin is so alluring here.*

Feeling physically and emotionally drained, Steven stretched out across the bed and slept through the night. But as soon as he awakened, thoughts of Rosa returned. He began to doubt that the plan to rescue her was even possible.

*Perhaps God intends for me to rescue another girl rather than Rosa. But how would that work? What if the girl didn't want to leave, and then she reported me? No, I will not get any girl other than Rosa. It's too dangerous, and it could risk the lives of too many other people.*

# CHAPTER 62

## STEVEN MEETS ROSA

STEVEN RETURNED TO THE LOBBY early the following day to check on Rosa's availability. Of course, no one knew her as Rosa. The name under her picture in the book was *Luscious*.

He approached the check-in counter and was relieved to see a different lady working there.

"How may I help you, sir?"

"Well, I was wondering if I may look at the escort book."

She smiled and handed him the book. Having learned his lesson the day before, he took some time looking at the pictures. When he came to Rosa, he inquired about her with less enthusiasm.

"Is this one available?" he said in a casual tone.

"Sir, I will look." Then she replied, "Actually, she will be free later this evening. She had a cancellation."

Trying to contain his excitement, he said, "What time will she be available?"

"Our evening service starts at six p.m. Is that what you are wanting?"

"Yes. I would love to have this one as soon as she is available."

"How many days are you requesting her?"

"How much per day?"

"Three hundred a night."

"I would like her for three nights."

"Well, that means she will be leaving you in the mornings and returning in the evenings. Or would you like her to accompany you all three days?"

"Oh, how much would it costs to have her for the full days and nights?"

"Sir, that is five hundred for twenty-four hours."

"Okay, I would like her for three full days and nights."

Steven handed over the money, which didn't leave much for the rest of the trip. But they had to get this done soon.

The thing that concerned him, though, was the knowledge that someone always watched his activities. If he tried to get away with Rosa, there would be a chase to get free.

Steven tried to entertain himself as he waited for Rosa, hoping nothing would go wrong. He called the missionaries, and in code, shared with them what was going on.

Precisely at 6:00 p.m., there was a knock at Steven's door. He rushed it. In front of him stood a beautiful lady who looked just like a grown-up, yet a more attractive, version of the passport picture. She stood tall and straight, with long ebony hair hanging in soft curls to the waist of her tight white dress.

"Please come in," Steven said, after he caught his breath.

With one sauntering stride, Rosa stepped inside the door and flashed a smile, showing her pearly white teeth framed by plump red lips. Now he understood why her name in the book was *Lucious*. Her only flaw was that her big brown eyes looked cold and empty.

Rosa's beauty stunned Steven, and he hardly knew what to say. Should he just jump right in, telling her first thing that he was going to rescue her? For one, he had to make absolutely sure this girl was Rosa. He did have some doubt because she didn't seem upset to be there. Maybe she wouldn't even want to leave. Perhaps she had become content with this life.

He reached out. "May I take your bag?"

Without saying a word, she nodded and handed Steven her bag. He set it by the sofa, wondering what he should do next.

*Rosa doesn't act like she's afraid, but I'm afraid. I'm afraid to mention that I know anything about her. And I'm afraid to talk with her about why I'm here while we're inside the unit. We may be under audio or video surveillance. The only safe place to talk will be in my car.*

It was an awkward situation for Steven. He was eager to get Rosa off-premises, so he offered to take her out to eat. She was hungry, so they left to have dinner. He could take an escort off-premises, but they had to check back in before daybreak, according to the rules.

Once he had Rosa in the car, he began to ask questions. He had no time to waste, as the escape plan's crucial timing drew close to the end.

"As you know, my name is Steven Price, and I'm from America. Where are you from?"

"Costa Rica," she said. "Why do you care where I am from?"

"Well, since we are spending some time together, I was just trying to get to know you better. So how long have you worked as an escort?"

"For a long time. Don't worry. I have experience. I can make you happy."

Steven's heart ached, as he knew her story and wished he could get her to talk, but she wasn't about to say anything.

When they arrived at the restaurant, he looked around.

"Are there security men here that protect you?"

"Yes, they're everywhere," she said. "They know exactly where you take me. It's all part of the work. We are encouraged to take our clientele to certain places."

Afraid she had said too much, she added, "It's all for our protection."

Steven felt that she was covering up, and Jose was indeed holding her against her will. Somehow, he had to stir her emotions so they could talk realistically.

After a few minutes of silence, he started a casual conversation.

"I went to a hotel in town, trying to find a place to stay, but there were no vacancies. While I was there, I looked through the book of escorts and saw someone who looked a lot like you. You two look so much alike. Really. You could be sisters. Do you have a sister who works at a hotel run by a man named Jose?"

These words shocked her, and her wide eyes filled with tears.

"Are you okay?" Steven said. "Did I say something wrong?"

"No, I don't have a sister. But what was her name?" she replied in a passive tone, as though she was simply carrying on the conversation.

Steven shrugged. "I don't know her name, but she looked like she was about your age. And she is beautiful, just like you. Now that I think of it, she couldn't be your sister. When I asked about her, they mention that she came from El Cuá, Nicaragua."

Rosa dropped her fork on the plate. The color drained from her face, and her lips began to quiver.

Again, Steven said, "Are you okay?"

She looked up with eyes that pierced right through his.

"Who are you. And why are you here?"

With as much compassion as he dared to express openly, he replied, "I am someone you can trust. I will never hurt you."

Steven knew that he had the right person, but he also knew that he had to wait until they got back in the car before he could explain further.

The rest of their time in the restaurant was solemn. He had stirred the emotions that Rosa had suppressed for ten years.

# CHAPTER 63

## ROSA FINALLY TALKS

After dinner, Steven and Rosa got into the car to go back to the condo.

But before Steven started the engine, he said, "Rosa, I know all about you—everything since the day you and Anna left home."

Rosa fell back against the car door. "Who are you? What are you saying? After all these years, are you telling me that someone remembers Rosa? She died long ago!"

"No, Rosa. I saw that you are still in there. I know you want to get out of this."

"How can I escape? Yes, of course I have wanted my life back. But there is no way."

"Rosa, are you sure you want out of this? Or are you happy now because you are in a high-end escort service?"

"You are an American. You don't understand anything. Of course I am not happy. You don't know the danger here. Every day, even so-called *high-end* escorts face the possibility of torture or death. I have finally accepted my life for what it is. Even if I managed to get away from this place, I still couldn't go home. I don't have my passport to leave the country, and Jose would hunt me down like a dog."

Steven tried to comfort Rosa by telling her that God had a plan for her life.

"A plan? Well, he sure had a plan, all right. He took me from my family and allowed Jose to enslave me. That is some God, and some plan."

Rosa was so upset, Steven couldn't get her calmed down. Before they returned to his unit, he needed to tell her that a group of people had already implemented an escape plan. So he continued to drive around until he noticed headlights in the rearview mirror. One of Jose's men was following them, and it would look suspicious if he didn't take Rosa back to his unit. It became more evident to him that Rosa was right about one thing—he had no idea how difficult and dangerous an escape would be.

Steven put his hand on Rosa's hand to comfort her.

"We can't talk about this at the condo," he said. "We'll just go back and spend time together. But I want you to think about what I'm saying. Right now, we have someone following us. We have to act like a normal couple."

"Don't you think I know the danger of talking about this anywhere except in this car?" she said. "And I knew they would follow us. How do you think I can possibly escape?"

"Rosa, you know more than anyone about how security operates at this place. You must start thinking about some details that might help us get you out. Could you please write down anything that might help, and just show it to me?"

As soon as they pulled into the resort, the car that was behind them went on past. In the light of the moon, they sat silently for a minute in the car before opening the gate.

Then Rosa looked at him. "You still don't get it, do you?"

"Rosa, *you* don't get it. I don't want anything from you—no sexual services or anything. I am here to rescue you. Can you get that? There has been a lot of effort to get you out of here. Anna risked her life to get us your passport. Please consider this plan as your only chance, and don't let me leave here without you."

Rosa kept shaking her head in disbelief. "See," she said as she opened the car door, "there are cameras all over this place.

They know we are here. We can't talk about this anymore, inside or outside of your unit."

Once they got inside, Steven said, "Are you tired?"

"I am always tired, but I am here to serve you."

"Well, I'm going to go ahead and go to bed. You can join me when you're ready."

Steven knew that he had to act like he was using the escort service. Doing this would be tricky because Rosa had already confirmed that the guards monitored the units' activities with listening devices.

"Are you feeling okay?" he said. "I'm feeling a bit sick to my stomach. Probably something I ate. I think I'll just go to bed and get some sleep. We can play tomorrow."

"Are you sure? You have paid big money for me and this place. I don't mind. I'd rather entertain you than anyone else."

"Seriously, I'm calling it a day. Goodnight."

Rosa knew she had to at least sleep with him, so she followed him into the bedroom and lay on the empty side of the bed.

Steven was a single man who had lived a rough life before becoming a Christian. That's why the missionaries had chosen him to go in and try to rescue Rosa—because he was rugged and street smart.

Steven *was* street smart, but there was a lot he didn't know about himself. Now, in the still of the night, he had a beautiful woman lying beside him, willing to do anything he asked, and this situation was an unexpected temptation.

He knew nothing about what the future held for Rosa—or him—but he would soon find out.

# CHAPTER 64

## DAY OF DECISION

STEVEN AWAKENED NEXT MORNING before the stars had faded from the sky. Rosa was still sleeping soundly, so he quietly showered and dressed. By the time he finished, she was awake and waiting for her turn to shower.

"When you get out, we'll have breakfast," he said. "And then I'll take you to the beach."

After getting back into the car, Rosa said, "You know Jose's men will follow us to the beach."

"I know. But they can walk only so close to us. I'm hoping that you will change your mind and start helping with the plan to get you away from these evil people."

"I keep telling you...I want to get out of this place, but I know it is hopeless. I have thought about ways to escape all these years, but I realized none of them would work in the end. The chain around my neck is invisible, but it is there, nonetheless."

"Rosa, you could not do this alone. Listen to me. You needed help from the outside, and that is why I'm here. We have a plan, and God is already working miracles."

Steven tried to convince her that she was young enough to start her life over. She could make it back home to see her parents. If they were still alive, they would still be wondering what had happened to her.

Again, her eyes filled with tears at the mention of her parents.

"Don't talk to me about it anymore," she said. "How do you think it would make me feel for my mom and dad to know that I have spent all these years working as a prostitute?"

"I know you feel ashamed, but this isn't your fault. Your folks would never feel anything except guilt for letting you leave. Besides, Anna is hoping you will be able to escape and come with her. She risked her life for you. You owe it to her to at least try."

"And how do you know all this?" Rosa said.

"The missionaries told me all about how miserable Anna's life has been with Jose in that terrible motel. They told me how she has managed to retrieve the passports Jose took the day you arrived at the hotel. And they said she continues to put her life on the line to get herself and some young children at the motel rescued." He put his hand on shoulder. "Rosa, think about it. Anna put her life on the line to retrieve your passport so you could leave and go home. You must now do everything you can. I know your life is bad, but Anna's life is so much worse. She will not want to escape without you. You know the ropes, and you can help me get you out of here."

"You have bought a service," she said. "You need to use it."

Steven left her alone on the beach as he walked around the condo, silently praying that God would help him because time was running out.

He decided that maybe the best thing to do was simply to make her love being with him. Perhaps she would then be more convinced that someone could simply enjoy being with her, and that she could experience true love one day.

Returning to Rosa, Steven held her hand as they walked in the frothy water, up and down the beach. Afterward, they ate lunch and spent the rest of the day just getting to know each other. They went shopping, tried on clothes, ate ice cream, and laughed a lot. It was a perfect day, considering the circumstances. The guards watched them all the time, but they had no clue what was happening between them.

That evening, Rosa climbed back into Steven's bed. He was still concerned that Jose had the room bugged, so he thought he should show her some affection. He took her in his arms and began kissing her. She kissed him back with passion. He wondered if she was developing real feelings for him, or if she was just doing her job. He had never been with an escort, so how would he know? Either way, he couldn't help himself. He was falling in love with her.

The next morning, they got ready for the day—the day Steven would either rescue Rosa, or he would not.

They drove around for a while without any conversation. His heart was in his throat, and he didn't want to express what he was feeling. He was sure that her beauty had smitten many men, and he didn't want her to think he was only one of those men.

Steven was deep in thought when he felt her hand on his arm. She leaned over and looked into his eyes.

With a softness in her voice that he had not heard before, she said, "Don't leave me. I will go."

"Thank you, Rosa. We have worked so hard for this day. I need you to tell me everything you know. We're going to need as much information as we can to escape. So what do you know about all the security around here?"

She said, "There is a small window of opportunity when the guards change shifts. During these few minutes, no one will be monitoring the cameras, and it will be our only chance to make a getaway. If we do get away, we will have to drive as fast as possible on terrible roads. You'll need plenty of fuel because there aren't many gas stations."

"I'll fill up last thing before we go back tonight," he said. "And I assure you that I am capable of driving off-road, especially in this Jeep."

The couple stayed out on the beach, on a blanket, the remainder of the day. They watched the ocean, all the while planning their escape. Intermittently, Steven would kiss Rosa and show affection. In his mind, he kept telling himself that it was part of the game plan. But in his heart, he knew it was something else.

That evening at the condo, Steven reported again to the missionaries. They asked if he was having a good time, and he told them that he was having an excellent vacation. So good, in fact, that they were planning to get up early in the morning to take full advantage of the beautiful weather. His words signaled that he and Rosa would attempt to escape early in the morning. The plan was to make a mad dash for the House of Hope, the mission camp on the county's eastern side.

Steven knew this message would initiate the other two escapes: Juan with Isabella, and Lucas with Marcos. These escapes must happen before Jose learned of the plan to free Rosa—whether she managed to escape or not. Jose knew where everyone was, and his guards would apprehend them.

That evening, Steven and Rosa went to bed, as they had before. But this time, they remained fully dressed.

At 3:00 a.m., they slipped out of bed without turning on a single light. After closing doors softly, they hurried out of the condo and to the car. Without turning on the headlights, Steven backed out of the garage and used his code to open the resort gates. They sped through, and the gate closed behind them.

Just as Rosa had said: no one was at the gatehouse at that time, and it appeared that no one had a clue they had left.

Steven had already mapped out the roads, so he drove as fast as he could. Headed out of town, he continually looked in the rearview mirror to see if anyone was following. Every time he saw car lights behind them, he feared someone was in pursuit.

They drove without slowing down, taking no chance that some other security guard along the way had fallen in behind them. The two counted down the miles in their minds as they got closer and closer to the mission camp. Even one mile away, they still did not consider themselves out of Jose's grip.

The sun was just beginning to rise in front of them when they first saw the shadowy forms that comprised the missionary camp. It appeared the guards never realized they had slipped out. And the getaway that had seemed so impossible turned out to be incredibly easy.

Steven pulled the car into the camp and rolled to a stop. The fresh morning light dispelled the darkness they had left behind. It was a sign that happiness lay before them.

*A new day is dawning, and maybe, just maybe, a new life is dawning for Rosa...and for me as well.*

At the thought of that possibility, Steven reached over and drew Rosa into his arms. She returned his kiss, and for the first time in ten years, a radiant smile spread across her face. There really was something of the old Rosa still alive inside of her.

"I can't believe it!" she said as she settled back in her seat and looked around. "I'm free! At last, I am free! I thank you, God. And thank you, Steven. Thank you for risking your life to rescue me. Thank you for caring about me. I don't know why you would, but I thank you. And as soon as I can, I want to find Anna to thank her. And...and I want to see my parents."

"Hold on, Rosa. Hold on." Steven held up his hand and winked. "I'll take you anywhere you ever want to go. But I think we need to get some food and rest first."

# CHAPTER 65

## ANNA'S LAST CHANCE

WHILE ROSA WAS SAFE THIS MORNING, time was running out for Anna. Isabella was due back at 6:00 p.m. the next day. When she did not return, the situation would go downhill quickly. As soon as Jose realized the child was missing, he would go into the safe and check on her passport. When he discovered it was gone, he would know Anna was responsible. At the same time, he would also find that Anna's and Rosa's passports were missing, and realize there was a plot for all of them to escape.

Jose, who was already delusional, would explode in anger at the discovery. Someone needed to rescue Anna at once. But the missionaries had no one else to play the role of a client requesting an escort. Their only option was to make another fake passport for a local man, but that presented another problem. Jose or one of the guards might recognize a local. If they did recognize him, then both lives would be on the line.

After much discussion and prayer, the missionaries sought help from area churches. As God would have it, someone suggested a man named Ricardo Manuel. He was an associate youth leader at a church out in the country, about fifty miles away. When the missionaries informed him about their rescue plot and the need for someone to go in and get Anna, he immediately agreed to help.

The missionaries made a fake passport showing Ricardo was coming into Costa Rica from Spain. He could easily pass as a Spaniard. Though his father was Costa Rican, his mother, whom he more closely resembled, was from Spain. Ricardo stood only five-feet-eight, but he was extremely muscular. He could take care of business if there was trouble.

As soon as Ricardo got his passport, he went to the motel to request Anna as an escort for the day. No one was at the desk when Ricardo arrived, so he approached an enormous guard standing in the lobby.

"Good morning, sir. I've just arrived from Spain, and I would like to book an escort for the day. Would you know if any are available?"

"We don't have any today," the guard said.

Ricardo pulled out a wad of bills. "I bet you can find someone for me. And if she's really good, I'll give you double when I bring her back."

The guard maintained his staunch, stone face without saying a word. Ricardo pulled out a few bills and stuffed them into the man's shirt pocket. With that, the guard turned and walked off.

"Follow me," he grunted. "I'll do my best."

For the last few days, Jose's state of mind had slipped deeper into obsessive suspicion, and the guards had now lost all loyalty toward him. They saw this weakness and no longer considered him top dog. They felt they could move in and do a better job running the business than he was doing. But if they didn't do something soon, there would be no business and no jobs for any of them.

A second guard fell into line behind Ricardo as they went to the backside of the motel. When they arrived at the office, there was Jose and Anna. Ricardo knew it was her from the description the missionaries had given to him, and he could already see things were not going well for her. The office was a mess. It looked like someone had turned everything upside down. Papers lay helter-skelter everywhere.

"So who are you?" Jose snapped, like a rattlesnake ready to strike.

"My name is Ricardo Manuel, and I would like to purchase an escort for the day."

Jose spewed a stream of profanity. "I guess you would!"

Jose had just learned of Rosa's escape. And as predicted, he suspected Anna was at the root of it. He was going to get to the bottom of this, no matter who was in his office.

He slammed his fists down on the desk, and snorting like a bull, headed for the closet where he kept the safe. Anna knew she was about to become the object of Jose's violent temper. Her gaze met Ricardo's, pleading for help. She didn't know who he was, whether a client or one of the missionaries, and he had no way of telling her.

Jose didn't know who he was either, so he ordered the guards to grab him. The guards rushed forward, one on each side, and dragged Ricardo out of the office.

"Look, I don't want anything to do with this mess," Ricardo whispered. "I'll give you more money if you'll just get me out of here. I have thousands in my car if you will just let me out of this joint."

The big guard stepped back into the office, leaving the door half-open. Ricardo heard him try to intervene. It wasn't that the guard cared a whit about what happened to Anna. He cared only for himself, and he knew Jose's business was going broke, so that meant his livelihood was at stake. Somehow, he had to keep Jose from chasing all the clients away.

"Boss, I don't think you have to worry about this dude. His passport shows he's from Spain. He knows nothing about you. You're going to lose all your business if you don't get it together. So we lost Rosa. We've lost others along the way. I will deal with Anna. Just let me get this man out of here before the authorities come looking for him."

"Go ahead and get rid of him," Jose said. "*I* will deal with Anna." And with a cynical laugh, "I hear the crocodiles down at the river are hungry."

The guard came out of the office, grabbed Ricardo's arm, and told the other guard to join Jose and Anna. The big guard then escorted him out of the motel and to his car, pretending to be mean and rough with him in case Jose was listening. He planned on getting the big bucks this man had offered, without arousing suspicion.

"Wow! What's going on in there?" Ricardo said. "That was one beautiful escort. I really would like to have her, but I don't need any trouble, if you know what I mean."

The guard said, "Don't worry. The boss is just a little upset because one of our girls quit and took off. It hurt his feelings."

"That's too bad," Ricardo said. "But look, that women back there is hot. She's exactly what I wanted to take out on the town tonight. You think you could still work a deal for me?"

"Man, I just saved your life! You said you would pay me to get you out of there. Now, where's the money you promised? Either you hand it over, or I turn you over to Jose."

Ricardo handed him five hundred dollars from the money the missionaries had managed to scrape up.

Shaking his head, he said, "That's all I have on me. I'll have to go get more, but I'm not sure this escort is worth the trouble or the expense."

"I can assure you," the guard said, "she's well worth the price. In fact, she's the boss's main squeeze. That should be proof enough."

Ricardo stretched to his full height and straightening his shirt.

"I just gave you big bucks up front. If you can deliver her to me, I'll give you more. If not, I'll just have to use another escort service. One that has less drama."

The guard realized he had already made more money on the side that day than he had in the last week working for Jose. Believing the business at the motel was about to go under, he saw a new job opportunity where he could make a lot of money.

"Okay," replied. "I'll get her for you tonight at eleven. Meet me down behind the bar on the beach at the end of this street. But you must have her back at the motel by sunrise because Jose will be up by nine. He'll want to see her first thing. Remember, my life is over if he discovers I did this for you."

"I'll meet you, but what's the price," Ricardo said. "Remember, I'll only have her for a short while."

"You can have her for two hundred. And that's a deal for her."

It was difficult for Ricardo to walk off and leave Anna at the motel, but he had no choice. He had to entrust her to God's care for the remainder of the day.

# CHAPTER 66

## JOSE'S DISCOVERY

THE GUARD RETURNED TO THE MOTEL and found Jose in the closet on his hands and knees, rummaging through the safe's contents. He tossed papers, cash, guns around the room.

"I know they were in a yellow envelope. I haven't touched them for months. Now where are they!"

Finally, he located the envelope under a pile of papers. He ripped it open and dumped the contents on his desk. After shuffling through all the passports, he discovered three were missing.

In a seething rage, Jose stood and got in Anna's face.

"How is it that the only passports that are missing are yours, Isabella's, and Rosa's?"

Before Anna could speak, Jose grabbed her by the throat.

"I'm going to kill you!"

The guard Ricardo had paid off tried to get Jose to release Anna, but he couldn't loosen the stranglehold. It wasn't until Anna collapsed to the floor that Jose relinquished his grip. And even though she lay unconscious, Jose began kicking her in the ribs.

Again, the guard stepped into the fray. He knew he couldn't get any money for a dead escort.

"Look, boss, you need to let me take care of this ingrate... this traitor. That dude from Spain knows something is going on here, and he may alert the authorities. If they find her dead, you'll be the prime suspect. You just keep your hands clean and let me take care of her."

Red-faced and panting, Jose replied, "You're right for a change. I've got to protect my reputation, and killing her now is too good for her. She will suffer before she dies. Lock her up until the morning. Let fear consume her during the night. In the morning, I'll torture her before I kill her. Then I'll go into town to establish an alibi. After that, you can take her bloody body to the river."

The guard picked up Anna's limp body, carried her to Room 120, and laid her on her bed. Out of frustration, he applied a wet washcloth to her face, trying to revive her.

*Now what am I supposed to do.* He paced around the room. *I've made this deal to sell her, but Jose will kill me if he comes to torture her in the morning and discovers she's missing.*

Drenched in sweat, he continued to pace. *Jose is a fool. He's a crazy man. Why do I spend my life worrying every day whether or not he will have me tortured and killed?*

Anna moaned as she regained consciousness, and the guard knelt beside her bed.

"Look, you have to get yourself together. Jose...he has gone crazy, and he's going to kill you. I brought you back here to get you away from him, but now I don't know what to do with you."

Though Anna could hardly speak without coughing, she mumbled through swollen lips, "Please. Please don't let him kill me. I beg you. The missionaries will pay you if you get me out of here."

The guard now had two reasons to keep Anna alive, but he could only deliver her to one person. This client seemed to be well-to-do, so he decided to continue with Ricardo's offer. The guard convinced himself that he could still make it to the bar on the beach to meet this client on time.

Anna was still too weak to walk, so he picked her up again and opened the door. There in the hallway, Jose lay face down, passed out from another overdose. He would be out for the night. His kingdom was finally falling apart.

The guard stepped over Jose, exited the back of the motel through, and headed for his car. A smile spread across his face as he laid Anna on the back seat and drove to the bar at the beach.

As planned, the guard found Ricardo standing under the dim streetlight. But he stopped short and pulled into a dark parking lot nearby. Leaving Anna in the car, he stepped out and whistled for Ricardo to come to him.

"Look, man," said the guard, "I need as much money as you can give me. I can't go back to the motel ever again. So if you want her, you're going to have to give me those thousands you promised. Otherwise, I will have to sell her to someone else. I have another offer for her."

"That five hundred dollars I gave you is all I have on me." Ricardo exposed the contents of his wallet to prove it.

The guard shook his head. "I need more than that. I just lost everything by doing this."

Ricardo couldn't believe he was so close to rescuing Anna, and only a few hundred dollars stood between her life or her death. Shaking his head in disbelief, he happened to look down at the gold ring his father had given to him. It was worth at least several hundred dollars.

"Here," he said. "Take my ring and watch. They're worth about another five hundred. That's all I have."

The guard was not happy about the deal, but he put the jewelry in his pocket. He then rubbed his hands together, pretending to cleanse them of the dirty deal.

"Good riddance!" He snorted. "She's been a lot of trouble."

Ricardo opened the car door, and the overhead light came on. It wasn't until he saw Anna in the light that he realized how severely she had been beaten. Her face was so badly bruised and swollen that he barely recognized her, and the front of her dress was bloodstained from her busted lip. She wasn't moving, so he wondered if she was even alive.

*I can't believe this. I could see that Jose fellow was cray mad. I should have never left her! She must still be alive, or the guard wouldn't have brought her to me. But if she doesn't make it, it will be my fault!*

"Look...Man, you couldn't sell her in this condition, anyway. Now what am I going to do with her?"

"Just get her!" the guard said. "I've got to get out of here."

Ricardo opened the car door to get Anna. At the sight of him, her eyes widened with fright. She thought he was a regular client who had run away, leaving her at the mercy of Jose. Even though he hadn't laid a hand on her, Anna felt he was partly responsible for her beating.

As Ricardo picked her up to put her in his car, she drew back.

"Who are you? Where are you taking me?"

Ricardo put his finger to his lip, signaling for her to be quiet. Then he put her in his car, and the guard sped off into the night.

"Anna, don't be afraid. My name is Ricardo. The missionaries sent me to rescue you. I'm taking you to the east coast, to the missionary headquarters. You will be safe with them. I'm going to drive as fast as I can to get you help. And when you're better, they'll drive you home. Your real home, Anna, to El Cuá to be with your family."

With all her strength, Anna sat up as straight as she could.

"Where are the children?" she said. "Where is Isabella? I want to see her."

"Right now, Isabella is safe at the resort where the other missionaries are staying. She's not due back at the motel until six p.m. tomorrow, but as soon as Jose finds out the guard has done something with you, there's no telling what he'll do. I have contacted the missionaries to let them know that I have you so they can get Isabella and Marcos out of town first thing in the morning."

"They need to leave now," Anna mumbled through her bruised and swollen lips. "Jose will kill them now that I'm gone."

"The guard said Jose won't know you're gone until nine a.m., when he goes to get you. So they need to wait until morning. If Juan took Isabella out on the town in the middle of the night, it would look suspicious to the guards who are watching.

They need to attempt their getaway early tomorrow. Although Marcos has a week to return, Jose will also come after him as soon as he finds out you're missing. So both of them are going to try to make a break for it at the same time."

Anna broke down and sobbed. While she and the children weren't completely free of Jose, all of them were at least out of the motel.

"Thank you. Thank you, Ricardo, for getting me out of that prison and away from Jose. I will never be able to repay you, but I know my God will. Please tell me, do you know anything about Isabella and Marcos?"

"Anna, it will take a miracle for both of them to escape and get to the camp safely. But from what the missionaries have told me, God has worked a lot of miracles in the last few weeks."

"Yes, I know my God. And I know that if he saw fit to deliver me, he will surely deliver these precious children."

# CHAPTER 67

## ANOTHER DASH FOR THE HOUSE OF HOPE

RICARDO CONTACTED THE MISSIONARIES with the good news that he had managed to rescue Anna. The missionaries then informed both Juan and Lucas that they needed to make their getaway with Isabella and Marcos first thing in the morning. This news confirmed the message Steven had already given to them. Both parties prepared to make a simultaneous mad dash for the House of Hope.

At 7:00 a.m., Lucas and Marcos left their room, ready to make a run for it. But as they walked toward the car, Lucas realized the guards were watching them, so the pair talked loud enough for the guards to hear them, about where they were going to eat breakfast.

Lucas took Marcos to a restaurant in town to make it appear that everything was normal. One of the guards followed them and posted up in a parking lot across the street from the restaurant, waiting for them to come out.

In the meantime, Juan and Isabella went out on their balcony. They pretended to look at the birds and take in the scenery for the last time before Isabella went back to the motel.

"Isabella," Juan said loud enough for the guards to hear, "today is our last day in this wonderful place. How would you like to go for a walk on the beach this morning and play in the sand one last time?"

Isabella jumped up and down, clapping her hands. "Yes. Yes. I love to play outside!"

She made so much noise, there was no doubt the guard heard their plans for the day. So the pair put their blanket and bag of food in the car and drove to a parking lot near the beach. The same parking lot where the other guard was watching Lucas and Marcos at the restaurant.

Soon, the guard who followed Juan started talking to the guard that had followed Lucas. They were so intent on discussing their problems with Jose's drug abuse and failing business that they became distracted.

As the guards huddled in conversation, Juan saw the opportunity he was waiting for. He snatched Isabella up off the blanket and raced toward the parking lot. After just a few long strides, Juan jumped into the open door on the side of a waiting van driven by Cruz. Maya and Lola helped Juan and Isabella as they tumbled in. Juan told Isabella to stay hidden on the floor while he lay there with her out of sight.

The guard heard a sliding door slam shut and the surge of a motor, so he scanned the beach to see if Juan and Isabella were still there, and realized they had disappeared. Then he saw the van speed off. Although Juan's car was still in the parking lot, the guard knew they had to be in that van, so he followed them. His only hope was that they wouldn't go far. If they escaped, Jose would retaliate with a cruel vengeance.

Marcos and Lucas had also been watching the guards, and they saw what had just taken place. So while their guard watched the scene on the beach unfold, they left the restaurant and jumped into Lucas's car.

"Marcos, I hope you're ready. This could get rough."

"More than ready."

Lucas handed Marcos a sheet of paper. "Your father made out this map for me to follow, so you're going to have to direct me once I lose this guy."

When Lucas pulled out of the parking lot, the other guard realized that the people he was supposed to be watching were also making a break for it. His tires squealed as he raced out of the parking lot in pursuit of Lucas and Marcos. He caught up with them, and the two vehicles sped down one street after another until they got outside of town.

The bumpy dirt roads made steering difficult, especially at high speeds, but the blinding dust Lucas kicked up as they drove worked in their favor. The cars continued to race bumper to bumper, until on a straight stretch of the road, the guard pulled up beside them and made several attempts to run them off the road. He sideswiped their car and lost control, crashing into the side of an embankment.

Marcos and Lucas were happy to lose their pursuer, but they knew they had to continue making good time. Others could soon be coming after them.

# CHAPTER 68

## CLOSE ENCOUNTER

The van carrying Isabella continued traveling east. Juan was familiar with these roads, so he directed Cruz to take a few shortcuts. They zoomed down the road, hoping they had lost the guard.

As the van rattled and bumped along, Juan tried to keep Isabella from bouncing around in the back. Tired of the rough ride, she leaned in close to Juan.

"I'm scared," she whispered. "Anna didn't practice this part with me. Since you're my angel, can you tell me where we're going? I want to see Anna. Will I see her again?"

"Sweetheart, hold on. I think we'll see Anna soon."

They hit a hole in the road, and the back right tire blew out. The van fishtailed until Cruz got control and stopped on the side of the road. Everyone jumped out.

Maya and Lola ran with Isabella to hide several yards off the road in some bushes, while Juan and Cruz located the car jack and lug wrench.

The men yanked, tugged, and tapped on the rusty old lug nuts, but they would not budge. Sweat dripped from the men's foreheads as they struggled with the tire, on their hands and knees in the dirt. Still no success. Between their frustrated grunts and groans, they heard a car coming up the road behind them. Pausing momentarily to look over their shoulders, they hoped to see Lucas and Marcos pull up. The driver came in fast, slid to a stop in a cloud of dust, and jumped out of the car with his gun drawn.

"Put your hands up." He waving the weapon around. "Where's the girl?"

"Sir, what do you mean?" Cruz replied in a calm tone. "We're just trying to change a tire. Can you help us?"

"Shut up, you fool." The guard pointed the gun directly at Cruz. "You know who I'm looking for, so don't play games with me. Tell me where she is, or I'll shoot both of you."

Neither of the men moved or spoke. The guard stepped to the side of the van and looked in the open door. Finding no one inside, he became more hostile.

"I know you have her. You better call for her to come out, or I will kill you. And then I'll kill her."

The guard pointed the gun at Juan. "You. You know where she is. Tell me where she is. Now!"

"Please, sir, you haven't told us who you want us to get for you. You have searched the van, and you can see there is no one here but the two of us. You can see...we have a flat tire."

Lucas and Marcos, traveling the same route, caught sight of the disabled van and the guard's car while the scene was still a considerable distance ahead of them.

Marcos said, "Lucas, that's the missionary's van. Looks like the guard caught up with them."

"You're right. Instead of rushing in and risking the guard firing at someone, I think we should try to sneak up on him."

Lucas pulled off the road, out of sight. He and Marcos got out quietly and advanced on foot the rest of the way. They almost made it, when the guard heard a rustle and whirled around in time to see the two of them coming at him.

"What are you doing here!" he shouted. "You *all* are going to die if you don't give me the girl."

Motioning with the gun, the guard ordered the four of them to stand at the rear of the van. Then he cocked the gun and began pointing it at each of them, saying he would torture the girl when he found her if they did not hand her over. The men stood still, silently praying, while anger mounted in Marcos. He hated the abuse he had suffered, and he wanted Jose and his men to pay for it. He had vowed to kill them many times, and now was his chance...if he could just get his hands on that gun.

*If anybody dies today, it's going to be this man, not us.*

While Marcos wrestled with the idea, he glanced at his father, standing beside him, just inches away. He had hoped for the day when he would see his father and mother again—but not like this. He knew he had disappointed them. But he couldn't bear the thought of them getting killed because of him.

Marcos stepped forward with his arms out for the guard to handcuff him.

"Here. Take me, but leave the others alone."

The guard smirked and stepped closer to grab Marcos. The idea of returning to enslavement evoked rage in him again. He would rather die than return to Jose. What did he have to lose? What did any of them have to lose? Jose would kill all of them, anyway.

Marcos threw his arms up and knocked the gun out of the guard's hand. It went up in the air and fell to the ground with a thud. Both the guard and Marcos scrambled in the dust to get possession of it.

Juan jumped on the guard. "Run, son! Run!"

The guard managed to get the gun, and fired a shot, hitting Juan in the shoulder. Still, he continued to fight the guard. A second shot rang out, and Juan fell motionless in the dirt. As the guard stood triumphant over his bleeding foe, Lucas grabbed the tire iron and hit him in the back of the head. Lying on the ground was the unconscious guard and Marcos's wounded father.

Marcos collapsed on his knees beside his father.

"Dad, please don't die." He sobbed. "I'm so sorry. Please, please, God, don't let him die."

Cruz tore off his shirt and applied pressure to stop the blood flow, while Lucas checked the guard's pulse. Seeing he was only knocked unconscious, Lucas dragged the man back to his car and handcuffed him to its steering wheel. It was just a matter of time before some of Jose's other men would be on the scene. Besides, the guard probably had the key to the handcuffs in his pocket.

Lucas then put Juan in the back seat of his car. Lola and Maya hurried to get in with Isabella. They hated to leave the van behind, but that could work in their favor. Leaving it and the injured guard could throw Jose's pursuing men off-track. Most likely, they would think everyone was fleeing on foot and hadn't gotten far.

Marcos and Lola tended to Juan as they sped the last few miles to the House of Hope, where there was doctor on-staff. Upon arrival, Isabella watched as everyone rushed inside with the wounded patient. It had been a long, traumatizing day. From her vantage point, someone had shot her angel. Even worse, that mean guard shot him because he was trying to protect *her.*

Her world was upside down. She was alone and afraid, not knowing where she was. Isabella hadn't been this sad since the day Javier took her from her home in Miami.

Then a mob of excited people rushed out to greet her. They pulled her from the car, smothering her with hugs and kisses, praising God for the miracle of getting everyone out of Jose's prison. Then the crowd began to part, and Isabella caught a glimpse of Anna running toward her with arms wide open. As sore as Anna was from Jose's beating, she picked Isabella up and squeezed her in a bear hug.

With tears streaming down her face, the only words Anna could say over and over were, "Thank you, Jesus."

"Anna, I was afraid. We didn't practice that part, but I kept pretending anyway."

"You did? What did you pretend?"

Isabella lowered her eyes as though she were ashamed to say.

She whispered, "I pretended that you were my mother, and that I was on my way to see you."

Anna tilted her little chin up. "Isabella, I *am* your mother in a very special way. You were born in my heart the first time I saw you."

"Oh, thank you, Mother." Isabella laughed.

"Just don't ever forget—you are God's special gift to me."

# CHAPTER 69

## FREE AT LAST

DESPITE THE PHYSICAL AND EMOTIONAL TRAUMA of the last two days, Anna awakened the next morning long before the sun stretched forth its glorious beams of light. She was ecstatic because this day was monumental. It was her first day free of fear. Everything seemed surreal—almost too good to be true. At the same time, her heart swelled with praise for answered prayers. And she was grateful to all those who surrendered to God's call to help set them free from a bondage of the worse kind. She also took great joy in knowing that her precious Isabella was safe beside her.

It was too early to awaken anyone, but the first thing Anna wanted to do was to find Rosa. It was much too late last evening to find her, but she knew they would reunite today. Anna was eager to see how life in captivity had been for her dear friend.

Anna continued stroking Isabella's hair while she watched her sleep. In the stillness of the moment, memories of her parents flooded her mind. She had suppressed thoughts of them during her imprisonment because thinking about them hurt too much. But now, the prospect of seeing them again warmed her heart. She dared to free her thoughts.

*I can't believe I'm finally going home. I wonder if Father and Mother are still in good health. Maria may be married. Does she have children? I can't believe I'm free. Thank you, God.*

Isabella lay sound asleep as Anna finally slipped out of bed to get ready. While walking down the hall, headed to the shower room, her body ached with every step from Jose's beating. The warm water that flooded over her washed away blood, sweat, and tears. She began to feel like the old life was behind her, and a new life was ahead.

Once Anna finished getting ready, she looked in the mirror—but she still saw *Anna the maid*. She couldn't face all the realities of life right then, so she turned away from her reflection. Even though she was free from imprisonment, she recognized that it would take a long time for wounds to heal and scars to fade.

On the way back to the room, a lady who worked in the mission camp met Anna in the hall. Before Anna said a word, the lady wrapped her up in a warm hug.

"Our prayers for everyone's rescue are finally answered, she said. "We have been praying for a *long* time."

Words escaped Anna because she was overwhelmed with gratitude for everything the missionaries had done for them. Tears welled up in her eyes as she struggled to thank this stranger who appeared to know her well.

"By the way, my name is Margaret. I'm in charge of guest services here at the mission. And I'm happy to tell you that we are arranging for you to meet Rosa. She is getting ready, and can't wait to see you."

"I am beyond excited and grateful," Anna said. "I wanted to find her last night, but I knew it wasn't the time for a reunion."

Margaret excused herself, assuring Anna that she would come back to take her to breakfast. Anna rushed back to get Isabella up and ready for the day.

"Anna, are you going to leave me again?" Isabella rubbed her sleepy eyes.

"Sweetheart, I will never leave you. I promise. And guess what...today, you can even hold my hand as we walk to the dining room because no one will care."

Isabella jumped up. "Yay! I'm hungry. Let's eat."

As Anna was helping Isabella get ready, she began telling her about Rosa. Anna also wanted her to know that she hoped to go home to see her family. Isabella began asking lots of questions. There wasn't time to explain everything before they left for breakfast, but Anna knew they had to discuss what would happen now that they were free. That would be difficult for Anna to explain when so many uncertainties remained.

# CHAPTER 70

## A DIFFERENT DINING HALL

WAITING FOR SOMEONE TO TAKE THEM to breakfast brought back bad memories for Anna. It was a reminder of the guards always escorting her from one place to another. She never had the freedom to go anywhere on her own. And going to the dining hall, where everyone congregated, was especially painful because of the sea of sad faces that were always present.

Anna wanted to see Rosa, and she wanted to enjoy breakfast. Still, she dreaded the dining hall experience.

Thirty minutes later, Margaret knocked on the door and called out, "Are you ready?"

"Yes, we are!" Isabella replied.

The three of them walked down a long hall to the main cafeteria, where the room was full of happy people—not at all like Anna's memories of the motel.

She paused in the doorway, scoping out the bright and happy room, looking for her friend. Then her gaze met Rosa's, and they ran towards each other, weeping tears of joy. After a long embrace, they looked at each other with a mixture of happiness and heartbreak. Rosa had changed a lot, but Anna still recognized her beautiful face. They couldn't stop hugging and crying. It was a long-awaited day—one that neither would ever forget.

Soon, Isabella came up behind Anna and tugged on her

shirt, wanting to be introduced to Rosa. When Anna turned to grab her, she noticed that everyone was rejoicing with them. All around, people were taking pictures of this emotional reunion.

After breakfast, Margaret asked Anna if she could introduce Isabella to some of the other children while she and Rosa talked. Isabella was reluctant to leave Anna's side, until the children came up asking for her. She overcame her fears and left to go with them to the playground.

Anna and Rosa went to a separate room where they could talk privately. They had precious little time to share ten years of their lives.

Imprisonment had broken both Rosa and Anna. But as they shared their experiences, they agreed that their experiences were not alike. Anna had lived as a hostage in a rundown motel where Jose and clients had savagely abused her. Jose had also forced her to get involved in trafficking young children. Anna was so discouraged that she had become dependent on alcohol to get from one day to the next.

Rosa, on the other hand, admitted that her enslavement was not as horrible as Anna's and that she would never have survived the abuse Anna had experienced. But she told Anna how she had cried every night for years, keeping her diary, wondering what had happened to her, and praying they would see each other again. Every time she asked Jose about Anna, he severely beat her.

"Anna, do you still have those panic attacks?"

"Yeah, I still have them whenever someone covers my face or holds me down. I guess I'll always have flashbacks of that small limestone cave we discovered that collapsed on me. I couldn't move or breathe, and I would have died if you hadn't been there to pull me out. I owe you my life, Rosa."

"I think we're even now," Rosa said with a wink

During the reunion, Anna finally received an answer to a question that had haunted her for ten years. She learned that Jose had not raped Rosa their first night at the motel, as he had her. For that, Anna was grateful. Perhaps Jose recognized her own strong will, and he felt challenged by it, or even attracted to her because of it.

Anna and Rosa agreed on one other thing. Both believed that they were not entirely out of danger, even though they were out of Jose's prison. He had a broad network of people, and it was just a matter of time before he would learn their whereabouts. The missionaries also believed Jose would come looking for them. So the plan was to get everyone out of Costa Rica as soon as possible.

# CHAPTER 71

## ANOTHER TEST OF FAITH

JUAN PLANNED TO LEAVE COSTA RICA with his family and return to the States as soon as his shoulder healed enough to travel. He wasn't overly concerned about Jose because he believed a man as paranoid as he was would not try to detain them. An American news report on Marcos's abduction and abuse could become an international matter. And Jose certainly wouldn't want that at a time when he already feared the authorities were about to shut down his business.

On the other hand, Anna, Isabella, and Rosa needed to leave for Nicaragua as soon as possible. But Anna had something she needed to do first. She hadn't had the chance to speak with Marcos privately since she got to the mission camp, and she wanted to make sure she told him goodbye before she left to go back home.

After lunch, she pulled him and his parents aside, where they shed tears of joy and sadness, knowing they probably would never see each other again.

"Marcos, I want you to know that if I ever have a son, I hope he will be just like you. I believe God has great plans for your future. And I want you to remember that I will always love you."

"Thank you," he replied. "I love you. But I don't see how anyone could ever love me. I-I don't deserve it."

"Marcos, you are the same precious person you were before

this happened. You have a God-given talent, and he is going to bless the world through you. Trust me, you are not to blame for the terrible things Jose did to you. And as soon as you had the chance to change things, you did. In truth, you demonstrated great courage and faith. You saved lives back there. You are a hero."

Juan reached into a folder and pulled out the drawing and letter Anna had given to the maid that night at the hotel.

"Son, here is proof that God has given you a special gift. He would not have given you that talent if he didn't think you were worthy. He loves you, and your mother and I will love you always, no matter what you do, or what someone does to you. It'll take time, but we will get on the other side of this. I promise."

Later that afternoon, while Isabella was on the playground, the missionaries called a meeting with the survivors of Jose's prison. First, they discussed arrangements to get each of the escapees out of the country before Jose caught up with them. Next, they arranged for the ex-prisoners to connect with an organization in their area to get support.

Escaping imprisonment was the first step. Healing from the trauma would take time and assistance.

The missionaries made detailed travel arrangements for Rosa, Isabella, and Anna to go to Nicaragua. Sitting around a conference table, they thought through every aspect of the journey.

Early the next day, before Jose had a chance to come after them, one of the missionary couples would drive them across the border into Nicaragua, and help them find their families. The missionaries would pack all supplies and food for the journey.

*Across the border...we may still be in trouble.*

Crossing the border into Nicaragua was reason for alarm. Anna feared the border guard, or someone else, in authority could take custody of Isabella. The idea that this child's sad saga might not be over made Anna shudder. But was she morally obligated to alert the authorities to the child's situation and whereabouts? Or should she continue to treat Isabella as her own child? Had God delivered her from imprisonment for her to possibly suffer further abuse?

Isabella's mother had abandoned her. She might abandon her again. And her father had sold her. What would keep him from selling her again—maybe even to Jose a second time. They did not deserve to get her back. And how could she risk Isabella's life by handing her over to some government official who might not be trustworthy—someone on the take.

Worst of all, the authorities could return her to Jose. She could still end up as his sex slave after the missionaries had rescued her.

Anna couldn't bear the thought of now losing this child. Each of these scenarios was unacceptable. Anxiety mounted, and her heart rate increased just thinking about it. Anna realized she faced another test of her faith.

*Lord, you know that it takes more than a womb to make a woman a mother. I pray that you will allow Isabella to be mine forever."*

"Are you okay?" Rosa said, noticing Anna's heavy breathing and tense face.

"Yes...yes. I'm just finding it hard to believe this nightmare is finally over."

The meeting closed, and everyone got up from the table and left the dining room. Only Anna remained seated, looking at the passports spread out in front of her. She picked up Isabella's passport and flipped it open to look inside. Anna she noticed something she hadn't seen before. A shiver went down her spine, and goosebumps popped up all over her.

*I can't believe it. Isabella has a Nicaraguan passport. This is just what she needs to cross the border. Without it, the border police might detain her for questioning or take her away. But how can she have a Nicaraguan passport? Did she really come from the States, where she had lived with her father? After all, she can speak Spanish, and she doesn't look American. Why did Isabella tell me that she came from Miami?*

Anna rushed to the playground to get the child. As soon as she saw Anna coming, Isabella jumped up and ran to meet her. Hand in hand, they walked back to their room.

"Isabella, come sit with me on the bed. There are some important things we need to talk about."

With a look of fright, Isabella said, "Are these people going to take me away from you?"

"Isabella, I must ask you an important question. Now that you are free are, are you sure you don't want to…to go back and live with your father or mother?"

Isabella's lips quivered, and her eyes filled with tears.

"Please don't ever send me back," she said. "I just want to be with you, always. Please don't ever leave me. I will be a good girl. I promise."

She became so hysterical that Anna took her in her arms and held her tight. She suspected Isabella's home life was worse than she cared to remember.

Anna's heart ached for the child, and she would go to the ends of the earth to make sure nobody ever hurt her again.

"Isabella, I promise I will never send you away. And I promise I will always love you unconditionally. That means I'll love you whether you're good or bad."

After Isabella calmed down, Anna explained that they would have a long ride to Nicaragua, and that they would enjoy the journey home together. She also told the little girl that she would meet Anna's mother, father, and sister.

After a moment of silence, Anna looked down and saw that Isabella was frowning.

"Why are you so sad?" Anna said.

"That's where my mother lived."

"What do you mean?" Anna replied, trying to hide her shock. "Why didn't you tell me this before now?"

Isabella put her head down and refused to look up.

"I thought I was going to see her when that man took me from Father. But I never saw her. He took me to a camp and then drove us all night on a bus, and then in the trunk of the car to the motel. I was afraid you would think I needed to go back to that camp if you thought my mother was there. But she wasn't. No one has seen her since she left us. It was scary until I found you, Anna. I don't want to be scared ever again."

*That explains everything. Jose had a Nicaraguan passport made up for Isabella so Javier could fly her into his camp in Nicaragua. From there, he smuggled all the children into Costa Rico. Jose knew he couldn't smuggle children through the airport or border crossings. That's why so many of them were in the trunks of the cars that evening at the motel. Isabella never even knew she had traveled from Nicaragua to Costa Rica.*

All the pieces were falling into place, and Anna was seeing the bigger picture of what God had in view all along. She fell back on the bed, laughing hysterically.

"What's so funny?"

"Isabella, there's a verse in the Bible that talks about how God, who looks down on us from above, laughs at evil men and their silly efforts to dethrone him or ruin his beloved children. Isabella, I think he is laughing right now!"

"He *is*?"

"Yes, I think God is laughing at Jose and his men. They made up a Nicaraguan passport to get you here, but I think God is going to use it to get you out of here."

Isabella fell back on the bed and laughed with Anna. She didn't understand what was so funny, but she did love to giggle.

The she sat up straight, went for her backpack, and returned with her cross necklace dangling from her fingers.

"Is it safe to wear this now?"

"Yes, it is. Turn around so I can put it on you."

"Anna, I want you to have it. You are the nicest lady *ever*."

Anna swallowed hard a couple of times before she was able to speak.

"And you, Precious One, have the biggest heart of anyone ever. It would be a great honor to wear this necklace, but I cannot accept it. That nice lady at the airport gave it to you because God wanted you to have it. He wants you to wear it as a reminder of his deep love and continual care for you."

Isabella turned around so Anna could hook the necklace around her neck. When she turned back around, she promised to never take it off.

# CHAPTER 72

## THE JOURNEY HOME

ANNA SHOULD HAVE BEEN JOYOUS the night before they were to leave for Nicaragua. But the anguish in her soul kept her awake. For one thing, every time she closed her eyes, she saw the faces of Jose's other sex slaves. The children were especially haunting. Their desperate eyes pierced her soul, and she knew she could never get over leaving anyone behind.

*Why Lord? Why didn't you arrange for us to get everyone out? They are suffering, and their families are suffering because they don't know where they are. It doesn't seem fair.*

In a small voice, God revealed to Anna that she should go public with her story to appeal to people everywhere to help stop human trafficking. Yes, she was free, but she would continue fighting to save the children left behind, and prevent others from experiencing such a travesty.

The other conflict that troubled Anna centered on the principle of truth. Honesty at all costs was something her parents had taught her as a young child. And it was the principle she had held in the highest regard. But now, there was a tug of war deep inside. She still struggled with deciding whether or not she should come forward and notify the government officials that a young child once held prisoner was now free.

As crucial as honesty was to Anna, she had to confess that she had lied to Jose on many occasions to keep him from abusing her. It was a matter of self-defense. And now, she wanted to defend Isabella. Who wouldn't do everything possible to save a child from harm or death?

*Would God permit me to just keep quiet about this? I know he hates lying, and I have given my heart to live right. So how can I not bring this truth to light? Yet I believe God has delivered us from sexual enslavement, and that he has given Isabella to me through his providence. What should I do?*

Anna continued to struggle. She knew that God sometimes works his will directly, and sometimes he works his will indirectly, through his servants. Had God given Isabella to her, expecting Anna to protect this child from evil men?

She didn't know. The only thing she knew to do was to pray harder. And when she did, peace flooded her soul, once and for all.

*God has given Isabella to me until the time he sees fit to take her away. I have to trust God from day to day. Today I have her. Today, I will love, hold, and protect her.*

Anna no longer felt guilty for not going to the authorities. And if anyone should ever ask about their relationship, she would acknowledge the reality of the situation and be quick to speak of God's excellent mercy and grace in giving the child to her. But until then, she would simply enjoy Isabella as a special gift from her Heavenly Father.

*Whatever he chooses, I will accept.* With that thought, Anna fell into a sweet sleep.

When the rooster crowed, Anna's excitement was so high that she could hardly stand it. She patted Isabella on her back and started singing. Isabella sat up in bed, rubbing her eyes and yawning.

"Mother, you're singing. I have never heard you sing."

Anna realized that Isabella was right. She hadn't sung a single note since she left home. How wonderful it was to have a song in her heart again.

"Yes, you are right," Anna replied. "But today is one of the happiest days of my life. If the police officers at the border crossing ask us why we're going to Nicaragua, we'll simply tell them that we're going home."

Isabella said, "Yes! I'm going to see my new family."

"This is a big day," Anna said. "As soon as you're ready, we'll go to the dining room to eat breakfast. After that, we'll meet Jim and Rita."

"Who are they?" Isabella crawled out of bed.

"They are a couple who have worked here at the House of Hope for a long time. They want to drive you, me, and Rosa to Nicaragua. They know the roads very well, and they know some people there who can help us readjust to normal life and heal from the abuse we experienced."

"Yay! I hope Jim and Rita have children so we can play," Isabella said.

"I don't think they have children. Even if they did, there would be no room for them. The missionaries have packed the car with necessities, and the trip will be rough. But we'll do our best to have fun anyway."

After breakfast, Jim greeted them at the dining room door and asked if he could put their bags in the car. Rita added items to the growing bundle of clothes, food, and toys that the missionaries had already given to them. Anna tried to think of everything they would need for their journey.

Isabella was the happiest Anna had ever seen her. She placed her hand in Anna's and said, "Mother, we are finally going home."

"Isabella, I couldn't be any happier than I am right now. I can't wait for you to meet my family."

Rosa and Steven appeared, walking arm in arm. They were also saying their goodbyes to each other, and it was evident by the sadness on their faces that they did not want to part.

"Rosa, I found you once," he said, "and I will find you again. Don't worry. Jim and Rita will make sure I know where you are. I promise. I will come back after I take care of things back home."

Rosa reached over and kissed him on his cheek. "After all you've done, how could I not trust you? You just be safe, and don't wait too long."

# CHAPTER 73

## THE SEARCH IS ON

JIM AND RITA GOT INTO THE FRONT SEAT of the car, while Anna, Rosa, and Isabella sat in the back. Once everyone settled in, Anna reached over and patted Rosa on her arm, assuring her that everything would work out.

"Rosa, do you remember how excited we were the day we caught the bus to San Jose? I'm more excited today than I was then. I wanted to see the world, but now I can't wait to see Mama, Papa, and Maria. Aren't you excited to see your folks?"

"I had given up hope that this day would ever come." Rosa let out a big sigh. "And it would not have come if it hadn't been for you, Steven, and the missionaries. I just wish Steven could be with me. I fear that something will happen, and I'll never see him again."

"I don't think you need to worry about that. Steven seems like a pretty determined guy," Anna reassured her with another pat on the arm.

Rosa continued waving goodbye to Steven as Isabella and Anna waved at everyone. Isabella, who was sitting between the two of them, reached over and patted Rosa. This child didn't know much about falling in love, but she sure did know how to cheer someone up.

Before Jim started the car, he turned around and asked if they could pray before leaving. Everyone bowed their heads while he prayed for their safety, and for help in finding the girls' families.

After the prayer, Isabella added a hefty, "Amen!"

Anna couldn't help but smile, thinking about how this young child's faith continued to grow.

It took them about an hour to reach the border crossing. Once they did, Jim requested everyone to be quiet. He had nothing to fear, but it was always scary to go through security.

He rolled the window down and greeted the officer.

"Good morning, Jim. How are things going at the mission house?"

"Oh, God is doing great things. I hope you're doing well."

"Yes, very well. What's the purpose of your trip this time?"

Jim handed over the passports and explained that he was taking some friends back home to see relatives. The officer asked no further questions. He simply nodded, stamped the passports, and told them to have a safe journey.

Anna breathed a sigh of relief because she never had to answer any questions. Crossing the border went so smoothly, they acknowledged that God had answered their prayers, and now Isabella, Anna, and Rosa were headed home.

Jim drove several more hours, before they stopped to eat the sandwiches Rita had prepared for lunch. He pulled over on the side of the road, and Anna could see the coffee bean shrub-like trees growing on the distant slope. The sight brought hope that when they arrived in El Cuá, she would find that things at home hadn't changed much there either.

Anna was so anxious to get home that she willed everyone to wolf down their lunch. She didn't want to waste a single minute.

After lunch, they traveled a few more hours, before they pulled into the first coffee bean field where Anna and Rosa used to work with their parents. The girls jumped out of the car and ran to the rundown shack where the workers brought their beans after they picked them.

The place was empty. Then they realized that there were no workers in the field either.

The girls were shocked and disappointed that they couldn't find anyone, but they didn't lose hope. Coffee pickers were migrant works, so they would just keep looking for their families.

After running back to the car, Anna asked Jim to drive to the village a little ways down the road. Perhaps someone there would know where the workers had gone.

Isabella could see that Anna was disappointed, and she also became sad. Anna had hoped they would at least find someone who would know their parents or their whereabouts.

Once they arrived in the village, Rosa and Anna jumped out of the car again. They went from place to place, asking whether anyone knew anything about their parents. No one seemed to remember them.

As a last resort, Anna told Rosa that she wanted to try this old store farther down the street, where her father would sometimes buy necessities.

They entered the dimly lit store, and the jingle of a little bell on the door announced their presence. The store looked exactly like it did ten years ago—cluttered from top to bottom with every supply any patron could ever need.

From the back of the long, dusty room, a croaky voice called out, "What could you pretty girls possibly want from a rundown place like this?"

Anna said, "Sir, we're looking for some people who used to work in the coffee bean field down the road."

"Well, they're not there," he said. "That place closed down years ago. Everyone moved on, looking for other fields producing more fruit. I used to work there myself until I slipped on the side of a slope and broke my leg. Broke it so bad, I can't do much of anything anymore."

*They moved on? I can't believe my ears. Is God punishing me for having Isabella? Please God, punish me if I need it. But please don't punish Isabella. She needs a family.*

Anna proceeded to tell the man every detail about her parents in the hopes that he might remember them.

"Yep, I remember um all right." He rubbed his scroungy beard. "But I don't know where they went." He shook his head. "I do recall a lot of those folks went to work in a field just north of here."

With a hitch in his step, the man hobbled to the counter and scrambled to locate a piece of paper. His fingers, gnarled from years of picking coffee beans, grasped the nub of a pencil. As best he could, he began drawing locations of the different coffee bean fields in the area that were still in business. The girls thanked him for his kindness and rushed out the door.

"Good luck," he said. "If you find 'em, tell 'em Pops said hello."

# CHAPTER 74

## THE SEARCH CONTINUES

AS THEY CLIMBED BACK INTO THE CAR, Anna handed Jim the scribbled piece of paper. He nodded, then pulled back onto the road and began driving toward the nearest coffee bean field.

Anticipation mounted with every mile as they continued up the road, wondering if the map was taking them in the right direction. The few signs that still existed had faded and were difficult to read. Everyone was hot, tired, and emotionally spent when they finally saw an old wooden sign that said, *Coffee Beans.*

Jim turned down a winding dirt road that led to an old building. It didn't look promising, but then they saw people picking coffee beans on a nearby slope. Anna jumped out of the car before it came to a complete stop, and rushed to a nearby building where she thought there would be an office. No one was in there, so she followed the sound of voices coming from the back.

"Sir, I'm looking for my parents," Anna said to the first person she saw. "They used to pick coffee beans in this area years ago Their names are Carlos and Juanita Hernández. Do you know them?"

The man shook her head. "No. I'm sorry. We do not have anyone here by those names."

Weak and wilted, Anna returned to the car.

Rosa noticed her discouragement, and said, "We will find them. God has not forsaken us. We *will* find them."

Anna opened the car door, ready to climb in, when she heard her name called from the nearby coffee field.

"Anna? Anna! Is that you?"

Anna spun around. Someone was running from the field, toward her. In a matter of minutes, there stood a wide-eyed, breathless young woman in front of her. Anna's little sister!

"Yes! Yes, Maria. I am Anna."

The sisters hugged each other with tears of joy flowing. Rosa joined them, and the three embraced, jumping up and down. The thud of car doors slamming rang out. Jim, Rita, and Isabella joined the celebration of such a glorious reunion. In a few minutes, they realized the coffee bean pickers in the field had stopped their work and were standing up, clapping and cheering.

Jim located the manager to explain the situation, and asked if he could take Maria back to her family to have some time together. The manager was sympathetic and agreed to let her off work for the remainder of the day.

Maria climbed in the car with them, and everyone continued to talk over the top of each other. Maria gave Jim directions on how to drive to their little house not far down the road. Anna was thrilled to learn that Father and Mother were still alive. And Rosa was learning more about her own parents as well. Unfortunately, Rosa's father had died. Everyone felt her sorrow. She never had a chance to say goodbye to him or explain what had happened to her. But they rejoiced that her mother was still living, and their families were still close.

# CHAPTER 75

## END OF THE ROAD

AT LONG LAST, THE CAR PULLED INTO THE YARD where Anna's parents now lived. Everyone sat still for a few silent moments. There, in front of Anna, sat her parent's home, like a pot of gold at the end of the rainbow. The house looked similar to the one she grew up in, except it was a little more settled and in need of repair.

After getting out of the car, Anna advanced with hesitating steps. She had yearned for so long to get here, but now she was nervous. She knew the faces of her parents—etched in her mind since the day she last saw them at the bus stop—would not be the same after all these years. She worried about finding them in poor health. She also worried about telling them her story and introducing them to Isabella.

With one more step, Anna stood on the wooden platform that served as a porch.

*How can I ever explain to my godly parents about the debauched life I've lived? Will they still love me the way they used to? Will they ever find it in their hearts to love Isabella?*

Anna took a deep breath and eased the door open without knocking or calling out. The familiar smell of beans and rice was in the air. She heard the rattle of dishes, so she crept through the front room and stood in the kitchen doorway. There, silhouetted against the setting sun shining through the window, stood her mother at the counter. Her profile looked exactly like Anna remembered.

From the corner of her eye, Juanita caught a glimpse of someone standing in the doorway. She turned to look into Anna's face. After ten years of mysterious absence, her daughter's sudden appearance was almost more than she could take. She dropped the pan that was in her hand, and grabbed her chest.

"Anna?" she whispered. "Dear God, please let it be. Let it be my Anna."

"Yes, Mother, it is Anna. God has finally brought me home." She choked back years of suppressed emotions.

Juanita rushed to her daughter as quickly as her feeble frame could go. Enveloped in her arms, Anna never wanted to leave her mother's warm embrace.

"Anna...oh, Anna." Juanita wept. "What happened to you? Where have you been? We have missed you so much, and prayed every day for your return."

"Mother, I'm so sorry. I want you to know it was not my choice. Just know that I'm here now, and I'm never going away again. I'll tell you all about it later."

They kissed and cried until, at last, Juanita took Anna's hand.

"Come. You need to see Father. He's been very sick, but he never awakens in the morning or goes to bed any night without begging God to let him see his Anna before he dies."

Juanita led the way to the bedroom where Carlos lay asleep under the covers. He looked frail, a mere ghost of what he used to be. It hurt Anna to see her father's health failing, yet she was grateful that he was still alive.

She stepped to his side and pulled up a chair beside the bed.

Taking his hand in hers, she whispered, "Father, it's Anna. I'm finally home."

Carlos slowly opened his eyes and turned his head toward her.

In a weak voice, he said, "Anna? Oh, Anna. Please tell me I'm not dreaming."

"No, Father, you're not dreaming. I'm finally home. God has answered your prayers."

Carlos lifted his hand and rubbed her cheek.

"Anna, are you okay? I've wondered since the day you left what had happened to you?"

Anna choked back tears, not wanting to upset him.

"Father, God has answered prayers. We will talk more about it later. Just know that I'm home, and that's what matters now."

In a few minutes, Anna led her mother out to the porch, where everyone else was waiting. It didn't seem to be the right time to go into details about who everyone was and what had happened, so Anna simply introduced everybody by name—with one exception.

When she introduced Isabella, Anna proudly owned her as her daughter. Juanita bent over and enveloped the little girl in a hug.

"I finally have a granddaughter! Isabella, welcome home."

"Thank you. Mother told me all about you, and how you and Papa taught her about Jesus. Is it okay if I call you Grandma? I've always wanted a grandma."

"And I've always wanted to *be* a grandma." Juanita chuckled.

Anna and Isabella said their goodbyes to Jim, Rita, and Rosa so they could travel on to get Rosa to her mother.

That evening, Maria was happy to share her room with Anna and Isabella. And what was a tight squeeze at first, caused them to grow even closer in spirit.

As the days passed, it was amazing how contently Anna worked in the fields again with Maria and Rosa, regardless of the heat and hard labor. What she had thought was intolerable before, was now a sheer pleasure.

Juanita had grown too feeble to work in the fields, but she found joy spending time with Isabella. And Isabella seemed to have breathed new life into Papa. She spent hours beside his bed, telling him make-believe stories. She even taught him to pretend.

It took several weeks before Anna could tell her parents all that had happened to her. She hated telling them about the abuse, but she believed they had a right to know how God had worked many miracles to get her and others out of imprisonment. She even told them how Isabella had come to be her daughter. They deserved to know the truth—and God deserved the glory.

The story Anna told them grieved their hearts, especially Father because he felt responsible for letting her leave home. But they never blamed Anna for anything. Instead, they loved her more for the faith and trust she relied on to see her through. She was not only their beloved daughter—she was their hero.

Anna was now more at home and more at peace than she had ever been. Best of all, Anna's parents loved Isabella for the miracle she truly was—the product of pain, the fruit of faith.

# EPILOGUE

ALTHOUGH ROSA DIDN'T GET HOME before her father died, she was grateful for the early years she had with him, and the many good years she had with her mother.

One day, after returning home from the coffee bean field, she found Steven waiting on her front porch. He lived up to his promise of finding *and* marrying her. She had, indeed, found that handsome man she wanted so long ago.

---

Anna's father died just six months after she returned. But she had many good years with her mother. And Anna's desire to be a mother also came true. Isabella remains with her to this day. No one ever came looking for her, and no one has even questioned their relationship.

Isabella has grown up to be a beautiful young lady. She never speaks of her father, or those horrifying days in the motel. She has put it behind her as though it were just a bad dream.

Every day, Anna thanks God for sparing Isabella. Her only regret is that she couldn't rescue all the children. She still has haunting memories, but she has peace because she found God's purpose in her pain.

Today, Anna works with missions in Nicaragua and Costa Rica, trying to bring awareness to this escalating evil, as awareness is the number one way to prevent it.

"For ten years," she said, "I was imprisoned by a human

trafficker in the hotel business who forced me to service clients who sexually abused me. For that reason, they belittled me, calling me *the maid*. Today, I bear the title without shame because I believe God has called me to serve him in the work of preventing human trafficking and sex slavery."

# AFTERWORD

During research for my doctoral studies in business, I became aware of the alarming number of children worldwide who work under forced labor. It was puzzling how this travesty still existed in the twenty-first century. More concerning was the number of children who labor in some of the worst forms of employment, especially that of sexual exploitation.

According to the International Labour Organization (ILO), millions of children work under forced labor conditions worldwide. Child labor in the worst forms is more prevalent in developing countries due to poverty and lack of education. The US Department of State monitors human trafficking and child sexual exploitation, and publishes the information in an annual Trafficking in Persons Report (TIP). If a country falls to the worst level of Tier 3, the country may face sanctions from the US and the World Bank.

During my dissertation research, the TIP report verified that Costa Rica had been downgraded to a Tier 2 Watch List. That rating means it was on the verge of slipping into the Tier 3 category.

In my research, I saw a correlation between certain industries and the prevalence of human trafficking. For example, human trafficking occurred more often in tourist areas than it did in other places. Therefore, I sought approval from my dissertation board to conduct research concerning corporate social responsibility in the tourist industry concerning child labor and sexual exploitation. The completion of my studies inspired me to do further research that led me on a personal journey—to shed light on the wickedness of human trafficking and sex slavery by sharing stories of actual victims.

Coauthor Kay Bowling is a researcher and writer. As someone who has a heart for children, she is also a past participant in the foster care program, and the mother of two adopted children. Together, we traveled to Costa Rica to conduct interviews with people who had experienced the travesty of human trafficking and sexual slavery. Having obtained an inside view, we joined several interviews into one storyline. We hope *The Maid* will allow readers to better understand what is happening every day—not only in Third World countries—but also in our own communities.

The reader must let these stories speak to the heart, and compel them to do their part in stopping human trafficking and sex slavery. These stories bring awareness to the problem, which is the first step in change.

The second step is accountability. Those who are aware can hold those who participate accountable by not supporting businesses involved—directly or indirectly. Look at a corporation's core values, especially those in the tourist industry. See what steps they have taken to prevent human trafficking and abuse.

By hearing the voices of these children, we hope that you, the reader, will place yourself in these stories and feel the suffering of those who find themselves trapped in sexual slavery. It is a travesty that could happen to anyone, anywhere, at any time.

Thank you for being brave enough to take this journey toward the end of one of the worst forms of human suffering.

—Michelle Osborne

# ABOUT THE AUTHORS

## Michelle Flynn Osborne

Michelle is a university professor and also serves as Chief Deputy Commissioner in a North Carolina State Agency. Her greatest passion is helping children, protecting their childhood with the hopes of promoting a better future for the world.

Michelle's research studies include child labor in the worst forms. She acquired a Doctor of Business Administration from George Fox University, Newberg, Oregon and received her MBA from Campbell University. In addition, She has been an entrepreneur, owning several businesses. Her hobbies include composing music, traveling, and kayaking.

## Kay Mann Bowling

Kay is a former foster care parent, the mother of two adopted children, and grandmother of three terrific grandchildren.

Kay is a retired deputy clerk with the county district court and a retired administrative assistant with the state government. These days, when she's not writing, you will find her tending to her garden and caring for her beloved hand-me-down pets. She is passionate about life's second chances.

## CONNECT WITH THE AUTHORS:

- traffickedvoice.com
- twitter.com/traffickedvoice
- instagram.com/traffickedvoice
- facebook.com/traffickedvoice
- linkedin.com/company/traffickedvoice

## CHECK OUT THESE OTHER GREAT READS FROM TORCHFLAME BOOKS

*Songs for the Forgotten: A Psychiatrist's Record* combines pivotal moments from Julia Burns's Southern upbringing in the 1970s with case histories accumulated through three decades of treating psychiatric patients, particularly those drowning in the cultural epidemic of child abuse. This book is her journal of rupture and return.

The reader will follow the author's hard-won reconciliation. In telling A panoply of stories, including her own, Burns argues for the interconnectedness of humanity: when one child is hurt, our humanity is violated, and we are all responsible for undoing that damage. If no one steps up to save children, to show them they are worth saving, the cycle of abuse will continue.

*Songs for the Forgotten* offers a strong practical component, providing information about trauma and healing. Burns illustrates how hope and wholeness can come from remembrance and telling.

When the world turns away from the horrors of war, genocide, famine, and natural disasters, the stewards of humanity run toward the suffering. They stand as a thin line between life and death for thousands of people who will never know their stories. These stewards are neither heroes nor saints—they are ordinary people with ordinary struggles who rise to extraordinary challenges. They are beacons of light in the darkness of humanitarian crisis.

With an unflinching view into some of the worst humanitarian crises of our lifetime, author Robert Macpherson—US Marine combat veteran turned aid worker—tells the stories of the men and women who have courageously confronted evil and injustice from Somalia to Bosnia, Rwanda, Iraq and Afghanistan.

Throughout his narrative, Robert challenges us to consider our place in humanity and our own role as stewards.

CPSIA information can be obtained
at www.ICGtesting.com
Printed in the USA
BVHW032132010222
627858BV00004B/147